VARIANT

To Beverly, my wife and companion for twenty years, and to our fine sons Ari and Dov, this book is lovingly dedicated.

CHAPTER ONE

NORTHERN EUROPE, *April, 1985*

How the boy got across the border from East Germany to the West, or even how he got from Leningrad to East Berlin, was something that, in the confusion that followed, no one thought to ask. And if someone had asked, the boy wouldn't have replied. But somehow he did, perhaps endowed by his superb intelligence with a cunning that surpassed the border guards' vigilance . . . or perhaps it was the fact that his muscles had a strength and endurance that exceeded all previous experience, allowing him to perform beyond anyone's expectations and so take everyone by surprise. No border guard or policeman expected to be outrun by a small child or made to feel clumsy and foolish by his quickness. Certainly none expected to be bodily thrust aside or hurled roughly to the ground by a child less than half his size.

In any event, once across the border into West Germany, he began to run, having no money and no other means of transportation. In this his performance was superb. Six minutes to the mile, mile after mile, his legs tirelessly consumed the roadway. The weather was cold most of the time. This worked to his advantage, since it minimized the fluid loss from sweating, while he was able to keep warm by his exertions. Despite his diminutive stature—even for an eight-year-old he was short—he could often cover eighty or ninety miles a day. Even he was amazed at what he could do, and he realized that all the tests in Leningrad had never really pushed him to his limits. He was driven by hatred and fear—hatred of those in Leningrad and fear of what he knew was going to happen, was happening, to him.

Travel by the main roads was too dangerous to be risked, of course, and he had only an old road map of Western Europe to guide him, so the route was rather circuitous. Food was a problem, too, since it had to be stolen along the way. Even superhuman muscles needed energy, and every mile used up 120 calories, so his food requirements were enormous. No small number of workmen and farmers later complained to the police about a strange-looking child, appearing like a tiny old man, who would steal their lunch boxes and then run off at incredible speed. An occasional rural housewife reported that a burglar seemed to have taken the entire contents of her refrigerator and pantry but left the silver untouched. Some grocers lodged similar complaints. He had nearly starved to death, though, by the time he reached Paris.

Because of the speed with which he moved, no one really got a good look at him. Descriptions of the boy varied. Everyone, however, agreed on several points. He was small, a child seemingly no larger than a six-year-old, yet if you could catch a glimpse of his face it was that of a sixty year-old man. That was the most striking feature—the little boy with an old man's face, sad and weary. His very strangeness

8

Copyright © 1988 by Dr. Alan Engelberg
All rights reserved, including the right of reproduction in whole
or in part in any form. Published in the United States of America
by Donald I. Fine, Inc. and in Canada by
General Publishing Company Limited.

Library of Congress Cataloging-in-Publication Data

Engel, Alan.
Variant.

I. Title.
PS3555.N3877V3   1988   813'.54   88-45419
                    ISBN 1-55611-114-2

Manufactured in the United States of America
10 9 8 7 6 5 4 3 2 1

VARIANT

A NOVEL

ALAN ENGEL, M.D.

DONALD I. FINE, INC.
New York

served to protect him. Occasionally motorists would stop to watch him run, or even accost him, but his appearance made them shrink from him. Often embarrassment, the embarrassment felt, for example, when confronting someone with a disfiguring skin disease, kept people from reporting what they had seen to the police. When descriptions were given, they agreed, other than in his aged appearance, only in that he was bulkily clad in frayed, drab clothing, had a small knapsack on his back and was carrying what appeared to be a rolled-up magazine clutched tightly in his left hand.

Adequate shelter was difficult to find, and the boy spent some cold, shivering nights huddled in lonely misery against his knees, curled up against storms that rolled across Europe from the Atlantic coastline. A barn was a welcome sight when evening came around. Near Cologne he was able to steal some blankets from a clothesline, and after that he was more comfortable. Still, most of his nights were spent in tears; no strength of body or mind could overcome the fact that he was only eight years old, frightened, and alone.

Evading capture was the first and the most difficult priority. At eighty miles a day, even a tortuous backcountry route from Leningrad to Paris wouldn't take too long, but many hours of daylight had to be wasted in hiding. River crossings posed the greatest dangers. Only once was he able to steal a boat. Other rivers he crossed on bridges, either late at night when he might be alone and, hopefully, unobserved, or during the day, fearfully relying on the anonymity of a crowd of pedestrians. Russian was his only fluent language, though he knew a little English, but he dared not ask for directions or assistance for fear of being captured and sent back to Leningrad. Only death awaited him there, and it was to try to escape this fate that he had run away in the first place.

Once in France he began to steal newspapers and magazines to familiarize himself with the language. As soon as possible, he stole a radio and listened intently to the strange sounds, imitating, practicing. He'd have to learn French to communicate with those he hoped could save him. In a moment of daring he crept into a bookstore and made off with a Russian-French dictionary and a French grammar text, and after that his hours of hiding were more productive. He made rapid progress. The functioning of his brain, like that of his body, was far beyond any normal human expectation. He had only to look at a page of the dictionary for several minutes to memorize the words on it. Within a week he could speak passable French, although his pronunciation remained awkward and clumsy.

But he aged even as he ran. He could feel it happening, see it in the occasional glimpse of himself in a reflecting window or pond. The exhaustion and privation of the journey made it worse, of course, made the aging process accelerate even more, but he knew he had no choice. It had begun at least a year before, but the changes had become more obvious and ominous in the last several months. The aging changes that a normal man might experience over many years, slight cumulative losses of strength and agility, little lapses of memory, even diminution of the urgency of sexual desire—these the boy had experienced compressed into the space of several months, a foreshortening of life that made each moment, each quantum of time, the more urgent and demanding.

The magazine he held so tightly was a Russian journal of biochemistry, a special issue devoted to abstracts of a recent international conference on the biochemistry of aging. In it were articles from around the world. But there was one article that the boy had read and reread dozens of times, the article that held the only shred of hope he could find in all the world. It was an article by Dr. Irene Sailland, the noted French geneticist, entitled "The Genetics of Aging." A footnote to the title gave Dr. Sailland's address as the Institut de Biologie Moderne, 11 rue de Montpelier, Paris.

It was to this address, and to Dr. Sailland, that the Russian boy ran.

10

PARIS, *May 21, 1985*

The man crouching in the basement morgue of the Hôpital des Enfants checked the time by shining his tiny penlight for an instant at his wristwatch—one A.M. He had waited long enough. He stood up slowly from the floor, rubbing the kinks out of his back; he'd been sitting on the floor since five o'clock, when he had darted unobserved into the morgue just before it had been closed and locked for the night. Crossing the floor silently on rubber-soled shoes, he listened at the door for a full five minutes, assuring himself that there was no one in the hall outside. The occasional blare of a distant horn from the street upstairs was the only sound that penetrated the stillness. Satisfied, he snapped his penlight on again, and despite its feeble beam it provided all the light his already dark-adjusted eyes required.

A hospital for children had little need for a morgue, so the room was small, not much more than eight by ten meters, and it was kept very cold to help retard decay until burial could be arranged or an autopsy performed. The bodies were laid out in plastic bags with zippers down the middle, one on each of three tables.

When he had been given his instructions no one had been able to tell him what the child looked like, since no one in the Soviet Embassy had ever seen him. They said it wouldn't be a problem, though. He would be the size of a six year-old, weighing about twenty-five kilos, but he would look old, with the sunken features and shriveled skin of an old man. It would be so striking, they said, that he couldn't miss it. The difficult part of his task would be to get the body out of the building.

He approached the first table cautiously, almost as though he half expected the cadaver to start moving. Though—as an agent of the KGB—he had killed men before and could do so with no qualm of conscience, the sight of a body always made him feel queasy, and these, after all, were children. The illumination provided by the penlight couldn't penetrate the frosted, semi-opaque plastic bag, but after a moment's fumbling he found the zipper and opened the bag down the middle.

No luck. As the narrow beam of light picked out one feature after another, it became obvious that this wasn't the one he sought. This body was a girl, about six years old. She must have met death quietly and bravely, he thought, for her face still held a gentle repose, and only the bulbous glands in her neck and the massive swollen knot in her abdomen marred her appearance.

"Merde," he said, vexed that he didn't find the body he was looking for on the first try. He zipped the bag shut angrily and turned around with another muttered curse, inadvertently knocking a pair of scissors onto the floor. The clatter sounded a loud alarm, and he froze breathless for a full minute, listening, before going on.

His second try was also unsuccessful, but on the third table he found what he was looking for. The wrinkled skin and balding skull were apparent as soon as he shined his light on the child's face, and the alien effect caused a spurt of fear that made him step back and wait several minutes for his heart to stop pounding. As he approached and looked again, he saw that, except for a large and bumpy forehead, the features weren't misshapen or distorted like those of a dwarf or midget. They were merely pinched and old, completely incongruous with the child's light, frail body.

His orders had been explicit. Steal the cadaver and get it back to the embassy by any means possible. If he could do so without discovery, so much the better, but the matter was considered so important that they were willing to abuse their privilege of extraterritoriality if the cadaver could just be brought onto the embassy grounds. The essential thing, he had been reminded over and over again, was not to allow the French to perform an autopsy.

He was trying to stuff the body into an oversized duffel bag when the police burst through the door, snapping on the overhead light, momentarily blinding him.

"Arrêtez-vous!"

Reflexly, not thinking, he ducked behind the table. Jerking his pistol from its shoulder holster, he began firing . . .

LOS ANGELES, *May 24, 1985*

"God damn it," George Mulligan snapped. He grimaced when the centrifuge stopped spinning and he got his first glimpse at the result of his labors. He'd made a mistake somewhere, and instead of the crisp clear lines of protein separation he'd anticipated, his gel electrophoresis was a blurred mess. It would have to be redone. Mulligan didn't tolerate frustration very well; like all scientists he hugely preferred the brilliant rapier flash of insight to the plodding revelations of systematic methodology. He especially hated having to do things over. "God damn it," he repeated a little louder.

"You swear too much, George," his friend Aaron said, chuckling, from the other side of the laboratory they shared. The laboratory was large but seemed smaller because of the chaotic clutter of beakers, pipettes, incubators, heating blocks, reagent bottles and other paraphernalia that covered its workbenches. Using a microtome, Aaron was cutting the brain tissue of a recently sacrificed white rat into ultrathin slices prior to fixing them to slides for staining.

Mulligan laughed too. It was an old joke between them. In lighter moods Mulligan loved grand and puffy overstatement, and he'd always stoutly maintained that profanity was the great safety valve of the psyche, without which Western civilization would surely founder. "I should never have let you talk me into this," he complained to Aaron. "If I'd stayed in medicine I could be a rich and happy internist today instead of the miserable little associate professor of biochemistry I let you talk me into becoming."

Aaron laughed again. "But then you'd never win the Nobel Prize," he said.

"You and your goddamn Nobel Prize," Mulligan groaned, his expression one of annoyance and amusement at the same time. The Nobel Prize was another running joke between them. It was the holy grail of modern science, and in the minds of thousands of researchers it bore the same relationship to genius and effort that the original grail bore to purity and chastity. He remembered the day when one of his professors of biochemistry had remarked that, no matter how old you were when you won the prize, the work that won it for you was always done before you were forty. Three years to go, Mulligan thought. He wondered for the thousandth time if he had let his ambitions subvert too entirely the rest of his life. Striving for the Nobel could easily become too much of a preoccupation. Mulligan smiled to himself at his vanity.

His complaint to Aaron was an old one. Though often repeated, it was never really serious. Ten years before, Mulligan had been a second-year resident in internal medicine at Bellevue in New York when Aaron Rosenberg, his closest friend from their undergraduate years together at Cornell, had approached him and said frankly, "George, you're too smart to be a doctor." At that time Aaron was a graduate student in neurobiology.

"That," Mulligan had rejoined promptly, "is one of the great snob statements of all time, right up there with Niels Bohr's contention that an interest in organic chemistry is the mark of a second-rate mind. What the hell do you mean I'm too smart to be a doctor?"

"You are," he'd insisted. "It's a waste of your talent. All a doctor has to have is a good memory; he never really has to think very hard. Nothing creative about it. You should be in research. Biochemistry research. Neurobiochemistry. You know you've always really wanted to do that. If you stay in medicine all you'll get is rich and overworked. But . . ." Aaron concluded, and a warm enthusiasm glowed in his normally parched Hebraic scholar's face, "if you go into biochemistry and work with me on studying the brain, I can practically guarantee that we'll win the Nobel Prize."

"We've had this discussion before," Mulligan had said. "Why bring it up again now?"

"Because I'm moving to California, to UCLA." Aaron had answered with an urgency in his voice that gave Mulligan the sensation of a last opportunity slipping away. "They've offered me an assistant professorship. This is probably the last chance I'll ever have to talk you into changing your career. There'd be no problem getting you into the graduate school. I'm sure of that. Besides, I hear the girls are prettier and easier in California, anyway."

Why does a man spend long years training for one career and then change to another? There may be dozens of reasons, any one of which might suffice. "In my case," Mulligan explained years later, "it was because some jerk seventeen year-old kid decided that I'd be happy practicing internal medicine for the rest of my life. The kid was wrong. And the fact that I was that seventeen-year-old kid doesn't make any difference."

What really happened was that, as the end of his residency neared, the prospect of an office practice seemed less and less appealing. Its gentle and kindly paternalism—listening to the elderly complain about how tired or constipated they were, doling out pills for hypertension and colds, sympathizing with the endless grievance against arthritis—was a lukewarm attraction. The stark dramas of medicine, when illness swept patients to the chasm and their doctors, nimble and clever at the edge of catastrophe, struggled to prevent their falling in, would be few and far between. That was the problem; Mulligan had been disheartened at the way older doctors' descriptions of their practices lacked excitement and eagerness. Maybe Aaron is right, he'd thought, his self-esteem not burdened by excessive modesty; maybe I am too smart to be a doctor.

The solution was to stay in academic medicine, to be on

15

the faculty of a teaching hospital. To do that, though, he'd need more education. By 1975 academic positions in medical schools no longer were awarded simply on the basis of clinical excellence. Increasingly, advanced training in the basic sciences, particularly biochemistry, was demanded.

So when he finished his residency, with little more than mild and occasional regret George Mulligan enrolled at the UCLA graduate school of biochemistry. He never went back to clinical medicine. He became trapped . . . trapped by a theory that occurred to him in his first year in graduate school and which had been the driving force of his life ever since, an idée fixe, an obsession—a theory about the genetics of human intelligence.

"Speculations on the Biochemical Nature of Human Intelligence" was the title of the paper he'd brashly published in *Science* in 1976. His ideas were then and remained controversial. Everything he'd done since that time, every new technique mastered, every new experiment designed, everything read and learned . . . all of it had been aimed at proving his theory.

So he stayed in biochemistry. Unlike many of his new colleagues, though, whose attitude toward doctors was a mixture of scorn and jealousy, Mulligan retained his admiration for physicians. He signed all his papers, "George Mulligan, M.D., Ph.D.," and he didn't love medicine less for having left it. Every so often he would stroll through the UCLA Hospital in the early morning to watch the residents on their rounds. There was an inherent fascination to human pathology, to physiology warped by disease, that he never lost. Patients whose kidneys no longer functioned, or whose heart rhythms were wildly chaotic, or who had cancers seeping through their bodies—Mulligan watched the struggle with a bittersweet nostalgia.

He was intense, ambitious, a man whose devotion to his work led him to exclude much else from his life. Curiosity, too, possessed and pushed him forward. Mulligan's was the sort of intellect that would follow a line of inquiry with the

16

same mesmerized fascination that makes a fish follow a shimmering bit of metal dangled in the water. Knowledge already acquired left him with a vague dissatisfaction. The fun was in the process itself, in the venturing into the unknown to extract its treasures.

And the human brain was among the greatest of unknowns.

He devoted little thought, though, to the social consequences of his discoveries. Knowledge was knowledge, pursued for its own sake. But it was one of those consequences that now, ten years later, led to his work being interrupted.

There was a soft knocking on the door of the laboratory. Mulligan and Aaron both looked up. Behind the frosted glass they could see the shadow of a man standing with his arms still poised to knock again.

"Probably a messenger from the Swedish Academy to tell us that we've won the prize at last," Mulligan said to Aaron. "Would you mind seeing who that is? I've got to throw this crap away."

He took the spoiled electrophoretic strips out of the centrifuge and walked with them to the special lead-lined trash receptacle for radioactive material. He'd returned to his bench and was starting to set up new gel panels when Aaron walked back into the lab, his normally stern expression wrinkling with amusement.

"I always knew you'd get into trouble, George," Aaron said, trying not to laugh, "but I never figured on anything like this."

Mulligan's interest was piqued. "Figured on what?" he asked, looking up.

Aaron gestured to the man walking into the lab behind him. He was a large man, bulky rather than tall, whose face looked as though it had been wrenched into a permanent scowl. There was a heavy, plaid-lined raincoat draped over his left shoulder. It suggested that he'd just arrived from a climate colder and wetter than that of southern California, and a vague aura of travel weariness that seemed to confirm the impression surrounded him.

"This fellow says he's from the CIA," Aaron said. Amusement turned up the corners of his eyes and mouth again. Aaron was enjoying this.

"What? From where?" Mulligan's voice was incredulous. An unexpected visit from the CIA could strain anyone's equanimity, whatever poise he'd acquired. The phrase instantly conjured up images of furtive men skulking about engaged in electronic eavesdropping, secret codes, bribery, and sexual blackmail. What could these jerks want with me? he wondered.

The large man brushed past Aaron and extended his hand, though his politeness seemed forced and artificial. "Brent Ridgely, Dr. Mulligan." He reached into his inside jacket pocket and produced a plastic-covered identity card after they shook hands.

Mulligan took the card and examined it carefully, pretending he knew what he was looking at, stalling, then gave up the attempt. "I'm afraid I wouldn't know a CIA identity card from a Japanese driver's license, anyway," he said. "Are you serious?"

"I'm always serious, Dr. Mulligan," Ridgely replied wearily, looking as though he meant it. "Anyway, I'm too tired to try to be funny. I have the right man, don't I? Dr. George Mulligan? The . . ." he stumbled over the word, "neurobiologist? I have a paper, a reprint, of yours here in my briefcase." He hoisted a battered attaché case to the laboratory benchtop and rummaged through it. "Here it is. 'Spéculations sur la nature biochimique de l'intelligence.' This is the French version, of course. But it is your paper, isn't it?"

Mulligan nodded slowly, perplexed. "I didn't know I was so famous," he said. "French translations and all. But, yes, that's mine. Why?" And what sinuous turn of events, he wondered, had led it to wind up, in French, in the hands of a CIA agent who couldn't even pronounce the words?

18

"Just trying to make sure we get the right man before committing ourselves," Ridgely answered.

Mulligan saw the smile disappear from Aaron's face.

"That's the real George Mulligan," Aaron said cautiously, edging around the bulky man to stand nearer his friend.

Ridgely noticed the tone of caution in Aaron's voice and turned toward him. "Nothing to be worried about," he said soothingly. He turned back to Mulligan and, reaching into his pocket again, produced a folded sheet of note paper. "The dean of the medical school said I'd find you here," he said, extending his arm.

"The dean?" Mulligan repeated. "How did the dean get into this?"

"He said to give you this if it would help you to make up your mind."

Make up my mind about what? Mulligan thought as he unfolded the paper. "George," the dean had written in longhand, "This man is what he says he is, a CIA agent. I checked. They need your help with something. He wouldn't say what it is, but apparently it's quite important. I've arranged for you to take a leave of absence for as long as it—whatever 'it' is—takes. Henry."

Mulligan handed the paper back to Ridgely. "This is rather sudden and unexpected, isn't it?" he asked. He squared his shoulders and unconsciously drew himself up to his full six feet. "What can I do for you, Mr. Ridgely?"

Ridgely sat down on one of the empty lab stools and rummaged through his overcoat until he found a pack of cigarettes. "May I?" Mulligan nodded. Ridgely wore a blue shirt with too tight a collar, and the veins in his neck stood out in purple abstract bas-relief. Mulligan was tempted to tell him that his appearance suggested someone straining to have a bowel movement, but Ridgely didn't seem the sort to take a joke. His nose was bulbous, with pitted scars, marred by a rhinophyma that undoubtedly condemned him to a reputation for alcoholism, deserved or not. But he had pale,

19

glaucous eyes that were cool and steady in their appraisal of Mulligan.

Mulligan endured Ridgely's inspection patiently. At thirty-seven he was still somewhere near the peak of his curve. The skepticism that was a professional obligation of a scientific investigator came naturally to him and was beginning to soften, with thin lines etched permanently on his forehead, an expression that sometimes verged on being too severe. Most women responded to that and found him masculine, steady and strong. His complexion was dark for someone with an Irish surname. He owed that to his mother, Italian by ancestry, and his slightly aquiline nose and gold-flecked brown eyes came from her as well. His eyes were piercing and intelligent, set deep in a lean face, and gave his gaze an intensity that sometimes made people around him wary and alert. Usually, though, his manner was the California one of relaxed and informal self-confidence. His black hair was as thick as ever, and where it was once looped slickly to one side in the best Ivy League style, it now lay loosely, California-tousled in easygoing disarray. When he'd left New York he'd vowed to abandon the necktie forever, and he was dressed now as he often was, in an open-necked blue sport shirt and gray corduroy slacks.

"We've had a request for your services from our French counterpart, the Deuxième Bureau," Ridgely said, exhaling a cloud of tobacco smoke.

Mulligan's face must have reflected his renewed astonishment, for Ridgely chuckled softly. "Everyone reacts the same way," he said reassuringly. "You've heard of the CIA and the Deuxième all your life, yet when you actually meet an agent you react as though we're characters out of comic books. There have to be real people, you know, staffing these agencies."

"You can hardly blame me for being a little surprised," Mulligan replied, slowly regaining his composure. "But you still haven't told me what you want with me."

People have at least several facets to their personalities.

Inside all American men slumbers an unfinished youth who yearns for the adventures he never had, who resents the relentless ordinariness of life. The slumbering youth inside George Mulligan now sat up, alert. CIA? Deuxième Bureau? This could be good, he thought.

Ridgely inhaled deeply. "You are, I am told, the only man in the world who can do certain . . ." he stumbled again over a word, "cytochemical studies on the brain."

"Which cytochemical studies?" Mulligan was momentarily puzzled. "There are many. And I'm not the only one who can do them."

"It must be the neurotransmitter enzyme assays, George," Aaron said. "They're the only ones that you do exclusively."

Ridgely scowled and blew a stream of smoke into the air. "I'm afraid I don't understand any of that," he said a little resentfully. "Could you explain what that is?"

"Sure. It's a radioimmunoassay." Mulligan tried courteously not to sound condescending or pompous. "Suppose you want to measure something precisely, very accurately, something that only exists in very tiny amounts and that can't be separated easily from other things. Like how much of a certain protein molecule there is in certain tissues. In this case what I measure is the amount of certain enzymes in the brain, the enzymes that make neurotransmitters . . ."

"Right," Ridgely said drily, nasally, interrupting Mulligan before the explanation went any further. He snubbed out his cigarette on his heel, a gesture of petty macho that Mulligan found irritating. "I'm not sure I understand any of it. Fortunately, I don't have to." He stood up and arched and rubbed his back. "How would you like to go to Paris?"

This gets better by the minute, Mulligan thought. "Same as anybody else," he replied. "I'd love to go to Paris. Depends who's paying."

"Guest of the United States Government."

Mulligan looked at Aaron and grinned. "Probability theory," he murmured, and they both laughed.

21

"What's that?" Ridgely asked quickly, annoyed.

"Sorry. An old private joke," Mulligan apologized, but laughed again. With Mulligan laughter was never far from the surface. His sense of humor was pervasive, wry and ironic. It readily detected human folly and on occasion had saved him from the mortal sin of taking himself too seriously. Only when he was angry or disturbed did it freeze into a caustic sarcasm. "Look," he said, "there are two possibilities here. You might be what you say you are, a CIA agent who pops up out of nowhere and wants me to pick up and go to Paris just like that. All this could be for real. On the other hand, you might be some sort of clever lunatic, and all this is an intricate joke. Which is more probable?"

"Very funny." Ridgely evidently failed to see the humor. "Look, there's a special autopsy to be done tomorrow in Paris, and your help has been requested. Something to do with those special studies you do. A Dr. Irene Sailland asked for you."

Mulligan chewed on his lower lip, a reflex gesture of uncertainty, for only a moment, then made up his mind. "And you're paying?" he asked again. It wasn't that he cared very much about the money; he just didn't have any.

Ridgely nodded again wearily. "Right."

"The ultimate luxury, then. Travel at someone else's expense. When do we leave?" He felt another surge of adventure.

"Today. Thank you for being so decisive." Ridgely looked at his watch. "It's ten o'clock now. Could you get a suitcase together by one? I've already made reservations for us on the three o'clock Air France flight from LAX. I think we can make it."

Mulligan returned to his apartment. Packing a suitcase posed few problems, since his interest in clothing was non-existent and his wardrobe scant. What do you wear to an autopsy, anyway? he wondered. The most impeccable taste might easily pass unnoticed. He threw in fresh underwear, socks, razor and toothbrush, then added tan gabardine slacks, several powder-blue dress shirts and, with some resignation, several ties. As a safeguard against an empty hour or two he added a few unread issues of the Journal of Clinical Investigation, but thought as he did so, what I really should be reading is "The Boy's Guide to Espionage in France." His brown tweed jacket with black elbow patches, a familiar friend, he draped on a hooked finger over his shoulder. He dragged from the depths of his closet an old and wrinkled raincoat which he folded into the suitcase. His passport was, fortunately, still valid, though it had been years since he'd used it. Curiosity and ambition left him little time for simple luxuries like foreign travel.

Ridgely had rented a car, so they drove to the airport. "What's in that paper of yours that makes these people in France ask for you?" he asked, making another attempt to understand what it was, though not taking his eyes from the freeway.

"Other than the immunoassay, you mean? I'm not sure. My theory, maybe." Mulligan wondered with some amusement what effect a leading statement like that would produce.

He found out immediately. Ridgely shot him a piercing glance. "What theory?" The CIA agent apparently had a sharp dislike for things he didn't understand and was deeply suspicious of men who made up theories.

Mulligan raised his hands in a pacifying gesture. A slightly mocking half-smile animated his lean face. "Don't get upset. Actually, the enzyme studies, the radioimmunoassay on the neurotransmitter enzymes, were developed to test the theory. It's a theory of comparative intelligence, why one species is smarter than another or one man smarter than another. It's fairly simple, really. The theory postulates that intelligence depends on two things: one, the numbers of cross-connections neurons make with each other, their numbers of axons and dendrites, and two, the speed and rapidity of signal transmission at the synapse. If your brain has twice the number of dendrites, it's twice as complicated, and you're twice as smart. If you can generate twice as many synaptic transmissions per second as someone else, you're twice as smart as he is. Simple enough."

"So simple even I can understand it," Ridgely said, not without a measure of gratitude. "But they can't want you in Paris just to explain that."

"I'd doubt it," Mulligan admitted. "Some people accept the theory and some don't. It's just possible, though," he added, grinning, "that I'm taken more seriously in France than I am here—like Jerry Lewis and Harold Robbins."

Ridgely wasn't in a mood for jokes. "How do these enzymes fit into the picture?"

"Good question. There's another part of the theory I haven't mentioned yet. That's what that paper you had was all about. That's this: the speed of repetition of the synapse is proportional to the concentration of neurotransmitter in the neuron. That, in turn, is proportional to the concentration of the enzymes that make neurotransmitters." Mulligan paused and looked at Ridgely. "I would have thought that you'd been told all this before."

Ridgely's dour expression relaxed, unexpectedly, the first indication of friendliness he'd shown. "We're not as efficient as you imagine. Anyway, this business in Paris came up quite suddenly. I don't know as much about you as you think I do. You're from New York, you're a neurobiochemist, whatever that is, you've been at UCLA for the past ten years. As of a year ago, at least, you weren't married, and I gather you're still not, since you would have mentioned your wife by now if you had one. But if it's any consolation, we're running a security check on you right now. I'll be able to tell you a lot more about you in a few days."

Mulligan was the sort of closet anarchist who instinctively bristled at invasions of his privacy, particularly if they came accompanied by a vague but assuming governmental authority. "Still not married," he said lightly, casually dissimulating his resentment.

24

They arrived at the airport. Ridgely was returning the car to the rental company when Mulligan asked, "What's all this about, anyway? You said something about an autopsy."

Ridgely looked around, evidently noting that a number of people were within earshot of them. "I'll tell you later," he said, and hoisted his suitcase out of the trunk, leaving Mulligan to do the same.

While waiting in the departure lounge to board their flight, Mulligan noticed that Ridgely stood with his back to the wall, positioning himself so that he could see the entire crowd, scanning it much in the way a security monitor scans the customers in a bank. Mulligan's questions met with only curt nods of dismissal or muttered half-answers, and the cryptic, evasive manner of his companion dampened his enthusiasm. He sat for half an hour in an uncomfortable silence, absorbed in second thoughts, wondering what he was getting into.

They were the last passengers to board the plane. Ridgely observed each passenger carefully, particularly staring at the one or two young women who looked for an inviting half second too long at Mulligan, at the lean, handsome man with the shock of unruly black hair and the intense troubling gaze. It was only when they were at last seated, presumably unwatched, on the airplane, and the airplane was safely in the air, that Ridgely finally ceased his vigilant circumspection. The high cabin seats and the murmur of voices around them seemed to ensure a private conversation. He ordered a drink, though, before he told Mulligan what he knew of the situation. "No particular reason not to let you in on everything," he said, stirring his bourbon with his index finger and staring at it contemplatively. "It's one of the odder events I've come across, and I've been in this business a long time. They told me to ask you if you knew anything about a disease called progeria."

Progeria? The name dredged from distant memory an impression of a disease he had encountered only once, in medical school years before. It was one of those diseases you had to see only once to remember forever—and hope you never saw again. Very rare, one of nature's more vicious aberrations, progeria was a genetic disorder that so altered the rhythms of life that a child aged at a greatly accelerated rate. Physiologically, childhood was finished by age four, followed by a grotesque and unsightly sexual maturation. By six or seven the changes of middle age—balding, sagging, wrinkling, perceptible slowing of reflexes—were clearly apparent. By eight or nine a true senescence had set in; the child, small for his age, now appeared like a tiny old man or woman, bent, fatigued, complaining of aches and pains. They died by age ten, sometimes younger, usually from a heart attack or stroke. Almost as a gratuitous cruelty, the child was feebleminded as well.

"It's a pretty rare disease," Mulligan said. "I've only seen one case of it, and that was many years ago. But so far as I know it has nothing to do with my work."

"Well, this kid seems to have had it, anyway."

"What kid?"

"The one that's going to be autopsied tomorrow. The Russian kid. About three weeks ago some weird-looking Russian kid shows up in Paris—that's what he had, progeria, I mean. The kid's dead now, of course." Ridgely stared out the window of the airplane for a moment, silent, watching the clouds slip by beneath them, then finished his drink at a gulp. "Amazing, dying of old age when you're only eight years old."

"Curve balls," Mulligan said.

"Pardon?"

"Curve balls. That's what we used to call nature's dirty tricks in medical school. Especially genetic diseases . . . the ones that seem particularly unfair."

"Medical school?" Ridgely looked at Mulligan quizzically. "They told me you were a biochemist, not a doctor."

Mulligan sipped his drink. "Past tense. Was. I'd finished my residency when I decided that what I really wanted was to study the brain, how it works. A simple obsession . . . the most easily explained psychopathology. I got interested in it, the brain I mean, and I wanted to find out how it worked."

Ridgely's eyebrows lifted again. After they'd been seated on the plane, he had loosened his tie and collar and his face had lost the choked expression it had had earlier. Sitting alongside him, Mulligan thought the man less imposing and intimidating, but more intelligent, than he'd appeared to be in the laboratory. "That happens in other fields, too," Ridgely mused, seeking some common ground to share with Mulligan. "That's what happened to me. I got interested in trying to find out what the Russians were up to."

"A simple obsession, then." Mulligan's smile faded slowly as he nodded. "I see. It was a *Russian* kid, wasn't it. But I still don't see what all this has to do with my work. My field is the genetics of intelligence."

"Where you fit in is this: this kid was smart, supersmart, smarter than anyone's ever seen before, according to what they told me. I think they want you to find out what made him tick."

Finally Mulligan understood why his presence had been requested. The child had been that rarest of creatures—an experiment of nature, when nature performed experiments that were either too difficult or too immoral for men to perform. Here was one such, a child whose intelligence was prodigious, vastly superior, and who had been considerate enough to die so that his brain might be studied. Evidently someone in Paris had read his paper, which explained its presence in French translation, and had thought that this would be an opportunity to prove or disprove his thesis, that the genetics of intelligence involved an increased concentration of neurotransmitter enzymes. But something was wrong.

"Smart?" he asked Ridgely. "That's not right. Children with progeria are retarded."

"Well, not this one." Ridgely signalled the stewardess and ordered another bourbon. He waited until it was served

27

before continuing. Mulligan began to think that the bulbous nose had been earned. "I'm told that this kid was really a phenomenon."

"Okay," Mulligan said, thinking the facts anomalous but accepting them for the moment. "Now we know where I fit in." He sipped his drink again and took a deep breath. "How do you fit in?" He asked the question without animosity but couldn't avoid letting a taunting edge creep into his voice. "It would never have occurred to me that the CIA was interested in neurobiochemistry."

"Not one of our usual concerns," Ridgely admitted. "But there's another part to the story." He lifted his head up, stretching his neck upward in a curious elongated maneuver, and swept another piercing gaze around the airplane cabin. Most of the passengers seemed to belong to a tour group and were clustered in the rear of the cabin. No one seemed to be paying any particular attention to them, and the gesture seemed to Mulligan to be laughably sinister. Ridgely lowered his voice further, assuring that it was inaudible to anyone in the seats ahead and behind. "We're interested in anything the KGB is interested in."

For a moment astonishment rendered Mulligan speechless, then he found his voice. "What is this, knee-jerk paranoia? Are you guys all crazy? What the hell's the KGB got to do with this?"

"Not so loud," Ridgely warned, a flash of irritation mobilizing the heavy features of his face. He tolerated Mulligan's contempt with a visible effort. "That's one of the things *we* want to find out."

CHAPTER TWO

Ridgely sat back in his seat, and, holding his voice low, related a tale that raised more questions than it answered. He knew only the bare outline of the story. A Russian boy, obviously a case of progeria, had mysteriously, seemingly from nowhere, appeared at the Institut de Biologie Moderne in Paris, asking for the French geneticist Dr. Irene Sailland. If what he said could be believed, he had run all the way from Leningrad to Paris. That was fantastic enough, but it soon became obvious that his intellectual abilities were even more fantastic, scarcely believable, far beyond anything in anyone's experience. He seemed to have been gravely weakened, though, by the privations and exhaustion of the journey. Its frailties unmasked, his aging body had succumbed and he died after having been in Paris for only a few weeks. The report was that a heart attack had finished him. Of course, they, the French doctors, wanted to do an autopsy, but the kid was so special that they wanted certain specific people to be in on it. Mulligan was one of them. While waiting for the experts to be assembled, the body had been placed in the hospital morgue of the Hôpital des Enfants.

"I still don't know how the KGB got into this," Mulligan said, finding his initital astonishment sliding into the allure of intrigue.

"Hold on. The plot thickens. I'm coming to that." While the body was lying in the morgue the night after his death, one of the night watchmen went down to look at it. Just a morbid curiosity, it seemed, to see this kid everyone had made such a fuss over. Fortuitous, though, because as he entered the morgue he heard someone moving about inside. At one in the morning no one was supposed to be there, and visiting the morgue without specific authorization was prohibited, anyway, so he beat a quick, quiet retreat and called the police. They didn't take long to arrive, but when they entered the morgue and called to the man to give himself up, he started shooting. One policeman was rather badly wounded, and the man himself was killed in the ensuing fire fight. "He was stuffing the boy's body into a duffel bag," Ridgely concluded, "like he wanted to take it somewhere."

"The KGB man?"

"Right. But that didn't come out right away." Ridgely finished his second drink, paused as though considering a third, then apparently decided against it and lit a cigarette instead. In an unconscious gesture of vexation, he blew the smoke out in a thin stream, unsettled by the thought of the rest of the story. "His identification papers said that he was a M. Jacques Martin of Grenoble, but when the Sureté looked into that it turned out that M. Jacques Martin was alive and well and, six months before, had reported that his pocket had been picked while on a trip to Paris. So he wasn't Jacques Martin."

"How did they discover who he was?"

"Who carries false identification? Criminals and spies, that's who. So the Sureté called in the Deuxième Bureau, and it didn't take them long to recognize the man as one of the KGB agents assigned to the Soviet Embassy in Paris.

The Deuxième watches everyone in the Russian Embassy, of course."

"Of course," Mulligan said drily. He had a momentary disagreeable sensation, as though he were trying to go through a door he had assumed was open, only to find that it was locked. Something dark and heavy was approaching. With difficulty, he shrugged off the premonition.

Intelligence gathering was a little like science, Ridgely went on to explain, obviously pleased with the analogy Serendipity—wasn't that the word the scientists used? Finding one thing when you'd been looking for another? Like the discovery of penicillin? The analogy to the methods of science was nearly perfect. You never knew where the next key to the puzzle would come from, and you could make up theories and test them by waiting to see if the next piece of information would fit. Information, though, might come from anywhere, any source, no matter how unexpected or obscure. That was why the Deuxième Bureau had informed the CIA of the incident with the KGB agent. It was standard procedure; Western intelligence services routinely shared such information with each other. You could never tell exactly where the next piece of the puzzle would come from.

"Just like science," Mulligan murmured, but the sarcasm was too mild for Ridgely to notice it. "Irene Sailland, you say?"

"Yes. Why? You know her?" Ridgely's eyebrows lifted again, peaked by sudden curiosity.

"Sorry to disappoint you," Mulligan said, noting that Ridgely's face brightened at the slimmest suggestion of conspiracy. "I know her only by reputation. But I can understand why a kid with progeria might seek her out."

"Oh? Why is that?" The large man leaned toward Mulligan, bulking over him, suddenly imposing again.

"Because of her theory of aging." Mulligan sat back in his seat and arched his back, feeling a need to stretch his muscles but unable to do so properly in the confined space. He disliked the sideways conversations of airplanes and was irritated at having his space invaded by the man sitting next to him. Partly to distract himself he tried to recall what he knew of Irene Sailland. He'd read her papers in the biochemical literature for the past several years. Now that he was about to meet her he spontaneously formed a vague mental picture of her as one of the aging, tight-lipped spinsters of science, an emaciated face continually puckered in disapproval. Not very appealing, but he'd admired her theory—it seemed as brash and insightful as his own. He wondered how to explain it to Ridgely.

"Think of it this way," he finally said. "Start with the premise, the fact, really, that aging and death are built into the system, that every living thing eventually ages and dies. Not by accident, you know, but by design. Nature wants us to get old and die. So . . . that must mean, that can only mean, that aging is genetically determined, that we have genes programmed for it."

"Depressing thought," Ridgely grunted, deflated, slumping back into his seat, "but hard to refute."

"The question then becomes, which genes? Sailland's theory is that it's those genes concerned with cellular energy metabolism, that something happens and not enough enzyme is made to serve the cell's energy needs. So the cells starve, so to speak. Your body's constantly tending to fall apart, you know. It needs constant infusions of energy for maintenance and repair. The theory's a guess, really, but a sensible one, energy metabolism being so basic. She's done some interesting experiments prolonging the life expectancy of cells in tissue culture by manipulating the genes involved. Nothing proven yet, of course, but it's the most sophisticated work ever done in this area. If I were a kid with progeria, I'd likely look to her as my only hope."

He didn't mention to Ridgely Sailland's contention that if those genes could be mapped, explored, understood, and their function controlled, the aging process might be retarded indefinitely. The suggestion of a biochemical foun-

32

tain of youth had met with general derision from the medical community, but if you were desperate enough, as a child with progeria would be, you'd grasp at anything.

Ridgely seemed to absorb the information slowly, mulling it over, but he looked at Mulligan with a new respect. The stewardess was passing out dinner trays, and Ridgely fell silent as he put his in place and snubbed out his cigarette. He ordered wine with his dinner but ate hungrily while waiting for it to arrive. "Thank God for Air France," he said, when the wine was finally poured. "It's the only airline that serves a decent wine with dinner."

"I should imagine you travel a lot," Mulligan ventured, pouring some for himself. "I mean, being interested in what the Russians are up to."

"One of the fringes," Ridgely said. He lifted his glass to the light, inspecting the claret carefully, then took a sip and savored it slowly. "Tell me some more about your own work. The genetics of intelligence, you say? How does that fit in with . . . neurobiochemistry?"

Mulligan dismissed the question with a nonchalant wave of his hand. "Biochemistry and genetics are so mixed together they can't even really be separated any more. It's all gotten more complicated than it used to be, more unnerving."

"Unnerving? That seems a strange thing to say. How's that?"

"Things don't hold still any more. Genetics used to be easy, at least in theory. DNA was the self-replicating molecule; it coded for protein molecules; the proteins performed either structural or enzymatic functions. It was a one-way street. Any kid could understand it. And only chance mutations, rare events like cosmic rays arriving from outer space, could alter it, could change the sequence of nucleic acids on the DNA and send life off in new directions. Things were solid; they didn't change very much."

"You mean that's not true any more?"

"No, no, that part of it is still true enough. But we've

33

learned a lot more, and now it seems that things are more complicated, more pliable, more malleable, less fixed. For one thing, it's not a one-way street any more. Somebody discovered an enzyme called reverse transcriptase that can make DNA from an RNA model. That opens up a whole new range of possibilities. Viruses have been shown to attach to human DNA, too . . . some cancers are thought to be caused that way. That's also something nobody ever thought of before. And chromosomes appear to be constantly rearranging themselves, exchanging genes, and the process changes the way genes are expressed and controlled. That's probably the explanation for that Russian kid, by the way . . . a chromosomal mutation, the kind of mutation that can alter the expression of many genes at once."

Ridgely looked at him closely, peering at his face intently for a minute, examining. "Why do I get the feeling that all of this bothers you? Is there something wrong with all this?"

He's more perceptive than I would have bet, Mulligan thought, but then I suppose you learn to be perceptive in his line of work. "Because it means things can be changed more easily than we imagined. The foundation of life is less stable than we've been taught. The ground under us is constantly moving."

"So?"

"So I don't know," Mulligan admitted, feeling sour and inarticulate. "I really don't know, but it does bother me. Maybe it's because I can't see where all this is going. We've learned so much so fast."

Ridgely finished his wine without saying anything else, and Mulligan wondered how much of what he'd said had been fully understood. It was hard to explain your uncertainties to people who weren't conversant with the science itself. The stewardess came and removed their trays. He looked through the tiny cabin window. The sky ahead was darkening as night and the airplane moved toward each other, and the cabin light dimmed as if in response to some unheard command. Ridgely fluffed a pillow for a nap, then nudged Mulligan in the ribs. "Anyway, let's get some sleep. We get to Paris about noon, their time, and we're going to have a long afternoon." He leaned the seat back and, half turning away from Mulligan, closed his eyes.

But Mulligan had trouble sleeping. He thought again of Irene Sailland and her theories, so very like his own. They might be speculative and controversial, but they were also why the Russian boy had run all the way to Paris.

They touched down at 11:35 A.M., Paris time. DeGaulle Airport was ultramodern, with chrome and tile and fluorescent lights, and voices over public loudspeakers doing their best to sound mechanical. Computerized message boards posted arrivals and departures. But with a little imagination the taxi ride from the airport to the city could serve as a journey through history in reverse. Epoques in French history surrounded the capital in concentric layers. The road took them first through the famous "red belt" of factories and working-class apartments that had grown up around the city since the end of the Second World War, populated by a French working class still petulantly loyal to the Communist Party. That layer behind, they plunged into the classical nonindustrial Paris of the eighteenth and nineteenth centuries, a jumble of sidewalk cafés, bulbous streetlights, elegant stores, massive public buildings and an occasional leftover cobblestone sidestreet. Finally they arrived at the medieval heart of the city near the Ile de la Cité.

Mulligan had visited the French capital before, though even if he hadn't, a thousand postcards and films would have made him familiar with its sights. Still, one's impression of Paris, like one's first impression of almost any modern city, could easily be overwhelmed and distorted by the automobile, which seemed even more noisy and noisome in a nineteenth-century than in a twentieth-century setting. Only in the central zone, where frustrated and furious drivers were forbidden to honk at each other, and where the narrowness of the boulevards and the density of pedestrian traffic slowed the rushing vehicles, could one capture some of Paris' grand nineteenth-century flavor. Stately stone-faced buildings, stuck side by side in weathered brown or gray, spilled their stairways onto the cement of cracked, root-uplifted sidewalks. Here and there one could discern behind the crowds a boulangerie or patisserie that had not yet succumbed to McDonald's or the *supermarché*.

Ridgely directed the taxi to the Hôtel Michelet-Odéon, a small, bland establishment that occupied a corner of the Place de l'Odéon in the heart of the Left Bank. Only two streets led into or out of the square. One side was occupied by the Théâtre National and another by a restaurant, both quiet during the day, so there was little car or foot traffic. "We like this place," he commented to Mulligan as they checked in. He left unspoken who "we" was. "No lobby to speak of, and the square is quiet. Anyone hanging around is sure to stand out."

They had an hour to shower, shave and change their clothes before going to the Institut de Biologie Moderne. Ridgely insisted on their having a cup of strong, bitter French coffee before going to the meeting. "We don't want to let fatigue make us miss anything," he said. "The autopsy has to be tomorrow—that's as long as it can wait. But we wanted to have a chance to hash things over before that got started. Our interest—mine and the Deuxième's—is simple. We want to find out what made the KGB so interested in this kid."

"And my meeting with the French doctors is going to help?"

"Maybe it will, maybe it won't. But it's worth a try."

Mulligan shrugged noncommittally. "Couldn't hurt."

They walked to their appointment, feeling the need for some activity after the long flight. The Institut wasn't far from their hotel. In Paris in May the trees were beginning to shade the streets again, losing winter's bareness as the new season's leaves came out. People, too, emerged from the huddled drabness of winter. In this neighborhood the

Left Bank was dominated by the Sorbonne, or rather by its students. Laden with books, appearing preoccupied, they hurried along the sidewalks or sat in animated conversation in the many cafés. City life was dominated by student life, and the students generated an atmosphere of eager curiosity that seemed to Mulligan too innocent to encompass espionage, too fresh to contain anything like the midnight theft of a mutant cadaver.

As they walked Mulligan reflected that you brought to cities the same preconceptions that you brought to everything else. On his previous trip to Paris, while he was an undergraduate at Cornell, his concerns had been with art museums and French girls. In medical school, though, he'd acquired a taste for medical history, an interest that, he found, helped him impose a sensible perspective on the tidal wave of technology that threatened to overwhelm the profession. For the physician, Paris, along with London, had been where medicine and surgery had begun the long vault from medieval superstition and bumbling to modern rationality and precision. Although the luminaries of medicine now lived on the other side of the Atlantic, and recent Nobel prizes had almost always been awarded to Americans, Mulligan thought of Paris as the home of Stephen Bichat, who performed twenty thousand autopsies, until he died in 1809 from the tuberculosis acquired from one of them; or René Laennec, who in 1804 got the idea for the stethoscope while watching boys play telegraph with a hollow log in the Bois de Boulogne; or Baron Larrey, who, as Napoleon's surgeon general, invented both the ambulance and the curved surgical suturing needle. Here Louis Pasteur pursued his explorations in bacteriology and led medicine to some of its greatest triumphs. Here Claude Bernard in the 1850s had defined the rules of experimental physiology.

The Institut de Biologie Moderne, situated several blocks north of the Luxemberg Gardens, was a series of gray stone buildings ringing a triangular courtyard, gravel covered and shaded by several old plane trees. Architectural harmony had been preserved by maintaining unchanged the exterior facing of the buildings, complete with statues and winged gargoyles, but the interiors had been renovated to provide modern office, library, and laboratory facilities. If physics had been the preeminent science of the twentieth century, biology here bid openly to be that of the twenty-first. The Institut was a major enterprise, visibly supported by massive funds, yet the atmosphere was one of quiet academic solidity. The experiments produced here, Mulligan sensed, would be characterized by the most rigorous methods, while the explanations of the results would have that passionate attachment to logic for which the French were so justly famous.

The second floor conference room into which Mulligan and Ridgely were shown conveyed the same impression. It was a large room, perhaps twenty by forty feet. Oak wainscoting set off light blue walls from which portraits of Pasteur and Bernard sternly looked down. They seemed to challenge you to match their achievements. In the center of the room a heavy oak conference table was surrounded by dark red leather easy chairs, into one of which Mulligan sank with gratitude.

They were joined shortly by two men and a woman. The first man was Pierre Legras, the Deuxième Bureau's man, a stout man of about fifty, with a ruddy complexion and a huge graying mustache. He puffed continuously on a dark meerschaum pipe, from which he sent up clouds of pungent but not unpleasant smoke. Dressed in a double-breasted tweed suit, he had the air, as only a French *fonctionnaire* could, of a man sartorially frozen at about 1896. Something in his manner reeked of admiration for Charles de Gaulle and of suspicion of anything not French.

Dr. Guy Lussac was the second man. Professor of pediatrics at the Hôpital des Enfants, he had been in charge of the medical care given the Russian boy. Lussac was a tiny man with a thin face and piercing eyes, bursting with more energy than his wiry body could contain. Even sitting, he

seemed constantly in motion, changing positions, folding
and unfolding his arms, a cascade of expressions constantly
altering his face. His courteous surface was broken by an
acrid impatience—a man of superior intellect who resented
having to slow the pace of his thought to accommodate others. He had a way of glancing frequently at his watch that
made you feel you were wasting his time, and, during their
talk, he seemed to regard the presence of the intelligence
agents as an annoyance, turning discussion away from the
true object of inquiry.

The woman was Irene Sailland. Her appearance was a
complete surprise. She was taller than most women, coolly
elegant and poised. She paused in the doorway for a second
or two as she entered the room, quickly appraising Mulligan
and Ridgely as they stood up. Her movements were graceful and faintly aristocratic, like those of a ballet dancer. Mulligan guessed her age as about the same as his own. Her face
was linear rather than round, with regular features. Olive-
tan skin suggesting a southern Mediterranean ancestry
stretched smooth and translucent over high cheekbones, setting off a narrow, straight nose and expressive mouth. Her
eyes were dark brown, enlivened by tiny irregular reflections of yellow and green. She cut her brown hair straight
and practical at shoulder length, and wore little makeup.
Her beauty was quiet and subdued, accepted, no attempt
made either to amplify or conceal it. In figure she was
slender but not delicate; a blue sweater curved gracefully
over breasts large enough to arouse involuntary feelings.
Mulligan found her powerfully attractive. This gets better
and better, he thought.

"*Enchanté, madame.*" Mulligan struggled to remember his
French as the introductions were made, suddenly conscious
that stumbling would make him appear contrived and ridiculous. "*Il me semble que je vous connais déjà.*"

She looked pleased and smiled at him warmly. The faint
fragrance of her perfume came to him and filled his head as
they shook hands. Her voice was a husky, melodic con-

39

tralto. *"Merci, monsieur. Moi, aussi, il me semble que je vous connais, j'ai tellement entendu parler de vous et de votre travail."*

"Speak English," Ridgely commanded curtly, annoyed. He turned to Mulligan. "You didn't tell me you spoke French."

"Only a little," Mulligan said, not taking his eyes from her, noting with relief that she wore no wedding ring. "You didn't ask." He sat down across the table from her, so that he could look at her without having to turn his head.

Legras presided and spoke first, in heavily accented English, in deference to Ridgely. He puffed on his pipe whenever he had to pause to think of the English word, which was often, and soon the air was filled with the odor of his tobacco. "What we want to know," he began, somewhat didactic at first, "is why, why the KGB would take such chances. What might be their motivation? It is most unlike them. Please keep this thought in mind." He reiterated the story of the KGB agent who'd been caught attempting to steal the cadaver. The way he told it, the tale seemed enmeshed in a heavy fabric of fatalism, a sense that it had all been ordained by an unseen intelligence for an unknown but sinister purpose. Ridgely had recounted the same events; but his version of the story had lacked that sense of predestination, favoring pure chance as the decisive element. Mulligan wondered who was right. Legras concluded with a strangely enthusiastic admonition. "An event like this can be a ray of light shining into the dark corners of the Kremlin."

"Wonderful," snorted Ridgely, unimpressed by the melodrama. "All we have to do is figure it out."

Dr. Lussac waved his arms vigorously, as though to clear the air simultaneously of both the clouds of smoke and the foolish yammerings of intelligence agents. "This isn't political at all," he protested loudly, jittery and nervous, pushing back his chair, slapping his fingers repeatedly on the edge of the table. "You don't seem to realize how extraordinary Ivan was. His importance is biological, not political."

"That's to be determined," Ridgely stated flatly, clearly

not going to allow himself to be influenced by a histrionic French pediatrician.

"That was his name—Ivan?" Mulligan asked.

"Yes. At first, you know, we thought he might die right away." Lussac addressed his comments to Mulligan, doctor to doctor. A fellow physician might appreciate what these thick-witted spies could never understand.

"Why? Was he ill?"

"Nearly dead. Totally exhausted, dehydrated, malnourished."

"Dr. Lussac stayed at his bedside continuously," Irene Sailland said. She spoke English easily, with only a slight accent. "He came here first, to the Institut, but we have no hospital facilities here, of course. Fortunately, the Hôpital des Enfants is nearby, so we put him there where he could be properly cared for."

"All the difficulties were correctable," Lussac continued, less irritated now as he recalled the child. "Except one."

"Age?"

Lussac nodded. "The one thing we can't overcome. No matter how clever we are."

"We saw right away that he had progeria," Irene Sailland said to Mulligan, "though later we learned it wasn't so simple. But what other disease makes a boy of eight look like a man of sixty?"

"He had one last burst of vigor left in him, though," Lussac interjected, raising a clenched fist, "one last grasp at life. The tenacity . . ." He hissed the words through biting teeth. "The tenacity with which he clung to life . . . that will to overcome the dumb animal passivity that slides into death . . . it was extraordinary."

Irene Sailland spoke again. Her beauty was distracting. "At first we knew nothing about him, of course. Not even that he was Russian. He slept most of the time, and ate. Only after several days did we begin to learn something about him."

Lussac resumed the narrative. "The first task was to keep

him alive, though our efforts were hampered by the fact that there was so much that frightened him. He was terrified most of the time. Delirious, really, at first. There was so much that was unfamiliar. Intravenous infusions, for example, sent him into a frenzy of fear and rage. He'd tear the needles out of his veins with absolutely no regard for any pain or damage he was inflicting on himself. But his strength! My God!"

"What's that?" Ridgely asked. "What's that you said? Strength?"

"It was incredible. Incredible! It took three men to subdue him. Only Dr. Sailland could calm him . . . almost like mother and child."

A crimson blush of embarrassment suffused her cheeks. "Not exactly. More like victim and hoped-for savior. He knew, you see, that he had a disease that would soon take his life. I don't know how he knew that, but he did. He hoped I could save him." She paused, and her voice dropped to a near whisper. "I couldn't, of course." An awareness of defeat hung heavily in the air. It was obvious that her interest in Ivan had been more than detached and clinical.

"Why would Ivan think that in the first place?" Ridgely asked, leaning forward, staring at her. His question was accusative, as though he suspected she had been party to something . . .

He already knows the answer to that, Mulligan thought, angry at Ridgely for playing the bad cop. What's he hope to gain by questioning her this way?

"Because, sir," Dr. Lussac answered for her, "Dr. Sailland is world renowned for her work in the genetics of aging. Ivan was carrying a Russian biochemical journal with a translation of one of her papers. The only thing he managed to say when he arrived was, 'Dr. Irene Sailland, Institut de Biologie Moderne, Paris,' over and over again, as though it were a beacon guiding him." Lussac's eyes darted nervously back and forth between Ridgely and Legras. "You know, when Banting and Best first announced the discovery of insulin in 1923, within weeks diabetics from all over the world had made their way to Toronto and were begging for treatment with it. When people are desperate they do desperate things. Obviously Ivan came to Dr. Sailland as his last hope."

"That's a clue, isn't it?" Legras asked.

"Clue to what?" Mulligan said, though he saw Ridgely nodding assent.

"Ordinary families don't subscribe to biochemical journals, do they? Of course not. So he must have been somewhere where a journal like that could fall into his hands."

"A university library, most likely," Mulligan said. "You'd be surprised, though, at the places biochemistry journals turn up. Thousand of students, for instance, might take it and leave copies almost anywhere. But, Dr. Lussac, didn't he say where he came from?"

"Never. Not a word. Only that he was from Leningrad. Nothing more. He never once mentioned the name of either a person or a place. Never."

"Why not?" asked Ridgely.

Irene Sailland ignored him completely. She gazed into space, and her eyes had the dreamy far-off look of someone whose mind is partly in the present, partly lost in memory. A slight frown tightened her lips. "I never could be sure," she said. "He was concealing something. He wasn't just being secretive, I'm sure of that. He seemed to want to answer our questions but didn't dare. I always sensed that it was for fear of betraying someone, someone he'd left behind, someone in trouble."

"Another clue?" Ridgely asked.

She made a gesture of vexation, rose from her chair and walked to the window, where she stood for a moment looking down into the courtyard. Her face was partly shadowed by her hair, and Mulligan could see in it the downward tug of dejection. She seemed to be struggling to overcome an inner barrier. He watched her with sympathy as she took a deep breath and sighed. "He was a *child*, you know," she said at last, initially speaking out the window, then turning to face the others, "a child, only eight years old. It's true that his ability to learn and to think was profound, astonishing even, but he didn't know enough when he got here to realize that I couldn't do anything to help him. The article of mine that he had read was pure speculation . . . theoretical . . . good only to indicate directions for research." She turned to the window again, her composure verging on dissolution. "He cried for hours when he learned that."

"When did you learn how intelligent he was? How?" Mulligan asked.

She smiled at Mulligan, grateful that he had changed the subject to one which provoked less discomfort. "After he got better, you know, when he wasn't delirious any more, we began to talk to him, to find out who he was, how he got to Paris, did he have a family—all the questions that had been bothering us about him. The extent of his intelligence wasn't obvious right from the start. It was more like one of those realizations that grow on one slowly until, with a snap, one becomes aware of them. The first clues came from his use of French. When he got here he could speak French only a little. What was astonishing was how fast he learned more. Once we provided him with reading material and a French dictionary his vocabulary seemed to increase by at least several hundred words a day."

"It was *more* than a photogrpahic memory," Lussac interrupted. "It was incredible. *Incroyable.* Much more than a perfect memory."

"How so?" Ridgely had leaned back and half-closed his eyes while Irene Sailland was speaking, and his voice rumbled out of a seeming inattentiveness.

"People with photographic memories can often recite whole chapters of books perfectly. That's no problem for them. But, ask them to integrate that with other information, to use it, and you see that their intelligence is really quite ordinary. Not so little Ivan. He could work with information, adapt it, be creative with it."

"True intelligence, in short," Mulligan murmured.

"Yes, yes." Lussac said excitedly. "We tested his IQ once, but it didn't do any good. We didn't learn anything useful. We gave him one of the standard IQ tests that all French schoolchildren are required to take. But we couldn't get a result that meant anything."

"Why not?"

"Because he didn't miss a single question. He was perfect. All IQ tests presuppose that you're going to miss a certain number of questions. We don't know how to score a perfect test. You could say he had an IQ of five or six hundred if you wanted to, though I'm not sure what that would mean."

Mulligan glanced briefly at Ridgely. The heavy features of the man's face were relaxed, his eyes nearly closed beside the bulbous red nose, contemplative as he listened to the description of Ivan. He doesn't understand at all, Mulligan thought; he doesn't see what this means. An experiment of nature like Ivan was a sudden and unexpected opportunity, a hole torn in the curtain of ignorance shrouding nature's secrets. Studies on a brain specimen from such an experiment could be more than a vindication of his theory; there could be a great leap forward in knowledge.

Irene Sailland sat down again across the table from Mulligan. She brushed her fingers through her hair once and then shook her head as though to clear it of foolish sentimentality. Still, despite her effort at objectivity, there was in her manner the same sense of awe and wonder Mulligan had sensed in Lussac, though made more gentle by a muted, hesitant affection.

"His courage never failed him," she said. "Even after he found out I couldn't help him. He persevered to the very end. Perhaps it was just desperation, the fact that he had nowhere else to turn. The body of human knowledge contains, you know, so very little concerning the biochemistry of aging. He set out to discover for himself what he needed to know."

Dr. Lussac interrupted her again, politeness pushed aside by rush and energy. His flinging hand gestures accentuated a voice already raised in emphasis, and his balding head bobbed up and down. "Dr. Sailland and I became his teachers. Never was there such a student! Never! We could scarcely keep up with him! Mathematics seemed trivial to him, trivial, the easiest thing to learn, mere symbolic deductive logic, child's play. That's really what made us realize we were dealing with a true intelligence. How many people have you met who can do cube roots of seven-digit numbers in their heads? When we taught him calculus it seemed a game, an infantile bit of mental acrobatics. He learned it in a week."

"But the math required for biochemistry isn't very hard," Mulligan said.

"That's true, that's true." Lussac took out a handkerchief and wiped his forehead of the small beads of sweat beginning to form there. "And because of that we never had a chance to see what he could really do. We didn't stay long enough with mathematics. Everything we did, you see, was focussed on the problem of keeping him alive . . ."

"Time was the great enemy," Irene said. "There was never enough time. He knew—we all knew—that unless he could find out what was wrong with him, unless we could suppress the genes that were making him age so fast . . ."

"Are you sure it was genetic?" The question seemed superfluous, but Legras asked it anyway.

"What else?" Lussac's contempt was withering.

"Time was the enemy," Irene repeated, unruffled by the interruption. "He read textbooks in molecular genetics as though they were novels, imprinting whole pages of information in just a few minutes. We were just starting to use the laboratory when the end came."

"How did he die?" Mulligan asked gently.

"He died one afternoon in the laboratory," she said. She paused a moment before continuing. A suggestion of a tear formed in her eyes, so that she shook her head again to clear it, and her hair swished gently around her sad and beautiful face. "Sitting on the laboratory stool, he looked like a small balding old man, a figure comical and grotesque at the same time, with large owl eyes that reached beyond his nose and chin. Suddenly he sat straight up and cried out, as though something had suddenly seized him. His hand went to his chest. 'Dr. Sailland!' he called out to me, 'Dr. Sailland!' He knew, of course, what it was, the fatal heart attack. He had fallen to the floor by the time I reached him. He couldn't speak, but I could see the agony in his eyes as the pain grew worse. The agony and the despair. Thank God it didn't take him long to die, only a few minutes and he was gone." She looked down at her hands folded on the table in front of her and then looked directly at Mulligan, although she sounded as though she were talking to herself. "I wonder sometimes if he might have succeeded if he had had more time, if he might have evaded that awful sentence of doom. It did seem to us that there was nothing beyond the reach of his genius."

Shafts of pale yellow light, a waning afternoon slant, came through the window, illuminating the chaotic and pointless frenzy of dust in the air. The sense of futility and loss echoing in her voice made Mulligan suddenly feel ghoulish. The experiment of nature had been, after all, a human being, a child; the impervious indifference one brought to the cytochemical study of rat brains crumbled at the touch of human vulnerability.

Lussac picked up the thread of the narrative. "After he died, we redoubled our efforts to find out where he had come from, how he had got to Paris, whom he belonged to . . ."

"Hadn't you done that before?" Ridgely asked.

"We had alerted the police, of course, when he first arrived, to ask if there had been any inquiries about lost Russian boys. Had any tourists, or children of Russian Embassy or trade personnel, got lost? Any missing persons reports? There was none. Then we consulted the Russian Embassy, but they didn't seem to know anything, either."

"That's how the KGB learned the boy was here, then,"

Ridgely said. "There are always several KGB men in every Russian Embassy."

"Actually," Legras said, "in this embassy there are seventeen." Everyone looked at him in astonishment. "I have counted them myself. It's a big embassy."

"Then why the delay?" Mulligan asked. "Why the three-week delay before they tried to steal the body? Or did they deliberately wait until he died before doing anything?"

"Probably nothing so sinister." Legras' mouth turned down at the corners and his hand wafted the air in a wry Gallic gesture of dismissal. "Nothing so devious." He rose to his feet and stretched. The movement conveyed boredom. "Espionage is like everything else, you know—hopelessly trapped in bureaucracy. Most likely it just took that long for the bureaucrats in Moscow to put two and two together. It probably went something like this: the Foreign Ministry received a low-priority report from their Paris embassy that a child with a strange congenital disease, apparently Russian, had surfaced in Paris. No one knew how he got there. Usually not much attention is paid to such reports."

"That's true enough," Ridgely concurred.

"It probably just took three weeks to correlate that report with whatever kind of missing persons report was filed wherever he came from. Then it took a while to decide what to do. By that time Ivan had died."

"But why the KGB?" Mulligan persisted. "Why steal the body? Couldn't they just come to you and say, 'Look here, this child was a Soviet citizen and we'd like to take his body back to the Soviet Union.'? Why not just do that? Isn't that a lot easier than sneaking around trying to steal cadavers from hospital morgues? What would they do if a member of a trade delegation died?"

"The obvious isn't necessarily easier." Legras relit his pipe and tamped it. "Not necessarily easier at all. Don't forget, this was a child and therefore covered by several stringent protections of French law. That could complicate things quite a bit. It wouldn't be enough for the Soviet Embassy just to say the boy was Russian, and therefore claim the body. We wouldn't release it on that basis. Especially considering how he got here. They'd have to show proper documentation of citizenship, for example, or proof of parentage."

"They *couldn't.*" Ridgely's eyes blazed with sudden insight and his voice crackled with the flat finality of conviction that tolerates no disagreement. "They couldn't document citizenship."

"What's that?" Legras snatched his pipe from his mouth.

"Don't you see? That's why they had to steal the body. It was impossible for them to prove he was a Soviet citizen."

"Why couldn't they?" Irene Sailland asked. "I still don't understand. Surely the parents could come forward."

"Maybe the parents knew nothing about it. Look . . ." Ridgely's excitement grew as his thoughts carried him along. "Suppose the kid was taken from his parents at an early age, as soon as it became clear that he was some kind of freaky mutation? That would make it hard to bring the parents back into the picture when the kid runs away to Paris. Suppose he lived in some kind of institution . . ."

"That would be understandable enough, I suppose," Mulligan said. "They'd want to study him, try to understand how it had happened, perhaps give him a special education and training, develop his abilities . . . "

"Not that," Irene Sailland interrupted him. "I don't think they ever did that. One of his resentments, one of the few things he confided in me, was that he'd not ever been allowed free access to any library where he might have learned things at will. You got the feeling that whoever raised him in Russia was afraid of him, took care that he never learned too much."

"That might account," Lussac added, "for why he seemed to know so little about where he came from and why he refused to talk about it."

49

Legras summed up. "At any rate, that will have to be our current theory. For some reason the Soviet Embassy was unable to claim the body through normal channels and therefore tried to steal it. The question, of course, is . . . why?"

Lussac said, "For the same reason we want the cadaver—they want to do an autopsy. To find out everything they can about how it happened, what the mutation was. That's just what we want to do." He turned to Mulligan. "You explain it to them."

"What Dr. Lussac is saying," Mulligan explained carefully, "is that if the KGB got involved it was only to steal the body back. The child himself had nothing to do with communist plots or the machinations of the KGB. You have to understand that a mutation like this is vanishingly rare. It is an opportunity to learn that we might never get again."

Legras had his pipe back between his teeth, biting on it fiercely, the gray curling smoke forcing a squint to his eyes. His head turned side to side in silent disagreement, and he spoke between clenched teeth. "You don't know the Russians the way I do. Anyway, it's a crime to steal a cadaver. And now one of their agents has been killed trying to do it. They have a lot of explaining to do."

"If you choose to demand an explanation," Ridgely mumbled, as though to himself.

"Why wouldn't you?" Mulligan asked.

Ridgely smiled beatifically, exuding parental concern. "Sometimes in this business we just pretend nothing has happened even when we know something has happened. It's a little game we play. Just to confound the enemy and see what happens next. Sometimes you gain an advantage by pretending you don't know something."

"Why, you sly old fox," Mulligan said sarcastically, unimpressed and annoyed that Ridgely didn't appear to understand the importance of the mutation.

"But this crime they *did* commit," Legras said. "Therefore, they must have been willing to run the risk, and we know the Russians hate to run risks, unless the matter is of very great importance."

"It doesn't make sense," Mulligan said, thinking aloud. "No sense at all. I'm sorry, Dr. Lussac, but I don't understand it either. Why go to such lengths, run such risks? Anything learned from Ivan's autopsy would be published in the scientific journals, anyway. The Russians would learn it nearly as soon as we did."

"They'd want to correlate the autopsy findings with the clinical observations," Lussac said, clinging to his theory. "Or maybe they'd be looking for something special."

"Still," Mulligan mused, "still, it doesn't seem worth the risk, unless . . ." His voice faded away as a suspicion chafed first at the edge of consciousness, then emerged. The others looked at him quietly. He bolted upright and looked around the table. "It *does* make sense," he announced, triumphant at having figured it out, "if you look at it this way. *They* don't want the body. They just don't want *us* to have it. They might know everything they want to know already, but they're afraid the autopsy will reveal something they don't want us to know. That's why they took the risk—to prevent our finding out whatever that something is." As he spoke Mulligan felt again an uncomfortable stir, a sense of apprehension and enclosure, such as a fish might feel when just becoming aware that a net has settled around him.

"*C'est ça,*" Legras nodded, unconsciously slipping into French. "*C'est ça exactement.*"

Once spoken, the thought became one of those self-evident ideas that made everyone wonder why he hadn't thought of it before. In the brief silence that followed a church bell could be heard striking five times; the day was nearly done. Outside, the shadows had perceptibly lengthened across the courtyard.

Lussac stood up. "Well, the autopsy is scheduled for tomorrow at 10:00 A.M. At the hospital. We knew it would be important," he said, directing his comments to Mulligan. "That's why we sent for you. We know of no one else who can do the cytochemical investigations you can."

Mulligan found the flattery embarrassing and waved it aside. "At least I get a free trip to Paris out of this. I can't do much here, though. Everything I need for the enzyme analyses—the antibodies, mostly—is back in L.A. What I can do here is to get the right specimen of the brain to study."

"You'll be here only a few days, then?" Irene Sailland asked. Was there regret in her voice, or did he make it up?

"I suppose so." He was aware again of her attractiveness and was traversed by a feeling of regret that he wouldn't be able to be with her longer.

The meeting adjourned. As they walked out of the conference room, Dr. Lussac asked Mulligan if he'd care to join him for an apéritif.

"Thank you, yes," Mulligan said. A drink seemed very welcome. He glanced at Ridgely, who nodded. Mulligan then looked at Irene. "Perhaps Dr. Sailland would like to join us as well."

"It's Irene," she said. "Yes, I would. Give me a minute to get my coat."

"Fine. I'm George, then."

When she joined them outside the Institut a brisk wind had risen and Mulligan regretted he had no overcoat of his own. They walked on the crowded sidewalk to a nearby café, Les Mouches Volantes, and sat at an inside table near the window. The café was crowded with people killing time over coffee or a glass of wine, waiting for traffic to subside before making their way home. Mulligan realized how tired he was and was grateful for the biting, stimulating taste of the Pernod that Lussac ordered for all of them.

"Not exactly ordinary events in my life," Mulligan said, confessing his boyish enjoyment of the adventure. The little needle of apprehension he felt only served to make it more delicious. He sipped the Pernod. "It's all bizarre. KGB agents, incredible IQ's, boys running all the way from Leningrad to Paris. Did he really do that, by the way? Did you believe it?"

"Oh, yes," Irene said. "No question about it." She nodded her head slowly, smiling, pleased by a memory. "Once you saw him run, you believed it easily."

Dr. Lussac put his glass down on the table. He seemed more relaxed without the intelligence agents around, with less of the twitching, avian wariness he'd had in the conference room. The memory seemed to please him, too. "You really had to see it, George. His endurance was phenomenal. We got to see it by chance, actually. We'd forgotten that he said he'd run all the way to Paris . . . I suppose we just didn't take it literally. One afternoon, though, he asked to go for a walk. It was a fine spring day, just after a rain, cool and invigorating. Maybe that's what inspired him, or maybe his muscles just needed the exercise. We went to the Bois de Boulogne. There's a jogging track there, a path really. Lots of French people have taken up 'le jogging.' Anyway, Ivan just started running. And he ran, and he ran. He ran for three hours, and I think he must have covered thirty kilometers by the time he stopped."

"So he had both strength and endurance?"

Lussac nodded brusquely. "Extraordinary. We've asked an expert in muscle metabolism to come to the autopsy, too." He looked at his watch. "I've got to go soon. My family sees too little of me as it is. What do you think of our spies?"

"Doctors in America have that problem, too. Legras and Ridgely? They're just doing their jobs, I suppose. Though, frankly, I don't think there's much chance we'll ever know what this is really all about."

"The autopsy should give us some clues."

"Maybe."

Lussac stood up and threw a twenty-franc note on the

table. "No, no," he said as Mulligan started to protest. "My invitation. But I have to leave. Until tomorrow morning, then."

"What about you, Irene," Mulligan asked after Lussac had left them. "No family to return home to?"

She looked at him steadily for what seemed a long time before replying, as though making up her mind whether or not to reveal anything of herself to him. In the moment of repose her face was elegant, delicate, then softened by a small satisfied smile. "My husband died two years ago," she said finally in her low voice. "He'd been ill for a long time, so we never had any children."

Mulligan flushed, chagrined. "I'm sorry . . . I didn't mean to pry."

"It's all right. It's natural enough to ask an acquaintance about his family. But what about you?"

"Afraid I'm alone in the world, too. Too ambitious for marriage, I suppose."

"Ah, ambition, the American disease." Her face relaxed into a mocking grin, warm and affectionate, and little friendly wrinkles appeared at the corners of her eyes.

"Perhaps we could discuss that over dinner," Mulligan said just smoothly enough. "It's a topic that can go on for hours."

She laughed aloud and reached her hand across the table to touch his arm lightly. "All right. I know just the place."

They left the café and walked toward the Seine, toward the Ile de la Cité. Evening had settled and it was getting colder, and they turned their collars up against the wind. Mulligan resisted an inclination to put his arm around her. As they approached the river he could see the great gray medieval bulk of Notre Dame Cathedral looming up out of the darkness. He thought, perhaps irrelevantly, that such a monument could not be built in the twentieth century. The forces of mystery and the unknown, inspiring obedience and worship, led in the twentieth century more readily to research grants than to Gothic cathedrals. They walked along the riverbank, on the broad esplanade where the bookstalls were closing up for the night. The cold wet stones of the cathedral seemed to emerge from and blend with the mist rising from the river; its walls were magically sustained and lifted by the soaring arch of the flying buttresses. Above the cathedral a few stars began to penetrate the glare of city lights. Though the remnant of a vanished mentality, Notre Dame could still inspire awe and dread, could still diminish the stature of a man.

"I know what you're thinking," she said, watching him observe the cathedral. "You're wondering how we got from there to here, from then to now."

"Do you always read minds?"

She laughed again and took her hand from the pocket of her overcoat and put it into his. "Only people I like."

The restaurant she took him to was nearly empty, and the cuisine favored quality over ostentation. They talked for a while about restaurants and cities, and Mulligan was immensely grateful she wasn't the snob most French people are about such things. Warmed by the wine and the dinner, she slowly lost the caution and circumspection she'd had all afternoon. The light from the dinner candle, as she picked up her wine glass with both hands and swirled the liquid slowly, made her skin appear a dusky bronze. Her beauty was deepened by character and intelligence and rendered him nearly helpless. He watched, entranced, as the lambent candlelight played over her face.

"I was thinking of what you said about being alone in the world," she said. An inner cord of sadness, beyond the reach of the wine and the warmth between them, appeared to shadow and trouble her. "Alone in the world. That's how little Ivan seemed. So alone. Not only the loneliness of the knowledge that he would die soon. More than that, George. He seemed such a stranger, a visitor from another world who wanted desperately to have a friend but who could find no one enough like himself to be friends with." Her eyes became luminous and moist, and for a moment he thought she would cry. Later, thinking about it, he realized that it was at that moment that he fell in love with her.

As they came out of the restaurant into the evening air something across the street caught Mulligan's eye. A darker shadow flickered within the shadow of a building. There seemed the fleeting glimpse of a face and eyes, too brief to be sure. A man? Someone following and watching them? CIA? KGB? *This is ridiculous,* Mulligan thought, and signalled for a taxi.

CHAPTER THREE

For as long as he could remember Mulligan had hated autopsies, an unprofessional distaste for which he'd had to apologize on more than one occasion. There were several reasons for it. An autopsy was, to a physician, a kind of test; it might reveal the presence of diagnoses totally unsuspected in life, which made it an unwanted reminder of fallibility. Death was, too, both insult and enemy, the stillness of the cadaver a silent reproach, the defeat and humiliation the physician always ultimately endured. But it was the utter helplessness of the dead that most prodded his aversion, the fact that you could take a knife and slice a body open as casually as fileting a fish; probe and pry, remove organs, and the cadaver would make no protest, no movement, not even a reflex withdrawal. Even under surgical anesthesia blood would spurt and flow, and muscles weren't so cold and slack.

The autopsy room was small and crowded and smelled badly of formalin. A single long tube of flat white fluorescent light was suspended from the ceiling, directly over the cold Formica table on which Ivan's body, partially wrapped in a plastic shroud, had already been placed. Along one wall were metal sinks and shelves with jars of formalin containing specimens from previous autopsies—a slice of liver studded with cancer nodules, a kidney distorted by a huge tuberculous abscess, or a section of lung hollowed out by emphysema.

Dr. Raymond Martin was the regular pathologist at the Hôpital des Enfants. His hands were already encased in rubber surgical gloves when they entered, so he didn't shake hands with Mulligan but merely nodded when they were introduced. Mulligan didn't mind; he didn't feel any impulse to be friendly to a man who made his living dissecting the cadavers of children.

He was introduced, too, to Dr. Marcel Gallieni, the muscle physiologist whom Lussac had mentioned. It would be Gallieni's task to define the mutations that underlay Ivan's strength, just as Mulligan's task was to determine those underlying his intelligence.

Mulligan stood next to Irene, to the left of the head of the table and watched as Dr. Martin lifted a hook-shaped knife, bounced it in his hand as though weighing it, then made a long inverted Y incision in the abdomen. He worked rapidly, expertly, his long, tapered fingers guiding the blade in a single stroke through all the layers of flesh at once, not going through one layer at a time the way a surgeon would. The open belly gurgled a little as he reached into the abdominal cavity to bring out the slippery intestines and lay them to one side.

Mulligan felt a wave of nausea pass through him and glanced at Irene. Clad in a long white lab coat, she stood motionless, her arms folded across her chest. Her face remained impassive, controlled and academically detached, though he sensed her struggle to suppress the revulsion provoked by the too-casual evisceration. The liver, one kidney and the spleen were removed in quick succession—each with no noteworthy gross pathology.

The pathologist muttered descriptions of the organs into a tape recorder as he sliced almond-sized samples of each and plopped them into beakers of formalin.

An assistant carefully labelled each specimen. Thin slices of tissue would later be stained and mounted on slides for microscopic study. The assistant handled the organs indifferently, as though they were lumps of clay or an assortment of objects to be placed in a store display window.

Dr. Martin finished with the abdominal organs and turned his attention to the thorax, extending the incision upward to the neck, cutting through the breastbone with the aid of a short-bladed handsaw. The saw made rasping and tearing sounds, and the sickening odor of cut bone quickly filled the room. Wide metal retractors were inserted under the cut edge of bone on either side and the pathologist grunted softly as he pulled the chest open. Several ribs cracked with a muffled pop.

Incision of the pericardium brought the heart into view. The heart attack that had caused Ivan's death was immediately apparent. The entire anterior mass of the left ventricle was infarcted, the muscle an angry hemorrhagic red that stood out sharply against the duller bronze-gray of normal myocardium. The aorta, the pulmonary arteries and the venae cavae were incised, and, sweeping his hand around the posterior side of the heart, Dr. Martin, with a quiet sucking sound, pulled it free from the chest. More careful attention could now be paid to the coronary arteries, and here, too, there were no surprises. The coronaries were thick, yellow and hardened with atherosclerosis, and a moment's linear dissection along one of them located the thrombosis that had occluded the vessel and ended the child's life.

Mulligan reminded himself that this was the heart of an eight year-old boy, an eight year-old who had died the death nature usually reserved for old men. Eight year-olds just don't die of heart attacks: they get run over, or maybe get leukemia or mostly don't die at all. But they don't die of heart attacks. Nature made all kinds of mistakes, he knew, and most mutations were deleterious, nature's failed experiments; but there seemed a perverse taunting cruelty about accelerated aging.

The boy's face was revealed for the first time as Martin shifted the shroud for the head dissection. Here the aging phenomenon was even more striking. Ivan's head was large, with an oversized and gnarled, bumpy forehead; but he had the shrinking features and receding hairline appropriate to a man of seventy. Skin yellow-gray, thick with deep wrinkles; his whole face was pinched and shortened, pointed forward, the nose beginning to hook downward to the chin, witch-like. The utter laxity of death sagged and sculpted his cheeks. And his eyes, closed but sunk deep in their sockets, imparted a slumped look of endless fatigue.

The pathologist wasted no time. It was desired to examine the brain in toto so the entire top half of the skull would have to be removed en bloc. The knife slithered through the scalp in a swift circumferential movement, the cut extending around the head at a level just above the eyes and ears. A small circular saw blade was used to cut through the bone, its whine and screech perforating the silence in the room, while the cut bone again emitted a nauseating stench. Dr. Martin raised his head briefly from his work and looked around the small room as though to apologize. Then, bending to his work again, he lifted away the entire top half of the skull and set it aside. It was like opening a box.

"Now we'll see if he had an extra lobe or something," Mulligan muttered to Irene as he leaned forward, looking intently for any deviation from the expected pattern of convolutions and convexities. Other than the enlarged size of the brain, no abnormality appeared. The cortical gray matter, the evolutionary afterthought that created the *sapiens* in homo sapiens, appeared entirely normal. It covered the cerebral cortex like a blanket and reflected light with a dull bluish-purple color.

Even in death the human brain seemed to Mulligan to radiate comprehension, and he felt a familiar awe and fascination as he looked at it. Here, somehow, embedded in this substratum, was the ability to remember, think, calculate, create. Intelligence was not a magic light ignited by divine spark. The woven circuitry of axons and dendrites, neurons sending each other the silent message of the synapse, received and sorted the raw information of the senses, then rearranged it, creating thought and memory. The urge to reveal this mystery was the force that dominated Mulligan's life.

The exposed brain could now be removed from the skull, although it had to be separated from the spinal cord by a slice through the medulla oblongata. Dr. Martin held it up to the light, turning it slowly in his hands and making descriptive comments. The gross anatomy was normal. No extra sulcus or gyrus could be found to account for the superlative intelligence that had, somehow, been contained within this organ.

The last step was to weigh it. Dr. Martin stepped to a balance scale and put the brain into a large pan, then added counterweights to the other side until it balanced. "Two thousand eight hundred grams," he said. "Six hundred grams more than the average for his age."

Huge, Mulligan thought, but not unexpected. Intelligence correlated nicely with the size and weight of a brain. The real question was what made it get that way.

Dr. Martin returned the brain to the cranium. He stepped back from the table and, without removing his gloves, lit a Gauloise.

He had finished. Except for confirming that a heart attack had been the cause of death, the autopsy had so far revealed little. If there were to be one, the clue to Ivan's intelligence would come from investigations far more subtle and esoteric than a mere inspection of the gross anatomy.

"Disappointed?" Irene inquired, tugging at Mulligan's sleeve.

"Not really. I wouldn't have expected anything different. The real tests will be the histologic studies and the enzyme analysis."

Dr. Martin concurred. "On the surface, except for its size, you can't tell this brain from any other." He looked at Mulligan. "What specimen would you like and what preservative should I put it in?"

"Cerebral cortex, frontal and parietal lobes, eighty grams, in formalin." The reply was crisp, brief, practiced. If an answer to the question of what made Ivan so smart were to be found at all, this was the tissue that would disclose it.

Dr. Gallieni took a large chunk of the quadriceps from the right thigh, leaving a bizarre, square-shaped hole in the muscle. He was an older man, balding and obese, whose perspiring face now grimaced in annoyance. "I wish I could do some of your immunoassay studies on this," he said to Mulligan. "I'd give a lot to know how much CPK this muscle contains. Dr. Lussac said the boy's strength was incredible. How much did you say he could lift, Guy?"

Dr. Lussac spoke from the other side of the autopsy table, looking up from where he'd been bending over the cadaver, scrutinizing something. "One hundred ten kilos . . . nearly two hundred fifty pounds. We tested him once."

"I can't do anything so accurate as your enzyme analysis," Gallieni continued, half apologizing, "but I ought to be able to give you at least a semiquantitative idea of how much CPK there is. Not precise, but some idea."

"What about structural studies of the contractile proteins?"

Gallieni smiled. "Out to prove your theory is true for muscle as well as brain, are you?"

"Why not?" Mulligan's theory postulated that the enhanced complexity of the brain that resulted in a more intelligent individual came from having more neurotransmitters present in the embryo when the brain was just developing. That was the link to the genetics of it. If the genes that made neurotransmitter-producing enzymes could be stimulated, then more enzyme and, hence, more neurotransmitters, would result. By analogy, the same thing might happen to muscle—it might be structurally altered, made better and more powerful by increased amounts in the embryo of the muscle enzyme CPK.

Gallieni assented. "We'll do all we can. Some electron microscope studies of the actimyosin, perhaps."

"I could make you an antibody against the CPK," Mulligan offered, "but that would take quite some time, and you'd have to purify some CPK to use as an antigen first."

Gallieni nodded. "Too time consuming. Maybe we'll save that one for later."

The remains of the cadaver would not be buried. Submerged in a formalin vat in the pathology section of the Sureté, they would be a source of tissue samples for future studies. So rare and valuable a specimen couldn't be left to rot uselessly in the ground.

The autopsy was over. Mulligan's specimen would be packaged for transport and could be picked up later that afternoon.

"Jesus!" Ridgely swore as the group filtered into the hall. "Am I glad to get out of there! I thought that smell would kill me. What is that stuff?" He lit a cigarette and deliberately exhaled through his nose, replacing, with evident relief, the stink of chemicals with the reek of tobacco.

"Formalin," Mulligan explained. "Like formaldehyde. It still preserves tissue better than anything else. Does take some getting used to, though. What now?"

Ridgely glanced reflexly at his watch. "Not much. You're not booked out of here until tomorrow, a direct flight from DeGaulle to L.A. Your ticket will be at the airport. So far as I know there's nothing planned for the afternoon. You're on your own."

"Maybe you'd like to see my laboratory at the Institut?" Irene asked. "You can see how we manage to do research without all those wonderful computers you have in America." An impish delight lit her face.

"Ah," said Mulligan, smiling back, "how the other half lives. Scientific slumming. I'm sure I'll be amazed you can do anything at all."

The tour would serve as a pretext for their desire to be together, but as they walked from the Hopital des Enfants to the Institut Mulligan found himself thinking how disappointing it would be if he was unable to explain what had made Ivan what he'd been. He ought to be able to identify and characterize the changes. In theory Aaron should find that the neurons had more cross connections than they normally did. In theory he, Mulligan, should find increased concentrations of both neurotransmitters and the enzymes that made them. In theory, in theory . . . never did theory seem more to be mere flimsy, tenuous speculation. The buoyant sense of adventure he'd had foundered beneath the prospect of defeat. What if the brain were merely bigger but otherwise quite ordinary? It would mean that his theory wasn't true. "There's got to be *something*," he muttered to himself.

"What's that?" Irene asked, reading his mind again. "Not losing faith, are you?" She had stopped on the sidewalk and turned toward him, and as she did so a breeze caught her hair and covered her face with it. Laughing lightly she brushed it back. "I think your theory is true, you know," she said. "That's why we invited you here."

Mulligan tried to put up a brave front but couldn't avoid looking pained. "Of course I have faith in my theory," he said. "But I think I'm just realizing what it means to be suddenly face to face with a chance to prove it."

"Don't worry," she said. "It's true—you'll see." They walked silently the several blocks to the Institut de Biologie Moderne. "I got a lymphocyte culture from Ivan's blood," she said as they entered the Institut, becoming cool and detached as she explained her work. "I'll need a tissue culture, of course, for the chromosome studies."

Everyone was agreed that Ivan had most likely been a chromosomal mutation, a translocation or reduplication of enough DNA to contain many genes. How else could such a mutation make sense? What she referred to was the fact that, in most cells, chromosomes closely concealed their secrets. At any given moment, only a few genes were functioning, and, when not producing something, chromosomes were clumped together, an amorphous ball of nucleic acid impossible to analyze. Chromosomes were elongated, spread out and individually visible only when cells were actively dividing. Only then could chromosomal structure be seen and studied.

For that, living tissue was needed.

Irene's laboratory, despite her joke about not having computerized equipment, was really quite up to date. Along one wall Mulligan recognized, among other equipment, the familiar form of the incubator, a metal-covered cube about eighteen inches on a side, with a heating coil and an inside thermostat set to maintain the exact thirty-seven degrees centigrade of the human body.

Irene opened the door of the incubator and took out a covered Petri dish, a plastic oval three inches in diameter and one inch deep, whose bottom-half contained a tan-colored gelatinous growth medium. "I'll show you what's left alive of Ivan," she said as she took the steamy lid off the dish and glanced inside.

"Mon Dieu!" she exclaimed, *"Elle est morte!"* When she looked up at Mulligan her face was a mask of horrified disbelief.

Mulligan grabbed the dish from her hand and looked into it. Instead of the yellow and purplish sheen of a healthy tissue culture, with no odor at all, there was on the surface of the gelatin only a large black stain of dead cells from which arose a stomach-turning feculent stink.

"What could have happened?" He handed the dish back to Irene.

"I don't know. I don't know what happened. I did everything just right, I'm sure of it . . . I . . ." She stared in dismay at the Petri dish, unable to go on.

"Probably had nothing to do with what you did or didn't

do," Mulligan said. "Probably the same biochemical defect that led to the progeria made his cells unable to survive in tissue culture."

She nodded soundlessly, staring at the dish for a long time before putting it down on the counter. The black spot in the center of the gelatin was a definitive, irredeemable termination. "Now we'll never know," she said, tears forming in her eyes. "We'll never know what kind of mutation it was." Her sorrow was as much for the loss to science as it was for the loss to herself. "The opportunity is lost forever."

"Let's get out of here," Mulligan said.

They spent the afternoon together, wandering aimlessly through the Left Bank, saying little, seeking solace in the sustenance of merely being together. Her mood was somber and solemn, and walking seemed a necessity, as though she were treading water in a sea of despair and would sink if she stopped.

"I had the feeling," she said at one point, "that if I could find out what it was, the mutation, I mean, that I could give some meaning to that terrible journey he made to get here. Even if I couldn't help him live any longer, it would make his struggle worth something. Now I can't do even that."

Mulligan struggled to maintain his optimism. Am I having fun yet? he thought bitterly. Toward late afternoon they drifted into the Panthéon, and, looking at the statues and busts of the great men of France's past, he had a sense of history leaning heavily on the present, conditioning and binding it, restricting freedom. Then he was annoyed with himself for having such uncharacteristic and unwanted gloomy thoughts.

The sky had turned a dark and threatening gray by the time they came out of the Panthéon. The melancholy of nature relieved their own, and Mulligan felt both his own and Irene's mood brighten as they were caught in the initial downpour and had to race for the shelter of a café. Inside, warm and dry, they looked through a window at the increasing traffic on the St. Germain and laughed at the awkward antics of pedestrians scampering over rain-slicked streets and sidewalks to avoid getting wet.

Mulligan ordered tea and a pastry for them.

"Where did you learn French?" Irene asked. The rain had made her face and hair slightly damp, and her cheeks were flushed from their dash to safety. Her eyes glistened brightly. She dried her face delicately with a napkin. Mulligan thought her indescribably lovely.

"In college," he said. "And then I spent some weeks here once, touring. Where did you learn English?"

She paused only slightly before replying, as she had done the night before, testing whether or not she wanted to trust him and tell him of her own marriage. She'd been quite young when she met Pierre Sailland, although they hadn't married until several years later. He'd been a rising star in the foreign ministry, a product of the elite École Normale Supérieure. She'd learned English to help him practice his own. Then, at age thirty, he'd contracted Hodgkin's disease, a young man's cancer. The illness lasted six years, the exacerbations and remissions doctors spoke about translating into oscillating cycles of bleak hopelessness and soaring delusions of a cure. He had died two years ago. She'd been saved from utter despair only by throwing herself compulsively into her research work. In a strange way, the recent events with Ivan had helped to restore her.

After the rain stopped they walked outside again. She took his arm in the old-fashioned way and leaned slightly against him as they walked, a gesture he found both quaint and endearing, unashamedly feminine. Evening had come and the streets had streaky illuminations from the headlights of passing cars. There were still streets in Paris that looked like Utrillo paintings, where the streetlamps threw an angled gold sheen over cobblestones and the gilt lettering in store windows gleamed with burnished reflections. It gave Mulligan a detached sense of being in another century, of transposition in time.

For dinner they found a small students' restaurant where

the atmosphere was noisy and unruly, but at a corner table the boisterousness around them created a bubble of privacy. The afternoon together had fortified the instinctive intimacy he felt with her. Mulligan found himself, for the first time in years, talking about his ambitions and how they had changed over the years, why he had left clinical medicine.

Irene mentioned surprising doubts. The investigation of the mutant child, she said, might verge on a moral and psychological edge from which some might withdraw. Knowledge might be dangerous, unwise.

"Don't be silly," Mulligan cajoled, protesting. "The last time a man hesitated before discovering something was when Adam approached the apple."

"*Exactement,*" she said, lapsing into French. "*L'innocence protectrice.* Lost forever."

Mulligan laughed warmly. "Surely you don't believe it, do you, that there's such a thing as forbidden knowledge?"

"No, not really." She sighed and toyed with her fork. "Not really. But I can't help having doubts. Let me ask you this: Do you think the early atomic physicists ever imagined a hydrogen bomb? Would they have continued their work if they could have known it would lead to Hiroshima?"

The question was troubling, and Mulligan felt grated by an indefinable suspicion. "I'm not sure," he answered finally. "Curiosity always wins."

She sipped her wine thoughtfully, then put the glass down and, leaning forward, rested her chin on interlaced hands. Her beauty made him feel helpless again, and on irresistible impulse Mulligan reached across the table and stroked her cheek. "You're very beautiful," he said.

"*Merci, monsieur,*" she said without blushing. She took his hand in both of hers and looked at him steadily for a long time.

The end of the evening came too quickly. "I'll have to go back to Los Angeles tomorrow," Mulligan said. His voice revealed his regret. "All the antibodies and special equipment I need are there."

"Can you return when you're finished?"

"I'll make up a reason," Mulligan said. "I'll tell Ridgely I have to consult with you on some chromosome studies or that I need another specimen, or something. If worst comes to worst," he laughed, "I'll pay for the trip myself."

"I'd like that," she said. "I'd like to see you again, George."

He felt an aching loss when the time came to put her into the taxi that would take her back to her apartment. She had turned the fur collar of her overcoat up against the evening chill and the frame it formed with her hair made her face seem more beautiful than ever. He kissed her on the lips, gently at first, then in a more passionate embrace. She responded by pressing herself tightly against him. "I'll be sure to return soon," he murmured.

On the airplane returning to Los Angeles Mulligan sat with the brain specimen in a tightly stoppered jar on his lap, feeling self-conscious, like a child shielding and hoarding a new gift. He felt rather paranoid, too, and found himself looking around the airplane cabin suspiciously, imagining himself the object of staring eyes. He hovered ever more closely over the valuable specimen.

Ridgely had set him on edge before he left Paris. "Watch yourself," he had intoned in a semicommanding manner. "Be alert. I'll see you in L.A. soon, but there are some things I have to attend to here first. A few more inquiries."

"Watch out for what?" Mulligan flared. "KGB agents? You think they'll tempt me with fabulous offers of wealth and women to give away national secrets?"

Ridgely's face had reddened with squelched anger and he had jabbed at Mulligan with a thick forefinger. "You don't know what they'll do. Rule number one is this: never underestimate the enemy."

"That would be a sort of inverse hubris, I suppose."

"Lesson number two," Ridgely persisted, oblivious to the sarcasm, "is to always assume that his motives are the worst imaginable."

"The famous worst-case scenario?"

"At least that way you won't get caught with your pants down."

"So to speak."

"So to speak." Ridgely's anger subsided, lapsing into a sincere if truculent admonition. "Look, if you guessed right, you may shortly discover something that the KGB has just got through trying very hard indeed to prevent us from finding out. We don't know what it is. I don't understand it myself, but obviously somebody thinks it's valuable."

He handed Mulligan a plain-looking business card with a telephone number on it. Nothing else, no names, just the telephone number.

"At least it's a toll-free 800 number," Mulligan quipped.

"Cute," said Ridgely. "Look, if you need help, call this number. Don't pay any attention to the nonsense the girl who answers will say. She'll shut up long enough to take your message. Just say you want to talk to me, then give your name and a number where I can reach you. If you need help urgently, say so. Okay?"

Mulligan slipped the card into his wallet. "Sure. If you insist."

His sense of foreboding was brightened by thoughts of Irene. He felt like an adolescent stricken by love, and he was astonished that he had such feelings. Sentimental rubbish, he told himself, half of him hard headedly aware of the utter impracticality of the romance. Still, he couldn't get over a happy feeling when he thought of her. He had known her only briefly but felt that he had known her for a long time. Like an intimacy with an old friend who returns from a long absence, it was resumed rather than initiated. In the restaurant, her skin glowing in the candlelight, a dust of perfume softening the air, leaning slightly toward him as she spoke, her smile seemed one of those bright woman's smiles that could dispel grief from the dark corners of the world. In another flush of adolescent sentimentality he thought that he couldn't live without seeing that smile again. When she had held her arms around his neck and thrust her thighs against him in their embrace . . . he knew his memory of that moment was a lure that would surely draw him back to her.

His mind was, as well, rippling with speculations about the Russian boy. It was incredible. How was it possible? An IQ of five or six hundred, Olympian strength and endurance, yet early death mandated by the grim genetic flaw. Irene had said that Ivan had seemed uncannily bizarre, alien, more than human and less than human at the same time. Awe and pity mixed in his feelings, overlaid by a tinge of revulsion, an instinctive recoil from creatures both like and unlike oneself. What a loss to science, he once again thought, that the lymphocytes had died. Now they would never know what chromosomal changes had produced the mutation.

Why had the child been so secretive, refusing to answer any of the dozens of questions one might think to ask? Where had he come from? Leningrad—that's all he would say. Where in Leningrad? An institution? Did he know he was a mutant? Probably—he knew at least that he had a lethal disease. How had he learned that? How did he get hold of Irene Sailland's paper? How much else did he know? What of his parents? Had he really *run* all the way from Leningrad to Paris? He ran to Irene Sailland, but what was he running *from?* And, most disturbing of all, the question that Ridgely had put in his mind, the question that recurred again and again until Mulligan grew impatient with his inability either to answer or forget it—how could a child, however remarkable, become an object, a pawn in the invisible underground tug of war of spies and counterspies?

How the hell, Mulligan thought wryly to himself, did I ever get into this? Two days ago the most cunning plots I ever hatched were only about how to get bigger research grants from the NIH. Here I am today sitting on this airplane with eighty grams of mutated brain in my lap, possibly watched by the KGB, and smitten with a woman who lives eight thousand miles away. Terrific!

71

VARIANT

It was Sunday when he got back to L.A. Mulligan went to his apartment to clean up first, though he was anxious to get to Aaron Rosenberg's house. Aaron's wife Claire was a schoolteacher. They hadn't yet had any children and lived like overgrown graduate students, a style Mulligan found pleasantly free from the pretensions that seemed to overtake and possess so many people.

He telephoned ahead first. "You'll never guess what I've brought back from Paris."

"Of course I can guess," Aaron said. "A brain."

"How did you know?"

"George, the CIA wouldn't ask you to go to Paris to pitch for the embassy softball team. You're a neurobiochemist, you study the brain. Obviously there was a brain there for you to study. But you need the antibodies you have here."

"Wise ass," Mulligan told his friend. "Don't be so damned smart. This one's really something."

When he reached their house he told them the whole story. Ridgely had said he could, since, in any event, Aaron would be the one to do the histologic studies of the specimen. As he narrated it Mulligan realized how outlandish and fantastic the story must seem. No embellishment was needed to stupify. He tried to leave out only the intensity of his feelings for Irene, but Claire saw through him immediately.

"You fell for her, didn't you, George?" she said. "Well, it was bound to happen. When do we meet her?"

"As soon as you can come up with the plane fare," Mulligan laughed. Claire had the kind of affection for him that she might have for a wayward younger brother; she regarded him as imperfectly matured until he married.

Aaron's interest had nothing to do with Irene. A lively enthusiasm seized him as he realized, at once and fully, the opportunities opened up by such a specimen. "George, it's perfect—perfect! We've gone through all this effort to try to make a better brain. Look at how much time we spent try-

72

ing to make animals smarter by feeding them neurotransmitters. Jesus! Remember the pregnant rat, how we infused dopamine into her throughout her pregnancy to try to improve the fetal brain . . . God! Remember that?"

Mulligan nodded. "And the rat died, damn her little rodent soul. Ruined six months of work."

"The *real* experiment," Aaron continued, "was the one we've never been able to do. Altering the genes, making the fetus make more of its *own* neurotransmitters, and in utero at that. That would be the real test of your theory."

"I know. I know," Mulligan agreed. "The experiment we haven't yet figured out how to do."

"And now nature's done it for us!" Aaron said, grinning broadly.

"And now nature's done it for us," Mulligan echoed, grinning back, "and a human brain, at that."

Mulligan had placed the box with the specimen on the kitchen table and now Claire looked at it with some distaste. A worried frown appeared. "Human?" she asked, speaking more to herself than to either Mulligan or Aaron. "I wonder."

"Wonder what?" Aaron asked in surprise.

"How many mutations does it take before you're not human any more?"

"Don't be silly, Claire," said Mulligan.

"I'm not being silly," she insisted. "It's a good question."

"All right," Mulligan admitted, both to Claire and to himself. "It's a good question, but it can't be answered."

"No reason not to ask it," she muttered.

"Listen," said Aaron, still excited, "I'll do the histology and you do the enzyme studies. Just like we always do. In a few days we ought to know if your theory is valid or not. This is our chance, George!"

Mulligan again felt a twinge of anxiety. He'd feel stupid if, after all, his theory wasn't true. All the years of effort would have been so much wasted time.

The enzyme studies Aaron referred to weren't so easy to

perform, though the principle of the radioimmunoassay contained an elegant simplicity that was itself a delight. The enzyme to be measured—say, tyrosine decarboxylase—had first to be isolated in pure form. It could then be used as an antigen to stimulate the formation of an antibody. Herein lay the great specificity and precision of the technique. The antibody, once formed, would react solely with the antigen and with no other molecule. By attaching a radioactive "tag" to the antibody and then measuring the total radioactivity in the test system after the reaction had been allowed to take place, the amount of enzyme present could be measured. The technique was so precise and so sensitive that it allowed measurement of substances in quantities no greater than a nanogram.

To localize the antigen—the enzyme—within the cell, Mulligan had made a minor modification of the technique. After tagging the antibody with radioactivity for a quantitative determination, he tagged it with fluorescein, a compound that, when subjected to light of certain wave lengths, gave off a luminous green glow. An ultrathin slice of tissue, when fixed to a slide, could be bathed in an antibody-fluorescein solution. Antibody would stick to the enzyme antigen. Once dried, the slide could be examined microscopically with light of the particular wave length passed through it from below.

The results could be spectacular. Mulligan would proudly show his slides to anyone who said science couldn't be beautiful. Cells containing the enzyme lit up in green spidery forms, interlacing filigrees. If the enzyme was located near the nucleus of the cell, it might look like an aerial view of a volcano with green lava, or, if the enzyme was more diffusely scattered through the cytoplasm, like a green exploding nebula.

But it was Aaron who recorded the first success. Mulligan had never tired of watching his friend work. Since part of the theory asserted that each neuron had more connections to other neurons, this had to be visually demonstrated. A

neuron was like a spider with a hundred legs and arms, fila-
mentous axons and dendrites, each one resting gently on the
body of another neuron, while allowing its own cell body
to be touched by the legs and arms of hundreds of others. If
you just looked at sections of brain under the microscope,
even properly stained tissue, it was all an incomprehensible
mess, everything impossibly tangled, and you couldn't tell
which filaments belonged to which cell, much less count
them.

Aaron had invented a way out of that difficulty, though
the technique demanded meticulous care and saintly
patience.

The specimen of Ivan's brain was brought out of the formalin. It was a grayish-tan lump of tissue with a few cerebral convolutions on the cortical side, the cut surfaces flat
and slick. Looked at sideways, from the cut surface, the
gray and white matter were clearly separable. The gray
matter, where the cell bodies of the neurons lay, would contain the answers to the mysteries. Aaron cut a small piece,
perhaps one centimeter square and one millimeter thick, and
placed it on a glass slide. This was the specimen he would
use, and he put it in an incubator held at exactly thirty-
seven degrees centigrade so that the tissue would have the
proper degree of fluidity. At body temperature the brain
had the consistency of warm jello.

Aaron's technique involved injecting single cells with a
water-soluble dye, a visible tracer, that would in time be
distributed throughout the entire cell, diffusing by osmolar
gradient down each axon and dendrite, enabling all the arms
and legs of that particular cell to be seen and counted.
Through the years he'd worked out just the right number
and pattern of injections into a given volume of tissue to
determine the brain's complexity. With the tissue counterstained and examined in serial slices, all the hundreds of
dendrites of a single nerve cell could be counted.

A micropipette, its bevelled tip only several micra in
diameter, was placed in a vertical clamp and set over the

brain specimen on the slide. It was then lowered very slowly by a series of reduction gears in units no greater than a hundredth of a millimeter, until the point pierced the tissue and lay within it. Then a drop of dye, the tiniest imaginable drop, a drop no bigger than the size of the tiniest bubble created by splashing a pool of water with your hand, was injected. With luck, the point of the needle would come to rest within a neuron, so that the dye would spread within that single cell.

Aaron repeated the process several dozen times, approaching and piercing the tissue from a variety of angles.

The specimen was placed again in the incubator and heated now to forty-five degrees to assist in the dispersal of the dye. It was left there for thirty-six hours. At that point the tissue was removed from the incubator and embedded in paraffin, sectioned into serial slices, mounted in order on slides and counterstained.

Aaron slipped the slide onto the microscope stage and focussed. His practiced eye took only a moment to discern the difference. "My God," he whispered, not speaking the words so much as having them forced from him.

They were alone in the laboratory. In the quiet Mulligan could hear the awe, fear almost, in his friend's voice. He looked up from his own work. A sudden pallor accentuated the gauntness of Aaron's face.

"Find something?"

Aaron pushed his stool back from the microscope and stared at it. "I'm not sure I believe it. It's incredible! Come and look at this, George! Just come and look!"

Mulligan crossed the laboratory quickly and, bending down, peered through the microscope. It took a moment to orient himself in the field, but then he could see it. Aaron had succeeded in finding a section in which the bulk of the cells were laid out in a two-dimensional array, so that their branchings and connections could be more easily counted. He blinked several times, unsure the microscope was properly focussed. It was astonishing. The neurons had at least ten times the usual number of dendrites, a dazzling array that far exceeded anything he had ever seen before.

"Do you see it?" Aaron paced excitedly and nervously behind him. "Do you see it? My God, George! It's like the difference between a pocket calculator and a mainframe computer!"

So it's true, Mulligan thought. This much, at least, of the theory is true. The years haven't been a waste after all. He uttered a sigh of thankful relief.

Then he realized how inadequate his feelings were. He should have been shouting, jumping in triumph and elation, pounding Aaron on the back. Instead he felt another wave of apprehension. He looked through the microscope again. This was more, much more than he had ever imagined possible. There was an indefinable sense of something wrong about it. Nature had been violated too much.

He recalled what Irene had said about Ivan's being so alien and Claire's question about how many mutations it took until you weren't human any more. "It's as if it's not a human brain," he said quietly. "It's as if this brain belongs to another species."

"But it doesn't," Aaron said, excitement overcoming his initial stunned reaction. "It is a human brain and it proves the theory. This is Nobel stuff, George. We've got to get a paper out on this right away, before somebody beats us to it."

"I wouldn't worry about that," Mulligan replied. "We're the only ones working with this brain. And we're the only ones who can do these kinds of tests. Let's wait until I finish my part before we start writing papers."

His own results came the next day, on June first. Over the years Mulligan had prepared antibodies against six of the enzymes involved in neurotransmitter synthesis. Now he tagged them with radioactivity and with fluorescein and allowed them to bathe the slides on which he'd fixed slices of the gray matter. The method was to coat the slide with the solution containing the antibody, allow it to react for twenty minutes, then wash it gently with buffered distilled water. To the naked eye nothing had changed on the slide, but the antibody, finding its antigen enzyme, would have bound to the tissue sample. Unbound antibody would wash off.

This was the moment of truth. He had difficulty controlling the anxious trembling of his hand as he put the slide into the counting chamber. Instantly the numbers on the digital readout began whirling. He watched the numbers mount with growing disbelief. The radioactivity of the sample was at least fifty times anything he had ever recorded in a normal human brain. And when he put the slide on the microscope stage and turned on the special lamp underneath, the cells sparkled with green dots as a mountain sky sparkles with stars. The visible evidence confirmed the radioactive count. The cells had many, many times more than the usual quantity of neurotransmitter enzymes.

With mounting elation he repeated the procedure with each of the six enzyme antibodies. The results were the same in each case.

This time he felt an unalloyed triumph. The theory was true, all of it! It was unequivocally confirmed. There could be no doubt. Nothing seemed impossible. The Nobel Prize seemed almost palpably within his grasp. He couldn't wait to tell Irene.

CHAPTER FOUR

His elation was noisily disrupted by the sound of breaking
glass and a muffled grunt. He turned to the noise just in
time to see Aaron being attacked by two men. The larger of
the two, a huge ham-fisted man, nearly lifted Aaron from
the floor with a powerful uppercut to the stomach, knocking his breath out, while the smaller man toppled him sideways with blows to the head and shoulders. The larger man
struck him again with an enormous fist as he went down
and even from across the lab Mulligan could hear the crack
of a snapping rib. Everything happened so quickly. Within
seconds . . .

The smaller man, shorter and thinner reached out to the
small slide-storage box in which Aaron's slides—ones dem-
onstrating the complexity of Ivan's brain—were stored, a
box labeled "Ivan: 5-31-85."

Aaron was curled up, moaning and retching on the floor.

"Ivan?" the man shouted, bending and holding up the
slide box where Aaron could see it. "Ivan's brain?" He pro-

nounced the name Ivan the way a Russian would pronounce it.

The larger man leaned backwards and, with the smile of a satisfied sadist, kicked Aaron viciously in the chest. Aaron screamed in pain and tried to crawl away, but the man stooped down and yanked him up by the armpits. "Ivan?" he repeated.

Aaron coughed and groaned, unable to breathe, unable to speak.

Mulligan, initially paralyzed by the sudden viciousness, now recovered his voice. "What the hell are you doing?" he shouted, lurching from his seat and scrambling toward the larger man. "Get the hell out of here!"

The larger man let Aaron collapse onto the floor again while the shorter one took the slides one by one from the box and dropped them to the floor, grinding the shattered pieces to fine shards under his heel.

As Mulligan moved, his eye was caught by the sight of the smaller man destroying the slides, so he never saw the fist that struck him, first a blow to the abdomen that doubled him over, then a crashing downward blow to the neck and face that sent him to his knees.

He felt blood spurt from his nose and tasted it in his mouth, but, still yelling, he lifted his head in time to receive a second blow to the face, and then a powerfully uplifted knee to the chest threw him backwards into the laboratory bench. He landed in a sprawl on the floor. Gasping for air, his head ringing, he saw legs step over him and walk quickly, purposefully, toward his own lab bench. He was dimly aware of snatches of conversation in a language from which he could cull only the words *"da"* and *"nyet."* Near him Aaron had struggled into a half-sitting position, his back to the bench, leaning on his right arm while with his left he clutched his chest, a taut grip of agony on his face. Mulligan watched in horror as Aaron coughed and spat frothy red blood.

My God, he thought, *they're going to kill us!* Still gasping for air, Mulligan heaved himself to his feet in time to see the smaller man peering intently at his equipment. The thought flashed through his mind that they must have been carefully instructed, must have known precisely what they were looking for, since with almost no hesitation the man located the lead container holding Mulligan's supply of radio-labelled antibodies. With these gone, his research would come to an instant halt; it would require months and months to make a new supply.

"No!" Mulligan screamed as the man emptied the glass vials one by one on the floor. Years of effort and study, the research tool that had made him unique among brain biochemists—gone, sacrificed to an instant's malice.

When he had finished, the thin man peered around, looking for something he couldn't immediately find. His face was narrow and dark, and his manner suggested a weasel ferreting out rabbit warrens. With a frown he motioned to the larger man to join him, then walked toward Mulligan. Mulligan stared at them dumbly through thickened vision as they approached. The thin man leaned his face close to Mulligan's. "Where is it?" he hissed. "Where is it? You know what we want, the brain specimen. Where is it?"

Even before Mulligan had a chance to reply the larger man had jerked him up by the shirtfront and slapped him, hard and quickly and expertly, forehand and backhand across the face. Mulligan felt his skin part as the man's ring gouged a furrow in his cheek. "Answer the question," he growled, striking Mulligan a third time. The sadistic smile spread again across the man's face.

It doesn't matter, Mulligan thought suddenly, a gleam of hope beckoning within him. It doesn't matter! They can destroy everything and it won't matter! We've already learned all we can from that specimen. But they don't know that . . . "Refrigerator," he gasped, nodding his head toward the corner of the room.

"Hold him," instructed the thin man. He ran quickly to the refrigerator. They'd only been in the lab for a couple of minutes, but their noise might already be summoning others. The man found the jar labelled "Ivan" and threw it into the air, watching its parabola before it shattered on the floor. Instantly the stink of formalin filled the laboratory, and the remnant of Ivan's brain, a lump of gray tissue the size of a walnut, lay exposed on the floor in a pool of fluid.

The thin man turned to Mulligan and his tongue flickered over his lips in a quick reptilian movement. "No more experiments on this specimen, Dr. Mulligan," he said, flattening the tissue under his heel. There was a soft squishing sound, as though the brain were feebly protesting its final obliteration. Then he nodded to the big man, who sent Mulligan reeling again with another powerful back-hand slap to the side of the head.

By the time Mulligan regained his feet the men were gone.

Aaron! he thought, and staggered toward his friend. Aaron hardly moved. There was a riveting agony in his eyes, his entire being concentrated on his right lower rib cage where his left hand held the broken rib. Mulligan could hear a scraping, crunching sound as the broken ends of the rib scraped each other with the movement of each breath.

"Jesus . . . that . . . hurts," Aaron gasped, his lips still coated with a bloody froth. Mulligan saw with horror that Aaron's fingertips were beginning to acquire a dusky cyanotic hue. My God, he thought, his lung's punctured; he must have a pneumothorax.

Aaron needed oxygen and a chest tube, and fast. The quickest way to get them was to call a paramedic ambulance. Mulligan staggered to the wall telephone and frantically scrambled through the emergency number, screaming to the operator when she answered.

The paramedics took only a few minutes to arrive, but those few minutes were almost enough to finish Aaron. He had developed a tension pneumothorax, a condition in which the lacerated lung acts like a valve. Air was being

82

sucked into the chest cavity through the laceration with each inspiration, but then it was unable to go back out through the lung as the valve-like laceration closed in expiration. The result was a relentless accumulation of a high-pressure air pocket within the chest but not in the lung, air useless for gas exchange, but deadly in its effect. Each breath made it a little larger, and when it got large enough, under high enough pressures, the air pocket began to compress the healthy lung, making it harder and harder for the lung to expand. It was like choking yourself to death. Aaron's gasping grew louder as his condition worsened, and sweat pouring from his forehead mixed with the blood on his cheek and lips. He turned blue and stared vacantly into space, the upper, conscious part of his brain fading from oxygen deficit, even as the lower respiratory centers reflexively drove the muscles of his chest and neck into ever-more frantic activity.

But even these efforts had begun to fail before the paramedics came rushing into the room.

Mulligan screamed at them. "He's got a tension pneumothorax! Give me the largest needle you've got. *Quick*, damn it! I'm a doctor. Now! The biggest one you've got!"

The senior paramedic responded rapidly to Mulligan's demand. He quickly found a sixteen-gauge needle in his kit. It was what Mulligan needed. A large-bore needle stuck directly into the air pocket would release the pressure and allow at least the unpunctured lung to reexpand. With extra oxygen, he could live on one lung for quite a while. Mulligan ripped off Aaron's shirt. This was no time for the niceties of sterility. The place to do it was in front, high up, just under the collarbone. The slumped and semiconscious Aaron offered no resistance. Mulligan shoved the needle into his chest. Immediately there was a soft hissing sound, and the air was rendered visible by tiny droplets of blood as it streamed out. With relief Mulligan watched Aaron's trachea move back to the right as the good left lung reexpanded. The blue color faded from his hands and lips after the paramedics put an oxygen mask over his face. His breathing eased.

Mulligan stood up. Aaron would survive. "Okay," he said, "take him to the ER. He still needs a chest tube and probably surgery to repair the lung."

The paramedic looked at him admiringly. "Nice work," he said.

Aaron's eyes fluttered. Through the plastic face mask Mulligan could see his friend trying to speak. He leaned closer. "Thanks, George," Aaron whispered. "It still hurts, though."

Mulligan looked on with relief while the paramedics put Aaron on a stretcher and took him away. Then a thought filled him with horror . . . *Irene!* What if they'd done the same to Irene?

He stumbled again to the telephone, cursing and wiping blood and sweat from his face and hands while the operator tried several locations until Irene was found at the Hôpital des Enfants.

"Irene!" Mulligan shouted when he heard her voice. "Are you all right? Some Russian goons just broke into the lab, smashed everything and nearly killed Aaron. Are you all right?"

She seemed not to have heard. Her voice was distant and hollow with strain. "Ah, George. I'm glad you called. I was just going to call you myself. *There's another one,* George. Another one. Another little Russian boy with progeria."

CHAPTER FIVE

WASHINGTON, *June 1, 1985*

Late spring may be the best time of the year in Washington, D.C. The air is cool, invigorating, not yet dampened and deadened by the humidity of a southern summer. New leaves emerge in a dozen shades of green, speckling the brown tones along the southern shore of the Potomac, shifting hues with every breeze. The cherry trees around the Tidal Basin open their blossoms to the warming sun, and vegetation not yet in bloom seems bursting with the promise and vigor of rising sap.

The pleasures of nature at this time of year play a seductive and treasonous role, diverting one's mind from the thought that Washington is the capital of the mightiest nation on earth. Dogwood and cherry blossoms invade the senses, occupy vision and smell, distract, tempt. Awareness of them seems light froth to thought of a nation locked in resolute antagonism with a powerful foe. Walking along the

Mall one can easily close one's eyes to capture the scent of the blossoms and feel the play of the breeze on the skin. Such moments shut out the buildings and the monuments and the sense of the heavy implacability of a massive government engaged in a massive enterprise. This year most of all, the city seemed too pleasant to be the nerve center of the Central Intelligence Agency.

Brent Ridgely was pensive. His thoughts drifted, as they often did on his visits to Washington, to the unwieldiness of the CIA. The agency frequently spun in clumsy pointlessness, oafishly going nowhere. Its flexibility and responsiveness were hamstrung by the mores of its bureaucracy. Thousands of faceless functionaries demanded, absolutely, unquestioningly and without exception—their insistence undisturbed by either foresight or reflection—that the proper procedures be followed. He sighed. It was the same everywhere, he knew. Bureaucracy was the inevitable tool of government, procedure the sticky conduit of service and authority, bureaucrats the drones who put the pieces into place.

His sudden recall to Washington had been, then, the more surprising. The agency could shake off the sloth of its inertia only when an unusually urgent or threatening situation developed. Then, but then only, could the clarion voice of authority slice through the bureaucracy, a lithe saber disregarding propriety and fairness, wreaking its will.

Ridgely had remained in Paris for several days after Mulligan's departure, in daily contact with the Deuxième Bureau. Events seemed at a standstill. He had heard nothing from Mulligan. Legras had been trying, so far without success, to penetrate the Soviet Embassy. Both agents assumed automatically that someone in the Soviet Embassy would know about what the KGB had wanted. But no further information about the boy could be gleaned from any of Legras' sources. If there were more information, it was bottled up tight. There was no next move; he simply had to wait for the doctors to issue their reports.

Under normal circumstances an agent of Ridgely's seniority would be permitted to exercise his own judgment, allowed to stay where he was as long as he thought it worthwhile. The peremptory summons to Washington darted little needles of disquiet in its suggestion that something was terribly wrong.

A summons to the Pentagon was, in addition, distinctly improper. Only at the very highest levels of authority did the CIA and the Pentagon interact. This was a matter of deliberate policy.

So Ridgely had been incredulous when told to report to the Pentagon. "General Alexander?" he asked the contact man in Paris. "General Joel Alexander?"

"That's what they said."

"Why? Did they say why? Why Alexander?"

"No. Don't ask. You'll find out anyway."

General Joel Alexander was legendary, not only for having kept his own military fiefdom locked in an iron grasp, but also for his ability to keep abreast of events within the CIA, even without official lines of communication. It was widely rumored that he had his own men planted there, spies inside the spy agency, playing the shadow game in the shade of the agency's own umbrella. Officially, Alexander's position was one of the most nebulous, yet potentially powerful, in the Defense Department: chief of the office of technology assessment. He stood a little apart from the usual military structure, with no official place other than his rank in the chain of command, no recognized role in the order of battle.

The vision of the office of technology assessment was focussed more on civilian than on military life. The task of Alexander's department was to discover and monitor any and all new civilian technology, in any field, American or foreign, with the aim of assessing its military potential. That was why he kept a close watch on the CIA, not trusting the agency to tell him about new Soviet developments. From Alexander's department had come such ideas as developing the laser beam as a range-finding device, the use of an in-board television camera to guide cruise missiles, the "smart" bomb. It was rumored that it had been Alexander himself, then still a major in Vietnam, who had had the idea of mounting a TOW missile on a helicopter, creating with that inspiration the world's most effective antitank weapon.

His originality and genius were rewarded by the independence of his office. High-tech products spewed out of American science and industry in an ever-quickening stream; and even the army, belying its reputation for thickheadedness, recognized the importance of an unbiased assessment of military potential. The legend was that Alexander was the smartest, and, hence, the most irascible general in the army.

Obviously, Alexander was interested in Ivan, though why, Ridgely couldn't guess. Yet as far as Ridgely was concerned, there had also been something eerie, something incomprehensible about the case from the very beginning. Any interest expressed by Alexander's department only added to his sense of unease. Ridgely shivered, sensing again the little needles of disquiet. He had never before heard of the KGB—or anyone else, for that matter—attempting to steal a cadaver. Then there was Ivan himself. The sight of the mutant body stinking with formalin had aroused in him an instinctive feeling of revulsion which he had suppressed only with shuddering difficulty. Whatever intelligence lay in that too-large head, whatever strength resided in those thin arms and legs, Ridgely thought the boy a twisted, perverse caricature. It was almost as though the cadaver had whispered to him, in sibilant, mocking laughter through yellowed lips, "Look. Look at me! I am what mankind prizes most—strength, intelligence. Yet how grotesque! How flawed!"

The doctors, too, unnerved him. The fuss they had made over the boy was incomprehensible. He remembered with some distaste the way they peered at the brain as the pathologist had held it to the light, growing visibly excited with anticipation when their tissue specimens were dropped into jars of preservative. Ridgely had always found it irritating and difficult to work with scientists. They played by different rules. People like Mulligan, with their quietly snide assumptions of superiority, had always triggered in him a reflex hostility. Ridgely regarded scientists of all kinds as necessary evils, much like highly trained animals who performed amusing tricks but who had to be watched closely every minute. You fed them research grants in the same manner, for the same purpose and with the same result as the seal trainer distributed his fish, coaxing from them the desired behavior. Almost to a man, they had half-baked, assinine political opinions. They couldn't be trusted. Their record of security leaks, not to mention frank treason, was a national scandal.

In moments of greater candor, though, Ridgely admitted to himself that much of his hostility was due to the fact that he had little knowledge of what the doctors were so excited about. He felt lost, inadequate. He knew what genes were, and chromosomes, but only in the simplest, most collegiate terms, and he'd had to go to a dictionary to find out that enzymes were protein molecules that made chemical reactions go faster. Patterns of enzyme behavior apparently governed much of life and evolution. Dealing with such unfamiliar concepts gave Ridgely the edgy caution of a soldier crossing a minefield; you might at any moment encounter an unpleasant surprise.

So now, back in Washington, Ridgely mulled it over as his taxi took him from National Airport to the Pentagon. At this time Brent Ridgely was forty-five years old and had been in the CIA for twenty of those years. His devotion was the product of a conscious realization that his life as a field agent for "the company" was ideally suited to his personality. Although as a rule he paid little attention to the state of his emotions, the dovetailing of work and character had made him, if not a buoyantly happy, at least a contented man. The rootlessness of the life soothed rather than disturbed. Espionage gave Ridgely a welcome sense of being an outsider, an onlooker, an observer but not a participant. So far as he could remember, he had been that way since childhood, often standing back from the other children at play, watching, making guesses as to the course of events. He enjoyed making predictions as to who would do or say what. Without realizing it he had become a shrewd psychologist, observing that behavior was rooted in character. The trick in spying was to be able to put yourself in the other fellow's shoes, to face the problem from his point of view and then, only then, to ask, "What do I want? What resources do I have to get it? What risks am I willing to take? What will I do if something goes wrong?"

The stumbling block to such predictions was that you could never know enough, could never penetrate anyone's stance or psyche deeply enough. Inevitably an opaque zone of ignorance was encountered where sequential occurrence lost its logical inevitability.

That was what made it exciting. It was the feature of espionage he loved the most and was why, after twenty years, he remained with the CIA. Events and motives were shrouded in a gray mist of uncertainty, a vision-obscuring fog in which vague shapes would appear and disappear with disjointed randomness, only seemingly unrelated to each other. To connect an image with an impulse, to discern the pattern, make sense out of the whole—that was the essence of it.

It was a game Ridgely never tired of playing.

In the current case, that of the boy Ivan, the job was made more difficult for Ridgely by his ignorance of biology. Mutations, changes in the DNA, seemed intangible, distant and abstract. There was nothing you could get hold of and look at, as you could with a new tank or airplane. There was, undeniably, something here of sufficient importance to impel the KGB to undertake enormous risk, but what it was was not immediately obvious. Ridgely had little intuitive understanding of what was meant by an IQ of "five or six hundred," as it was said the Russian boy had had. So what? he thought. What difference does it make? The kid's dead, anyway.

How this would interest the military was another mystery. The Defense Department, to be sure, was an ardent consumer of the latest in high-tech goods, seizing any advantage it could, but it seemed to Ridgely that a mutant child had about as much relevance as a new breakfast cereal. So far as he knew, the Army's only interest in biology was its flirtation with germ warfare.

The taxi stopped at the first security gate at the Pentagon, and, descending from the vehicle, Ridgely went through the laborious security checks required for entrance to the building. The army was the chef d'ouevre of all bureaucracies, and a black staff sergeant, his officiousness a masterwork of subtlety, put him through the routine. His name was checked against a long list on the sergeant's clipboard, the validity of his identity card electronically verified and the photo on the identity card compared to his appearance with suspicious and deliberately obnoxious scrutiny. His briefcase was opened and inspected. He was, finally, permitted entrance to the building and was conducted by an armed escort, under the watchful eyes of slowly rotating television cameras mounted high in the corridors, to General Alexander's office.

General Alexander received him promptly. His office was spare, spartan in the military style. It was furnished with a wide oak desk, a captain's chair behind it, and filing cabinets, at least two dozen filing cabinets, many of them padlocked. The privilege of rank was confined to a broad picture window that opened to a view of the Potomac and the Washington Monument beyond. The visitors' chairs, awkward and without arms, seemed designed for discomfort, to keep anyone from sitting in them for too long. That would keep interviews short, Ridgely presumed. Sore muscles tend to abbreviate rambling conversations.

Ridgely didn't know quite what to expect. Others, the

worse for wear, had said that an interview with Alexander was an intimidating cross-examination, that his intellect was an abrasive that scoured ideas until they shined free of falsity and illogic. But the general didn't seem at all, in appearance, to be the inspired genius of his reputation. He looked more mechanical than cerebral, a stocky bullet-headed man with close-cropped, steel-gray hair and a square face that contained more than a hint of bulldog determination. Bulky of shoulder, rugged and powerful looking, he had nonetheless the drawn look of the man of fifty who has to struggle to maintain the physical fitness that is effortless at twenty-five.

"I see you were in Army Intelligence once," Alexander said after the introductions were over, indicating with a nod a file on his desk. He stalked the room as he spoke, as though he had more energy than he could contain or more anger than was considered civil. The impatience of his manner set Ridgely on edge.

"For three years, General, in Saigon." So you've done some homework already, he thought—that was fast. He avoided calling Alexander "sir," somewhat archly rejecting the superior-inferior relationship the honorific would imply.

"Ever do any technological assessment?" Alexander asked. "Know what it is?"

"No." Ridgely answered both questions at once.

"I see." Alexander ceased pacing the room. He seemed lost in thought for a moment, staring vacantly out the window like an attorney going through the line of reasoning one last time. Then he turned to face Ridgely again. His tone was simultaneously challenging and patronizing. "That means you're probably wondering why you're here at all, why I sent for you."

"The question did cross my mind." Ridgely kept the sarcasm mild. "I'm sure you're aware it's against policy. Anyway, the army has its own intelligence sources."

Alexander began pacing the room again, as though he hadn't heard. On the wall behind his desk there was a large

Mercator projection of the globe with the communist countries conveniently colored in red, all except China, tinted a more hopeful pink. The vast extent of the Soviet Union loomed ominously, like an unstoppable advancing glacier, over Europe and Asia. For the thousandth time Ridgely gratefully took note of the oceans flanking and protecting North America. More powerfully than any words, the map conveyed a sense of the immense scale of the conflict between the United States and the Soviet Union.

"What's your view of war?" Alexander asked suddenly.

"Sir?" The question, completely unexpected, took Ridgely by surprise, and he was instantly annoyed with himself for having allowed it to trick him into saying "sir." "I'm afraid I don't quite understand the question. My view of war?"

"Yes. Your view of war." Alexander picked up a steel ruler from his desk and tapped it softly against his left palm. "In general, I mean. No specific war. How does war fit in with the rest of human life?"

For a moment Ridgely had an impulse to laugh. It was absurd, irrelevant. Asking one's view of war was like asking one's view of life; the question either required hours of discussion or was merely rhetorical, not meant to be answered. Ridgely had heard talk like this before, in officer's clubs in Saigon. Usually it was accompanied by reams of praise for the virtues of war. Only in extremis, it was said, did such qualities as honor, courage and loyalty reach their fullest expression. It was a view Ridgely could neither wholly accept nor reject. "I'm not sure," he said after some hesitation, wondering what sort of reply he was expected to give. "I haven't really thought about it that much." He hesitated again. "It's something men have always done."

"And always will," Alexander snapped brusquely, his face suddenly taut, intense. His mouth set into a thin, grim horizontal line. "Always will. Remember that. No matter what you hear about détente, someday we'll have a war with the Russians. That's how great nations are. That's

how man is. I'll tell you what war is," he said, sitting down in the captain's chair behind his desk. Alexander leaned forward on his elbows. "It's human life reduced to its bare essentials, men reduced to a level of necessity, nothing more. Nothing obscures your vision of the relation of the parts to the whole. Purpose is clear, defined. All the pretensions and frivolities have been stripped away. Only the most elemental urges persist. And the army provides for them. Men hunger, so the army provides food. They endure injury and disease, so the army has doctors and hospitals. Men need order and direction, so a chain of command is provided. They need entertainments and have passions, so we provide movies and sports and alcohol and allow prostitution. And finally, and mostly, men hate and fear and conquer and kill, so the army provides weapons. The very best weapons," he said, emphasizing the point by slapping the heavy ruler on his desk. "The very best weapons, using the very best technology." He put the ruler down and sat back. His face relaxed into an ironic half smile. "So we won't lose, of course."

"Isn't that obvious?" Ridgely hoped the question didn't seem impertinent. What was Alexander leading to? "I mean, isn't it obvious that in combat you'd want every advantage you could get?"

"Damn right!" Alexander's eyes glittered with a sudden flash of animosity which then slowly subsided. He heaved a sigh of resignation. "It ought to be obvious, anyway. And I suppose, in a general sort of way, it is. But you'd be amazed at what can get in the way of the obvious." He picked up a slim book from his desk and tossed it to Ridgely. "Ever read that?"

Ridgely turned the book over in his hands. It was General Gavin's memoirs of the 82nd Airborne during the Second World War, *On To Berlin*. "No," he replied, "I can't say that I have."

"No? Let me give you an example of what I'm talking about. When the division was first sent into combat, in Sicily in 1942, they made the drop carrying a new weapon, the bazooka. It was supposed to be a weapon small enough for a man to carry but powerful enough to stop a tank. There was only one problem—it didn't work. It wouldn't even slow down a Tiger tank. So here were these American paratroopers firing the wrong weapon against German tanks. It was okay against a truck or a half track or a staff car, but a tank just rolled right through the blast. But . . . the troopers did capture a German antitank weapon, the *panzerfust,* similar to the bazooka but more powerful. The *panzerfust would* stop a tank. So Gavin sent some back to army headquarters and said, 'Send us some of these, they work.' Do you know what the army did?"

"What?"

"Nothing. Absolutely nothing. Not only didn't they send him any then, or even later in the war in Europe, but ten years later—ten years!—Gavin was fighting in Korea with the same damn bazooka that hadn't worked in Sicily. We didn't get a hand-held weapon that would stop a tank until the TOW missile was developed."

Alexander's speech was slick and practiced, and Ridgely was sure he'd given it many times. The general's face had the seamed and weathered look of a man who has spent a great deal of time outdoors, and an element of tension ebbed from it as he acted out the compulsion to deliver the diatribe one more time. The ice-blue eyes above the leathery tan seemed a little less cold. He leaned back in his chair and looked at Ridgely expectantly. The point he'd been making seemed clear enough, but Ridgely still didn't see its relevance. What did antitank weapons have to do with neurobiochemistry or mutant children in Paris? "General . . . I still don't see what all this has to do with me."

The general made a small placating gesture, as though mildly admonishing a child. "Patience. I'm coming to that. There are lots of other examples of how the army failed to either develop or adapt technology for military purposes. But we're not *that* stupid. Among other things, whatever

95

else they do, armies reflect the societies that create them, and the United States prides itself on being a leader in technology. So in 1956 the army established the office of technology assessment, to evaluate new technology, see if it can be adapted for military purposes. So we can at least keep up with the Joneses and maybe get ahead of them a little. And that, Mr. Ridgely, is why you're here."

The general was deliberately being obscure, Ridgely knew. He was playing the game of "see if you can guess what I'm thinking," and when you couldn't it put you at a disadvantage. It was a trick he'd always found extremely irritating.

A hard edge crept into Ridgely's voice as he let his irritation show. "General, I'm not some congressional committee you've got to cajole funds out of, you know. I could answer your questions a whole lot better if you'd be a little more direct." Without asking permission he drew a package from his jacket pocket and lit a cigarette. "I don't know what you're driving at. The KGB tried to steal the body of a supposedly superintelligent boy from a hospital morgue in Paris. Superintelligent and superstrong, and he had some weird aging disease called progeria. Everyone agreed he was some sort of mutation. I was asked to escort a Dr. George Mulligan, a research biochemist at UCLA, to Paris for the autopsy. I assume you know all that or I wouldn't be here. But you'll excuse me if I don't see what all this has to do with General Gavin's problems with bazookas and German tanks."

Alexander made another small placating gesture but smiled the faintly smug and superior smile of a bridge player who has just successfully got through a double finesse. "How much do you know about genetic engineering?"

Ridgely knew he'd been had. "Nothing. Why?"

"Because that's what this is all about."

"How did genetic engineering get into this? I just told you everyone agreed that the kid was a mutant."

"So he was. So he was. I wouldn't dispute that." Alexander picked up the ruler again and drummed it impatiently on his desk, the general who couldn't tolerate thickheadedness in his subordinates. "Look here, I know only what you know about this business in Paris. But there are implications you haven't thought of yet."

"Such as?" Ridgely curled his upper lip down to blow out smoke in a thin stream.

"Such as this: the KGB tries to steal a cadaver. Extraordinary. Unheard of. Why the hell would they do that?"

"We discussed that," Ridgely replied. "The French said it was the only way they could recover the body if proof of Soviet citizenship or parentage couldn't be provided."

"But why would they want to recover the body in the first place? What can you do with a dead body? An autopsy, that's what."

"That's just what we *did*, General," Ridgely answered briskly. "And you're not so far ahead of us, you know. We discussed all that, too, at quite some length. The Russians pretty clearly wanted to keep us from finding out something, presumably from finding out just what kind of mutation the kid was. We figured they probably already knew, but didn't want us to know what made him so smart and able to run so well."

"Ah," Alexander breathed, his manner that of the satisfied teacher who has at last elicited the correct answer from a somewhat dense student. "Go to the head of the class. What made him so smart? Exactly. What made him so strong?"

Ridgely was dismally aware of a sensation of sinking, of floundering in dark waters while others, with access to special secrets, swam happily and brightly on the surface. Alexander was leading him by the nose. He felt droplets of sweat beginning to form under his arms and it was with difficulty that he swallowed his resentment. "All right," he conceded. "Granted, that's the question. Dr. Mulligan thought it was some kind of chromosomal mutation, though he couldn't be sure. But I'm sure you don't know the answer to that question any more than I do. Why is it, though, something that concerns the army?"

The general beamed with pleasure. "I thought you'd never ask. Because someday—not soon, but someday—the great technological breakthrough will be an improved *soldier*, not an improved weapon."

Ridgely stared. The man's mad, he thought. Three stars on his collar and he belongs in a mental hospital.

Alexander must have anticipated the reaction, for he grinned jovially. "No, I'm not crazy. Not crazy at all. Think about it. Think carefully."

"Think about what? Mutant soldiers?"

"Exactly. Exactly that. But don't imagine the wrong thing. Don't imagine an army of freaks and monsters crawling around on the ground. It won't be anything nearly so dramatic, but it's not nearly so farfetched as you think. Genetic engineering has already got to the point where certain specific changes can be made in simple organisms like bacteria. Did you know that? There are bacteria that happily manufacture insulin, human insulin, for which they have no need themselves. They've had the gene for it spliced onto their own chromosome—then they're just turned loose in a vat full of sugar and amino acids and off they go. Suppose, just suppose, you could make changes in people the same way."

"That's crazy," Ridgely said. "I still say it's crazy. Even I know that people are infinitely more complicated than bacteria."

"Don't be so narrowminded," Alexander said in a peevish tone. "The essence of the future is its unpredictability. If that weren't true we'd all make millions in the stock market. You have no idea what new things will be invented. High-tech stuff is always startling and unexpected. But I'm not talking about redesigning an entire species. You wouldn't need to do anything so complicated. You could make smaller, specific changes."

"Like what?"

"Like what?" Alexander mocked him, sure of himself. "Like almost *anything*. Any of the qualities that might make a better soldier. Suppose you had soldiers who could see better in the dark? Suppose you managed to modify their eyes so that they required less light to see? Imagine the consequences for military planning? Imagine the advantages militarily—one army able to see while the second army is blind? It would be almost like having a cloak of invisibility. The enemy would be as helpless as infants."

Alexander rose again and paced the room, punctuating his talk with gestures. Words and ideas tumbled from him. This was obviously a subject that excited him, one to which he'd given a lot of thought. "Another example. Imagine a pilot with faster reaction times. The average pilot takes 0.45 seconds to respond when he sees an enemy plane or missile coming at him. That's a quarter second faster than the average of all people. That's one reason he's a pilot in the first place. But suppose he were even faster? Really fast. Imagine a pilot who took only 0.25 seconds to react? Not a major difference, you might think, only a fifth of a second. But it's easily the margin between being shot down and shooting the other guy down. At seven hundred miles an hour an F-15 covers a lot of ground even in a fifth of a second. Talk to some of them. The pilots I've talked to all agree that they'd be unbeatable in dogfights with an advantage like that. And if you're invincible in dogfights you control the air, and if you control the air you win the war. Simple as that.

"Another example. Armies have always been limited by how much a man can carry. Suppose you had a soldier who could carry a hundred pounds and do it without getting tired? How much heavier a weapon could he carry? How much more firepower? How much more ammunition and food could he carry? In any given movement of troops you could cut the logictics problems in half.

"And just suppose," Alexander concluded, speaking more slowly now, letting the significance of his words sink in, "suppose it all hinges on some simple genetic change, some minor modification of the nervous system or muscle, just a few genes here and there?" He settled again into his chair. "I'm told, by the way, that this Russian kid could run twenty miles without stopping. And that he could lift nearly two hundred fifty pounds. Is that true?"

"That's what they told me." Ridgely answered quietly, beginning to realize the full range and awful potential of what Alexander was saying. The eerie sense of unreality that had troubled him from the beginning of the case crept into him again. Might men exceed and extend the limits set by nature, remake the mold? Here was dangerous and uncharted ground, yet his instinctive recoil was accompanied by an irresistible fascination. He shivered involuntarily. There seemed colossal risk in this, and a wonderful daring.

Alexander's voice interrupted his thoughts. "Are the French looking into that, too? His remarkable endurance and strength, I mean. That could be even more important than the kid's brain."

"They are. At least I think they are. There was a muscle physiologist at the autopsy, and he took a specimen for study. Dr. Mulligan took a brain specimen, of course."

"Ah, yes, our friend Dr. Mulligan," Alexander said cryptically. "We'll get to him in a minute. But tell me first about the autopsy."

Ridgely shrugged. "What's to tell? He was a sort of grotesque-looking child . . . weighed maybe seventy or eighty pounds . . . looked like a shrunken old man. Sort of like he'd been pickled. But the pathologist said that he couldn't see anything strange about the internal organs."

"Of course not," Alexander muttered, more to himself than to Ridgely. "The mutations would be more subtle than that." His brow furrowed in thought and he leaned forward on his elbows with his fingertips on his forehead. He scowled once at a passing idea, but then his expression brightened. "All right," he said. "Now for the good Dr. Mulligan. How much do you know about him?"

"Not that much. I haven't had a chance yet to do a really extensive background check. He's a research biochemist at UCLA. Neurobiochemist, really. He's from New York, but he's been living in L.A. for the last ten years. Supposedly brilliant, one of the top researchers in his field. The French asked for him specifically."

"Where is he now?"

"In L.A., I guess. At least he was on his way there the last time I saw him."

"I'd like him closer," Alexander muttered, "where I can keep an eye on him myself. The Russians will be watching him, of course."

"What's so important about Dr. Mulligan?" Ridgely asked.

Alexander suddenly glared at him harshly. "You haven't read his paper, have you?" he accused. "If you had, you'd know why he's so important."

Ridgely flushed with embarrassment. "And the Russians have?"

"*Of course,*" Alexander snapped. "If the French knew his work the Russians know it, too. It's unique. He's key to the whole thing. That's one of the problems with science, you know. It's all public information. All the Russians have to do is to get subscriptions to the right magazines. Everything's written down, right there. Remember when that high school kid in New Jersey announced he could build an atomic bomb—if he could get the uranium—with the information he could get from physics journals. He was right. He could."

"Oh, come on," Ridgely said. "It can't be that bad. We keep plenty of secrets."

"We do when we know there's a secret to be kept. Sometimes we don't even know that. You know, when the Germans Hahn and Strassman split the uranium atom in 1939, they actually published their experimental results. Published them! Right there where anyone could read it! Fortunately for us the Nazi censors didn't have the vaguest notion of what it was all about. But every physicist who read the paper instantly realized you could make a bomb from the stuff." Alexander paused and looked at Ridgely now in milder admonition. "You'll have to read his paper, you know."

"I probably won't understand a word of it," Ridgely said lamely.

"You'd have to read it first to know if you'd understand it or not, wouldn't you? I have read it . . . several times. That's my job. That's the job of my department. Technological assessment. I've got a staff of officers who've had advanced training in practically every field of science and technology, and they read everything. And every time they read something they ask themselves the same question: 'What might be the military applications of this?' We've been watching Dr. Mulligan's career ever since he published that paper." Alexander paused and added parenthetically, somewhat snidely, "He hasn't made a lot of progress, though."

"He did tell me about his theory of intelligence, though," Ridgely said apologetically.

"Oh? And what did he tell you?"

"Something about how intelligence was proportional to the connections brain cells made with each other and how much neurotransmitter there was."

"That's all he said?" Alexander smiled superciliously.

"That's all." Ridgely realized that he was about to be made to feel foolish again and braced himself for it.

"You missed the main point, then."

"All right." Ridgely sighed. "I'll bite. What's the main point?"

"The main point is this: Mulligan asked a very interesting question in that paper. He asked, 'What if it's all much simpler than we think?' An interesting question, that, one that grows on you. By that he meant that maybe much smaller genetic changes, involving just a few genes, could result in profound alterations. He asked if increases in the enzymes that make neurotransmitters might result in a sort of superintelligence. The trick was that these increases had to be present in the embryonic stage, when the brain was just forming, so they could influence its structure as well as its function."

Suddenly the light clicked on and Ridgely understood for the first time what it was all about, why everyone had made such a fuss over the Russian boy, why doctors in Paris had sent all the way to Los Angeles for Dr. Mulligan. "The experiment of nature," he murmured.

"What's that?" Alexander was attentive and probing.

"An experiment of nature," Ridgely repeated, louder. He looked directly at Alexander. "That's what all the doctors in Paris kept talking about."

"That's right." Alexander understood immediately. "Nature did for Mulligan what he couldn't do for himself. This gives him the chance to confirm his theory. And to explore the genetics of it."

"And if it's true?" Ridgely let the question hang in the air.

"If it's true, we're a lot closer to making smarter or faster, or whatever, people than we thought we were. It may actually be a lot simpler than we think. Maybe changing just one or two genes, at the right time . . ." the general's voice trailed off.

"But Mulligan said nothing about genetic engineering."

"Why should he? He's not interested in that. I am. Mulligan's only interested in discovering the biochemical basis of intelligence. He just wants to know what makes the brain tick. I'm the one who's thinking of making better soldiers."

Ridgely shivered again.

Alexander noticed the involuntary gesture. "Think it's disgusting?" he snorted in contempt. "Sure it is, but so what? Napalm is disgusting, too. So are chemical weapons. The purpose of a weapon is to kill somebody, not to tickle his fancy. There's nothing particularly aesthetic about having a leg sliced off by a piece of shrapnel, either, or getting

103

burned by an atomic fireball. Disgust doesn't stop us from using any of these weapons. At the very least you can always justify what you're doing on the grounds that the other side is doing it, too."

Alexander was right, Ridgely knew. Genetic engineering could be preempted for military use, like any other bit of knowledge or discovery. The Wright brothers had had visitors from the army almost as soon as they had got home from Kitty Hawk. Almost by its very nature, knowledge couldn't be left unused. When something became possible, sooner or later someone would actually go ahead and do it . . . and the argument 'better us than them' was a hard one to refute.

He glanced at the wall map behind Alexander's desk and was overwhelmed again by a sence of the colossal scale of the conflict between the United States and the Soviet Union. The ancient rivalries of Greece and Persia, Rome and Carthage, France and Germany seemed puny by comparison. Alexander might be right. War might very well be an inevitability, even if diplomacy had its periods of warmth and chill. Could anyone afford to ignore a potential advantage? But . . . undermine the genetic foundation of the species? Such a question had never been asked before.

Whatever its ultimate significance might be, the pieces of the puzzle were falling rapidly into place. The motives of the KGB now seemed obvious.

But another consequence seemed equally obvious. It was an ominous thought, but at least it put the matter in a diametric, pungent perspective. Someone, some Russian equivalent of General Alexander, had had the same idea. That was why the KGB had made the extraordinary if bungled attempt to steal the body. The enemy also realized that Ivan was an experiment of nature too precious and too rare to miss—that one might find out if things really were as simple, and as simply malleable, as Mulligan's theory had predicted.

Ridgely broached the subject carefully. "You realize,

General, that this same conversation has taken place in Moscow."

Alexander nodded. A thin, humorless smile flickered across his lips. "I told you, didn't I, that at the very least you could always justify things on the grounds that the other side is doing them, too. And that's also why you've got to keep an eye on Dr. Mulligan."

Ridgely stood up, trying to dispel by a physical movement the heavy sense of foreboding that had begun to settle over him. "I'd better get out to L.A., then."

"One thing about that," Alexander cautioned. "You haven't had as much experience as I've had with research scientists. They're positive fiends for publishing their results."

"So?"

"So the good Dr. Mulligan will expect to get at least one paper out of this. From his point of view it's almost miraculous that nature's given him this chance. He's probably got visions of the Nobel Prize dancing in his head."

Ridgely considered that carefully. "Will the Russians be expecting him to publish a paper with his results?" he asked slowly.

"Of course."

"Then it would give us a chance to ply them with a little disinformation, wouldn't it?"

"Keep going. I like where you're heading," Alexander said.

"Let's see first what he finds out. We'll see if there's a chance to mislead the Russians about this. Then maybe we'll write Dr. Mulligan's paper for him."

Another thin-lipped smile flickered across the face of the general. "I'm glad to see that you and the CIA take the same cheerful carefree attitude toward civil rights that we in the military do."

"Of course," Ridgely commented, "he'll scream bloody murder."

"So what if he screams? All the scientists scream when we

close in on them and tell them what to do or not to do. That's not important. These are questions of national security."

Strange, Ridgely thought, how events interlock once you understand their significance. A mutant child in Paris, a dead KGB agent, an obscure neurobiologist at UCLA—all catapulted abruptly to the level of national security by this monomaniac of a general who saw things in long perspective and with great imagination.

"Don't mistake its importance, Mr. Ridgely," Alexander intoned, threatening and commanding. "Don't mistake it for a minute. National security is at stake. Not immediately. Not this week or next, not even this year or next, not for several decades, perhaps. But eventually. Eventually there will come a day when the security, the very survival, of the United States may very well depend on our ability to create the right sort of mutant soldier."

"I'll be in L.A. tonight," Ridgely said.

CHAPTER SIX

All the way to Paris Mulligan thought, it's impossible, impossible, things like this don't happen. They just don't. The vast amount of neurotransmitter enzyme he had found in Ivan's brain could be explained in only one way, simultaneous mutation of many genes at once—an event of staggering improbability. One such might be believed, but two! Nature often teased and taunted, dangling the unlikely before wondering and uncomprehending eyes, but here Mulligan felt his sense of improbability stretching into blunt disbelief. He found himself simmering with annoyance. Maybe they're twins, he speculated, although the explanation seemed inane almost as soon as it occurred to him.

He had caught the 11:00 P.M. direct flight from L.A. to Paris, the earliest one he could make. The jetliner couldn't get there fast enough. The appearance of the second child could put Irene in frightful jeopardy. He felt the push of imminent danger, of hanging portent, as though he was on the edge of a cascade of terrible events. Malign forces seemed to be swirling and circling around him, and he remembered with a shudder the sight of Aaron gasping for air through purpling lips. Could the same happen to Irene? The Sûreté, or even the Deuxième Bureau would, he hoped, provide her with enough protection. She had promised to call them immediately after talking to him, to let them know that another Russian child had appeared.

"But there's been an attack here, too," she had said. "Today."

"Attack? Are you all right?" He had felt his heart pounding.

"No, no. I'm all right," she had reassured him. "Don't worry. I'll tell you all about it when you get here."

Too much was happening too fast. The KGB might realize, though, if their purpose had been to prevent anyone's learning the secret of Ivan's mutation, that there was no point in attacking Irene Sailland's lab. She might have been able to detect the chromosomal abnormality if the cells in her culture plate hadn't died. But they *had* died, and that failure might actually keep her safe. If the Russian agents who invaded his lab in L.A. had known enough about him and his work to pinpoint their destruction so accurately, then surely they would know that there was nothing to be gained by attacking Irene Sailland. They would know already that Ivan's cells couldn't be multiplied in tissue culture. Or would they? It seemed ironic that her inability to perform certain experiments might shield her from harm, that ignorance might be a form of safety. For no particular reason a memory of the dead boy's face came to him, a vague floating image of formalin-yellowed skin finely wrinkled and blistered as though by the passage of searing heat.

Through his fears, though, surged an enormous sense of vindication and triumph. His theory was confirmed. It was true! The years of effort and frustration, of unsuccessful experiments, enduring all the while the barbed and often nasty criticism of his colleagues, had not been a waste. Intelligence was, after all, determined by the in utero concentration of neurotransmitters. It was undeniable. Ivan's brain had been the proof. Mulligan smiled to himself as he recalled his original question: What if it's all much simpler than we think? It seemed to him now to have the penetrating elegance and simplicity of all the great scientific insights.

From the airport in Los Angeles he'd called the 800 number Ridgely had supplied. Ridgely had been right. The girl who answered the phone chattered a lot of nonsense about customers and orders but seemed to be taking down everything he said. Could she get a message through to Mr. Brent Ridgely, please? Yes, of course she could. It had all seemed reassuringly ordinary, until you recalled that the Russian agents in L.A. had been perfectly willing to commit murder. The message was from Dr. George Mulligan: Dr. Mulligan's laboratory had been attacked . . . by Russians, probably KGB. Also, another child with progeria had arrived in Paris. Just today. Dr. Mulligan was flying to Paris right away. He could be reached at the Hôpital des Enfants, care of Dr. Sailland. The girl said casually that she would see to it that Mr. Ridgely got the message, and hung up.

Mulligan carefully fingered the bandage on his left cheek. The gouge had been deep and had required a dozen stitches, and now it felt as though the skin were being parted with a sharp blade. He hoped the gauze had remained dry and didn't have any unsightly bloody splotches seeping through it. He felt conspicuous enough already.

Confinement in an airplane cabin had always made Mulligan feel uncomfortable and slightly claustrophobic. He resented his total dependence on the plane and pilot, and being shepherded around by professionally friendly stewardesses aroused a sense of rebellion that grated and scratched at his composure. It occurred to him suddenly, with a jolt, that there was very likely a Russian agent on the airplane. Surely he was under surveillance. It seemed the enemy put a greater value on him than his own side did. Had the great slovenly man behind him at the ticket counter actually been following him? Or was there no one on his tail, had they merely noted what flight he was on and then telephoned ahead to Paris? Easy to spot . . . the man with the bloody bandage on his face. He felt a rush of outrage and helplessness and got up to walk up and down the cabin. It was night outside, and most of the passengers were dozing, their heads nodding in those uncomfortable postures people assume when trying to sleep on airplanes. Here and there a man read quietly, illuminated angelically from above by one of the little seat lights. How could you tell a Russian agent when you saw one? Did he look sinister? Would there be anything so obvious as foreign clothing? He found the sensation of being watched an invasion of privacy, like having one's personal conversations overheard in an elevator, and he returned to his seat, now more angered than frightened.

The sensation intensified when he landed at DeGaulle Airport. As he waited for his suitcase, he surveyed the passengers. Faces, subtly altered by the suspicions he projected onto them, lost any semblance of conviviality: innocent mannerisms became threatening. For the first time in his life he felt a sense of inadequacy, like a wood chip in the waves, overwhelmed and crushed by the forces around him.

DeGaulle, like all great international airports, was a crossroads of the world, a compressed amalgam of humanity, dazzling in its variety of sizes, shapes and colors of people. It would be child's play, he thought, for a trained agent to follow someone unobserved in such a crowd. People scurried in all directions, paused to listen to loudspeaker announcements in several languages, lifted or dropped luggage with varying degrees of strength and agility, shouted and waved when friends or relatives came into view. British businessmen in three-piece pinstriped suits mingled with African diplomats resplendent in native costume; American tourists, carefree and relaxed, jovially glorying in the favorable exchange rates, rubbed elbows with surly Algerian immigrants. Who among these people could be Soviet agents? He had no idea. For a moment Mulligan toyed with the thought of trying to lose himself in the crowd, then rejected the impulse. Screw it, he said angrily to himself. Let Ridgely worry about security.

The return to Paris after a mere four-day absence, though, made him feel like a jet-setting commuter, with a commuter's comforting sense of familiarity. He sat in the back seat of the taxi an idly watched the city slip by. He hadn't slept at all during the long flight, and he realized how tired he was, how much his body still ached where the KGB agent had hit him. A last-minute glance into a mirror before disembarking from the airplane revealed that his face was bruised and swollen, as well as lacerated. He had a feeling of disorientation and disproportion, as though he'd been abandoned in an amusement park's hall of mirrors or bodily lifted out of one world and unceremoniously dumped into another. A month ago he'd been quietly pursuing his research in neurobiochemistry, solid and stable. Now he had a sensation that reality was sliding out from under him, a fugitive's sense of being uncontrollably buffeted by events. He found humiliating and infuriating the suspicion that he was being used as a pawn by other, more powerful men. Maybe I'll wake up soon, he thought, and find this has all been a bad dream. Then his cheek started throbbing again.

The taxi driver was one of those muttering Frenchmen who seem to be in a continual boil of anger. A thick Gauloise could be seen dangling, magically adherent to his lower lip. He turned his head to ask, *"Pourquoi vous allez à l'Hôpital des Enfants?"*

Mulligan sat upright in alarm. Reason said that the driver had been a random choice from the taxis clustering outside the air terminal and therefore couldn't possibly be a KGB agent. Fear insinuated the suspicion anyway. *"Je suis médecin,"* he replied, scowling and hostile.

That seemed to settle the matter and the driver resumed his self-appointed task of indiscriminately cursing all the other motorists in Paris.

111

The scene in the lobby of the hospital was again reassuringly ordinary. A two-way current of parents and children flowed up and down the broad steps from the boulevard, through the wide front doors and across the lobby. It was easy to tell who was coming and who was going. The parents with expressions of relief, whose children pointed and shouted with anticipation, were obviously leaving to go home; those with dour faces of concern, pulling silent, reluctant children with large tearful eyes, were leading them to the admitting room. He asked for Dr. Irene Sailland to be paged to come to the main desk, and stood to one side next to his suitcase, uneasy because he couldn't manage to find an empty spot on a wall to back up against. As he listened to her name being called over the loudspeaker, he again became self-consciously aware of his cut and bandaged face, although no one seemed to be paying him much attention.

He waited long enough to become worried about her and was just thinking of telephoning her home number when she was upon him. She rushed at him from the side, so that he didn't see her until she was there, her arms around his neck, covering his face with kisses.

"George, oh George," she murmured, holding him tightly, her face warm and moist against his. "I was so frightened, so worried."

In that instant he knew she cared about him and felt a flood of happiness tumble through him. "I'm fine, Irene, really," he said, loosening himself from her embrace and looking at her. A flush burnished the olive-tan of her skin, and tears poised perilously on her cheekbones. She dabbed at them unconsciously while other tears curled from her glistening eyes to the corners of her mouth. "I missed you," he said, realizing how much indeed he had.

"*Moi aussi,*" she said, then smiled through her tears. "It's so silly. I feel like a young girl again." She stepped back and eyed him critically, and a warm bubble of laughter rose from her throat. "You look awful." She reached out to touch with a gentle hand the bandage on his face. "Does it hurt much?"

"Only when I laugh," he said, embracing her again. "So don't say anything funny."

"Come on," she said. "There's a lot to discuss. I'll tell you about the dramas we've had here."

She led him to a small cafeteria the hospital maintained for its staff. Retelling his story helped Mulligan dispel his fatigue. He related again, in greater detail, the circumstances of the incident the prior day in Los Angeles, the rapidity and violence of it, how both he and Aaron had been stunned and overwhelmed. With just a trace of boastfulness he described how he'd saved Aaron's life with the chest tube . . .

"They must have known exactly what they were looking for," he concluded. "Exactly. Aaron's slides, my reagents, the brain specimen. They destroyed just what they needed to destroy, not more, not less. Very well coached."

"And your friend Aaron?" Her concern was genuine and troubled. He guessed that she, too, felt the menace that, like a sticky film, was wrapping itself around their lives.

"He was just coming out of surgery when I got on the plane, getting his lung sewn up. He'll be all right, but for the next month every time he coughs it's going to feel as if someone's stabbing him."

"Are you sure they were Russian?"

"Who else? I'm almost sure of it. I don't speak Russian, but it sure sounded like it."

"The well-known American ability for languages," she teased.

"The point is," he said, ignoring the teasing, invigorated again, "they were too late! Too late, Irene! We'd already proven it! The theory is true, every bit of it! The findings in the brain specimen confirmed it perfectly. Everything we looked for was there, just as the theory predicted it would be. Every neuron had at least ten times the usual number of dendrites . . . Aaron's slides demonstrated it conclusively.

And the concentration of neurotransmitter enzymes was at least fifty times greater than any I've ever found before." Mulligan clenched his fist and pounded it softly on the table. *"My . . . theory . . . is . . . true!"* He sat back and grinned even though it hurt to do so. "Aaron thinks the Nobel is in the bag."

"Fifty times?" Though she shared his excitement, Irene seemed strangely puzzled and disturbed. "How do you explain that?"

"I can't. Not yet." He looked at her and grinned again, suddenly relishing the challenge the unexplained phenomenon put before him. "But it was at least that much. It was uneven, though. Some cells had a lot more than others. Very haphazard and peculiar. I'll need another specimen, though, to demonstrate it again. The Russians ruined the one I had."

"You won't be able to get it," she said. The excitement on her face faded to a troubled and worried expression. "That's part of the news I had for you."

"What happened?" Mulligan asked, instantly apprehensive that he might not be able to prove his theory, after all. "Was Ivan's body kidnapped? Did they try again?"

"Not kidnapped. Burned. That was the attack I told you about."

"Burned?" His voice mixed incredulity and disgust.

"Someone set the morgue at the Sûreté on fire. An incendiary bomb, they told me. The morgue had a window opening onto a small side street, the rue des Curés, and they think it was thrown from there."

"When?"

"Just yesterday. Just before the second boy showed up."

"The same day my lab was attacked," he sighed, feeling another oppressive sense of enclosure. "They're well coordinated, anyway."

"The principle of surprise. It always works, doesn't it? The Sûreté were prepared to stop a man at the door, but no one thought of defending against a fire bomb through the window. By the time the fire was put out, half the building was gone and Ivan's body had been cremated. It seems indecent," she said, struggling to keep down an indignant abhorrence, "that there wasn't even anything left to bury. It won't happen again, though. Not here at the Hôpital des Enfants. Since yesterday it seems as though there are more security police than patients in the hospital."

"What about Dr. Gallieni?" Mulligan suddenly remembered that he wasn't the only one doing studies on tissue obtained from the now cremated body.

Irene turned down the corners of her mouth and shrugged, her hands raised in an expression of bewildered dismissal. "Nothing," she said. "He's fine. I spoke with him last night after you called." Her brow darkened with a disturbing thought. "You're the one they want, George. You're the one that's the danger to them."

"Ah, there you are," said a man's voice beside them. "I've been looking all over for you." It was Dr. Lussac, looking professorial in a long white lab coat, spilling over with excitement and eagerness, undaunted by the shadows of foreign intrigue spreading over them. "Irene told me you were coming back. Well!" he said, throwing his hands in the air in a grand Gallic gesture. "What do you think? There's another one of them!" He sat down to join them.

"I think it's impossible," Mulligan stated flatly.

"Impossible? Yes, of course! But there it is! The impossible remains impossible only until we learn how it works. Like a magic trick until you learn how it's done, eh?"

"I *know* how it works," Mulligan said, "and I still think it's impossible."

"You know how it works?" Lussac's eyebrows furrowed. "Ah, I see," he said, realizing. "Your theory. It's true, then, your theory about neurotransmitters?"

Mulligan nodded his head slowly. "Yes." He recounted again, briefly, the results of his and Aaron's experiments.

Lussac seemed puzzled again. "Then why is it impossible?"

115

"Because the mutation involves too many genes at once. It wasn't just one neurotransmitter enzyme that was increased, it was all of them. All at once. Do you realize what the odds are? There was probably something funny about his muscle enzymes, too. But that would make it even more enzymes, more mutations. Too many at once."

Lussac nodded in agreement. "You're right about the muscles. Dr. Gallieni called me this morning when he finished his investigation. Your original idea was correct. It was the CPK. He thought it was at least twenty times its normal concentration."

CPK, or creatine phosphokinase, was an enzyme essential for energy transfer within the cell. Mulligan knew little about muscle physiology, but he supposed that, in concentrations greatly exceeding normal, CPK could produce a rippling enhancement of muscle contraction. It would be like adding a more powerful fuel to an engine or running a chemical reaction at a higher temperature. In any event, the analogy to the brain was exact—an incomparable functioning of the organ had been achieved by increasing the concentration of an essential enzyme. But this thought drew him back again to the basic conundrum; it was too many mutations at one time.

"I know what you're thinking, George," said Irene, guessing his thoughts. "The only way you can get so many mutations at once is to have a chromosomal mutation—a duplication of part of one chromosome, or maybe of three of a certain chromosome where there should only be two."

"That's the only way I can conceive of it . . . unless the boys are identical twins."

"They're not that," Lussac stated with assurance. "You can tell that just by looking at them. But I can run some blood-typing tests, or even some tissue typing, to be sure, if you want."

"Please. The sooner the better." Mulligan felt his frustration mount.

Irene looked at him steadily. "We'll have to explain it

some other way altogether," she said evenly, anticipating his objections. "It's not the chromosomes. Definitely not. I haven't told you yet that I managed to get some lymphocytes from the boy who came here yesterday to divide once, just once, before they died. One mitosis only, but it was enough for a chromosomal analysis." She paused a moment. "The chromosomes are normal. I'm sure of it."

"They can't be."

"They are." Her look softened and affection crept into her voice. "Look, George, chromosomal analysis is my forté. These chromosomes are normal."

"But they *can't* be normal," he said again, foolishly, yielding to the temptation to cling stubbornly to false theory rather than be forced to face inexplicable fact.

"They *are,*" she reiterated. She reached across the table and covered his hand with hers. "We'll have to find another explanation, George."

"What if," Lussac interrupted, thinking aloud, "what if all these genes, the ones coding for these enzymes, were controlled by the same stop-and-go signal on the chromosome, and it doesn't know when to say stop? Suppose that's the mutation? Then one mutation could account for the whole thing." Lussac seemed delighted by the cleverness of his idea.

"Good logic," Mulligan rejoined, "faulty premise. These genes aren't turned on and off by the same signal. They can't be. Normally, in certain areas of the brain you find one neurotransmitter predominating and other ones in other areas. Serotonin and dopamine work mostly in hypothalamic functions, noradrenaline in the cortex. If the genes coding for the enzymes manufacturing these substances were all controlled by the same stop-and-go signal, their concentrations would be equal in all parts of the brain. Since it isn't, they are, therefore, governed by separate signals."

The logic was inescapable. Lussac drummed his fingers on the table. *"Rien ne va plus,"* he muttered.

So the mystery remained, obdurate and unresolved.

117

Nature buried her secrets as the Earth buried its gold, forcing men to dig. A moment arises in scientific inquiry when the observed facts no longer fit the mold intellect has created; then ignorance and creativity stand in bold confrontation. It was like taking all the gold from the mine that could be obtained by pick and shovel. To get more, a new method would have to be used.

No one spoke for what seemed a long time. Mulligan rubbed his forehead wearily. His back felt stiff and the laceration on his cheek was beginning to throb again. He wondered how hard it would be to find a bottle of bourbon in Paris.

"How do we know," he asked abruptly, as the thought struck him, "that this second boy is just as smart as the first? Has he said anything, or done anything, to show it?"

"No, not really, not so far." Lussac shook his head dolefully. "He's too sick, much sicker than Ivan was when he first arrived. I'm not even sure he's going to survive for the present moment."

"What's he got?" Mulligan asked.

"Pneumonia and renal failure," Lussac answered. He grinned suddenly, inspired by that charitable perversity of doctors, enthused by the presence of disease as a warrior is enthused by the imminence of battle. "Dehydration and myoglobin toxicity, from all the running. His muscles just broke down under the strain, and his kidneys couldn't flush it out fast enough. We'll take care of that, of course. We'll dialyze him. It's really the pneumonia I'm worried about. I have to keep reminding myself that he's not really a little child, that physiologically he's more like a man in his sixties."

"So you don't know for sure he's as smart as the first one."

"No, not for sure, but it's reasonable enough to assume that he is. The circumstances are the same: he's about the same age, he's got progeria, he turned up just as mysteriously from nowhere, he speaks Russian, he was looking for Irene. Everything's the same."

"And they're not twins?" Mulligan asked again. He was still grasping for straws.

"No." Lussac was definite. "Come and see for yourself."

Lussac and Irene led Mulligan through the hospital to the pediatric intensive care unit. The Hôpital des Enfants was much older than most American hospitals, a legacy of the 1880s, and the esthetics of the nineteenth century had long ago surrendered to the imperious utilitarianism of the twentieth. Through the corridors an overhead maze of heating ducts, water pipes and electrical conduits coursed seemingly at random. Gray stone walls, otherwise prone to echo the shrieks and cries of the children, were covered with sound-absorbing tapestries as well as pictures of zoo animals and clowns. One ward had been converted into a large play-room, a distraction from loneliness and pain, where convalescing children could be helped to turn their eyes away from the glazed faces and motionless bodies of other children on gurneys returning from surgery with IV bottles stuck up on poles, tiny reservoirs dripping fluid into tiny veins. Here and there a statue of the Virgin offered quiet solace.

The intensive care unit was at the end of a long hallway, a location which facilitated its security. At intervals along the corridor a uniformed, armed officer of the Sûreté sat quietly, stopping and questioning anyone who looked as though he didn't belong there. At the entrance to the ICU three of the policemen stopped them to inquire who Mulligan was before permitting his entry into the unit.

Lussac vouched for him. "The Sûreté insisted on these guards," he told Mulligan, "after the fire incident. This boy, at least, will be well guarded."

It seemed to Mulligan that it would take a frontal assault with at least a squad of men to get into the ICU.

The intensive care unit was a large room with beds laid

out perpendicular to the wall on three sides of the rectangle. There were no windows. On the same side as the door was the nurses' desk with its usual clutter of patients' charts, lab reports, and half-empty coffee cups. Within the room was assembled the vast armamentarium of modern medicine: sighing, hissing respirators drove air into the lungs of several inert young patients, constant infusion pumps delivered precise amounts of potent medications and cardiac monitors captured on oscilloscopes every erratic heartbeat, their wire leads emerging from under the blankets like electrical umbilical cords.

The Russian boy lay on a bed directly opposite the door. They approached the bed quietly, almost warily. Mulligan could see at a glance that Lussac was right, that the two boys couldn't be identical twins. The progeria imposed a surface similarity, but this boy was smaller, somehow more birdlike, bony with light, airy bones in bare arms that lay on top of the blankets. His muscles were lean, stretched and wiry, yet not the muscles of a boy, more like a miniature man's muscles, defined, hinting at strength beyond their bulk. A sandy thatch of thinning hair, streaked with gray, unkempt and matted, too long, imparted a look of primitive savagery. But it was the boy's face that drew attention the most, a face more worn and beaten than old, like a gnarled tree stump exposed to decades of inclement weather. He lay in a semistupor, struggling against its oblivion; and his dark brown eyes glimmered a ceaseless vigil, a darting sensory apparatus moving restlessly around the room. They seemed to imprint discontinuous mental pictures of the scene before them. Like Ivan's, his forehead was large, bumpy and high, and when the eyes focussed on him Mulligan could almost feel the power of the intelligence that lay behind them.

It was obvious, too, that the child was desperately, critically ill. His skin was like unglazed white clay, though flushed with fever. An unceasing cough jerked his body spasmodically, compressing his chest with a snapping bellows motion, producing a thick greenish phlegm that a nurse dutifully wiped from his mouth.

The probing eyes fastened on Irene when they saw her, and the child's face melted into an expression of bottomless yearning, of supplication and helplessness. It was the look of a hurt child stumbling home and seeing his mother, rushing forward with the expectation of miraculous cure. He strained upward, reaching a thin arm out to her. "Dr. Sailland." It was a cry wrenched through agony, rising from a throat unwilling to bear the pain of creating sound. A cough gripped him immediately and he fell back, exhausted by the simple utterance of the name.

The effect upon Irene could not have been more dramatic had she in fact been the child's mother. She took three hurried steps to reach the boy's side and, taking his hand in hers, stroked and patted it, murmuring, *"Dors, petit garçon, dors."* The boy murmured something unintelligible, then lay back, comforted for the moment.

CHAPTER SEVEN

Mulligan flushed slightly and looked away, feeling that he had intruded on a private moment.

"It was the same with the first one," Lussac whispered. "I suppose it's a result of the enormous effort they've gone through just to get here. It magnifies her in their esteem. She's become their personal savior."

It seemed a long time before the boy closed his eyes, the unrelenting surveillance surrendering at last to the body's need for rest. He fell into a sleep troubled only by the interminable cough.

"Look here," Lussac whispered again. "Look at this." He pointed to where the boy had grasped Irene's hand. Her flesh was white, bloodless, pressed so hard that Mulligan wondered she did not cry out in pain. "You see the great strength?" Lussac exulted. "Remarkable!" Mulligan had to exert considerable force to loosen the boy's grip.

"*Il ne veut pas me faire mal,*" Irene whispered to herself, "*mais il ne connaît pas sa force. Je reviendrai.*" She turned away and walked quickly from the room, wiping tears from her eyes.

"I'll stay here," Lussac said, although he was beginning to sound tired. "We're just going to start the dialysis. There's a long way to go if we're to save his life."

Mulligan found Irene in the corridor. Her expression was the oscillating mixture of anguish and horror of someone who has just witnessed a traffic accident in which people have been mangled and mutilated.

"Irene . . ."

"I know, I know." She waved her hand to ward off his sympathy. "I'm behaving badly. Emotional. Unscientific. But it's so horrible, George. So horrible! That boy actually ran, starving and cold and alone, from Leningrad to Paris because he thinks I can save him from that horrible disease he has. I feel so . . . responsible." Tears welled up again in her eyes.

"It's not your fault." He patted her on the shoulder, aware of the limp inadequacy of his attempted consolation.

"And you saw how sick he is. That cough. It's tearing his body apart."

"Dr. Lussac is doing everything he can. You know that."

"And if Lussac does save him, what then?" she burst out fiercely. "What then? He'll just die in a month or two from a heart attack or stroke or some kind of cancer. What's the use?" Her anger, futile, collapsed, and she fell against Mulligan with a sob.

He put his arm around her shoulder and they walked down the corridor. "Can we sit down somewhere?" he asked.

She nodded silently, still crying, and led him to Lussac's office. The office reflected Lussac's monomaniacal devotion to his profession. Stacks of pediatrics journals in French and English were piled high on the desk and floor. A reference book was left open to the moment of latest interest, and the handwritten draft of a research paper was scattered in scholarly disarray on the desk top.

123

Irene sank into a huge leather chair and, though still wiping tears from her eyes, began rubbing the hand that the boy had held.

"Do you think it's broken?" Mulligan asked. "Perhaps we should get an x-ray."

She shook her head. "I don't think so." Then she spoke in a harsh voice of bitter irony. "How could he hurt me? He's *only* a little boy. No, no, I'm all right, just upset, not cracking up." She seemd better after a few more minutes.

A telephone on the desk reminded Mulligan that he ought to make another attempt to reach Ridgely.

"Do you have to?" Irene asked when he told her he needed to call Washington. "I don't like those people."

"Neither do I, but I really haven't got much choice, do I? Just as you had to inform the Sûreté and the Deuxième that a second boy had turned up."

He telephoned Washington. The girl was unable to tell him whether or not the first message had been delivered, so he repeated it, adding merely that he was now in Paris, and hung up. While he was talking he watched Irene carefully. She had stopped crying but looked as though she might start again, and her mascara was smeared. With a nervous gesture she reached one hand to wipe her cheek but succeeded only in smudging it further. He took the hand in his and held it softly. He felt he loved her beyond measure.

"Irene, you know that there's more than just the life of the boy involved here. We can't make the world nice just by wishing it so."

He felt her shudder. "I know," she acknowledged. Her voice was barely audible. "I know."

Mulligan stood up and looked at his watch. It was six o'clock. "I'd better get a hotel. I wonder if there's a room at the Michelet-Odéon."

"Don't," she said abruptly, standing up.

"Don't what?"

"Don't find a hotel . . . Stay . . . with me. Why don't you stay with me?" The question was open and straightforward.

124

She was frightened and wanted his protection; she needed him and wanted him in her bed. Why not just ask? If her voice held any timidity at all, it was only in tacit recognition that the offer might, possibly, be turned down.

A great longing for her swept through him, merging with and overcoming his weariness. He felt a sensation of being at home, at last at home, as though he had just returned from a long journey. He reached his arms out and drew her to him. She looked up at him expectantly and he brushed back a wisp of hair that had fallen over her forehead.

"But I'm not even French," he murmured, smiling.

"In that case you might even like my cooking." She smiled back, then chuckled quietly. "We're a fine pair. Your face is all messed up and I've been crying like a schoolgirl whose boyfriend just jilted her. Come on, let's go."

He retrieved his suitcase from the cafeteria and they left the hospital. She lived, she said, in one of the many apartment complexes that surrounded the city. The best way to get there was by métro. Outside, the long spring day was winding down. The crowd on the sidewalk jostled him uncomfortably. The sense of being watched returned. His bruised face made him conspicuous and the suitcase made him awkward. With the prickly alertness of the rabbit sensing a hawk circling overhead he began to dart his gaze around, turning frequently to look behind them. He thought again that the crowd would conceal the pursuer more than it would protect the pursued.

Irene noticed his nervous movements and guessed its cause. "Do you think we're being followed?"

"I don't know for sure. I think so. It could be my imagination. I haven't actually seen anyone, but I've had the sensation of being followed ever since I left Los Angeles."

In the métro station the air was cooler, but the crowd thickened. At six o'clock the station was jammed with commuters, tired, self-absorbed people anxious to get home. A thin odor of cigarettes and sweat filled the air. There was a few minutes' wait for the train. Mulligan's eye absentmindedly took in the posters advertising Gitanes cigarettes, Carrera sunglasses, and the latest model Renault. A poster saying Dubo . . . Dubon . . . Dubonnet was covered with glass, and in its reflection he noticed a squarish man's face looking at him for what seemed a second too long, but when he whirled around the face had receded into the crowd.

On the train the crowd was even thicker, and Mulligan stood pressed against Irene, his suitcase bumping against his legs as the car swayed. The class divisions of Parisian society were reflected in the evening newspapers the commuters read: those in working-class blue shirts or company service uniforms read the communist *l'Humanité*, while the men in suits perused the more staid *le Figaro*. Different types of people got off the train at different stops as the subway made its slithering underground passage through the structure of society.

They left the train at the Place de la Cinquième République. The exit from the station was alongside a small traffic circle around which dashed Renaults and Fiats, and an occasional Peugeot, in rush-hour frenzy. The proscription on auto horns that kept the central city reasonably quiet didn't apply here, and a joyous cacophony celebrated the lack of inhibition. Several tree-shaded streets feeding into the traffic circle were lined with small shops and markets, and a number of men walked home with the bread for the evening meal wedged between arm and chest.

Her apartment was on the tenth floor of a new building, modestly but tastefully furnished, not overly neat. It conveyed a feeling of comfort and refuge. The living room had a brick fireplace and on the mantel was a photograph of a handsome man Mulligan presumed to be her husband. Her taste in furniture was light and functional, nothing heavy or overstuffed, and the walls had several prints by Dali and Degas. A small balcony looked toward the city, but the view was obscured by another building on the other side of a small courtyard.

Mulligan showered and shaved and changed his clothes while she cooked their dinner. He looked closely at his face in the mirror. The bruise and gash on his left cheekbone had swollen even more, though the sutures were holding nicely. He thought he looked a bit like a losing prize fighter.

"Are you sure you can stand a face like this?" he asked, coming up behind her in the kitchen.

"Sure." She turned and kissed him lightly on the lips. "I've seen worse."

He opened a bottle of the nouveau Beaujolais and poured two glasses, an unspoken assumption of domestic familiarity. "There's something I've been thinking about," he began. "Do you feel like talking about the boy?"

"You mean, will I start crying again? No, I won't." The task of cooking had restored her.

"It occurred to me that his situation might not be so hopeless after all. We know a good deal more about this one than you knew about Ivan. Assuming they're the same, of course. Which seems reasonable enough. What I mean is, we have a much better idea now about how the mutation works."

"The enzymes, you mean?"

"Yes, exactly. We know that he's got an enormous over-abundance of the enzymes involved in the production of neurotransmitters and at least one muscle enzyme. Let's assume that somehow, in some biochemical fashion we don't understand, this same overactivity of the enzymes is responsible for his progeria."

Irene grew more interested as she followed the line of his argument and saw where it was going. "So enzyme inhibitors could turn it all off!" She said this almost triumphantly. "It might work. It just might work. Unless," she added more pensively, "it's too late, if he's already got too much tissue damage."

"That's going to be a problem," Mulligan admitted, "but the idea fits in with your theories of aging, anyway, and it gives you something to work on."

"I always thought you were smart," she said affectionately, "even before I met you."

They sat down at the table. She'd prepared lamb chops, green beans, and a salad. "I haven't cooked for a man for a long time."

"I'm flattered."

"I think I'm a better chemist than cook."

"I'd say it's a toss-up. Did I mention that I'm crazy about you?"

"I know," she smiled.

While they ate she returned to the subject of being followed. "It makes you feel uneasy, doesn't it—I mean, to think that there might be someone just outside the apartment, watching us, keeping track of where we are and where we're going."

Mulligan sipped his wine and patted his lips with a napkin. "Not that I'm sure someone is following me," he said. "I'm not at all sure of it. It could easily be my imagination, maybe from that eerie sense of everything being so alien."

She nodded. "Like Ivan himself. Remember I told you how he didn't seem to fit anywhere."

After dinner she was making pralines, stirring butter and sugar together with almonds in a saucepan, when he approached her soundlessly from behind and kissed the back of her neck.

She turned around. "Don't you want some pralines?"

"Not now. Now I want you."

"All right," she breathed, and he saw the urgent assent in her eyes. "Let's go into the bedroom."

She retired to the bathroom to change her clothes. Mulligan turned off the light in the bedroom but left the door to the living room slightly ajar so that a hazy, muted light came through.

He had removed only his shoes and socks when she returned. She had changed into nothing but a translucent powder-blue nightgown that rustled slightly with the movement of her hips as she walked. Her breasts were half visible and swayed gently as she came toward him. Mulligan thought he had never seen a woman so lovely. She stopped in front of him and put her arms around his neck, her eyes already smoldering and her lips half-parted, and she stood on her toes to kiss him. He felt his heart beat faster and his erection rise as her lips parted further in the kiss. Her tongue flickered into his mouth and she pushed her thighs against him.

"I haven't been with a man since my husband died," she murmured, as though to apologize in advance for any awkwardness. Her breath was warm against his cheek and ear.

He looked down into her eyes and felt that he wanted to reach into her soul. "I want you," he said. "I want to make love to you, Irene." He reached his hand down to her buttocks and pulled her more firmly against him, wanting her to feel him, and he shuddered a little when he felt her knees bend and her thighs part slightly as she yielded to his embrace.

She stepped back and helped him to undress, unbuttoning his shirt and unfastening his belt and trousers. She took a sharp breath when his underwear came off and he stood naked in front of her. She stroked him lightly with both hands along the length of his erection, a caress at once of aching intimacy and yet not intimate enough. Her nightgown was tied loosely at the throat and Mulligan loosened the string and pushed the garment over her shoulders and let it drop to the floor. The curves of her body seemed wondrous, graceful shadows curving over soft ivory skin, and the musty fragrance of her perfume rose from between her breasts. He cupped one breast in his hand and bent to kiss the nipple, listening to her breath becoming faster and shorter. She continued standing in front of him as he sat on the edge of the bed, holding and kissing first one breast and then the other, while she reached under his arms and continued to stroke him, increasing even further his size and

VARIANT

rigidity. He pulled her closer, and with a swift and supple movement she sat on his lap facing him, her legs around his waist.

"Now," he murmured, "now." He leaned back a little, and she bent forward and down to kiss him again, and as she did so her hair fell across his face, forming a darkened cave, an impenetrable world of their own. "Now," he repeated, and she raised her hips slightly and, taking his erection in her hand, guided him into her. Their movements together were joined and flowing, flesh softened and kneeded by passion pressed against kneeded and softened flesh. He rolled her over so that he was on top as his urgency increased, and she locked her legs around the back of his thighs. As he neared his climax he felt himself clinging to her desperately, his arms around her holding her to his chest as tightly as he could. *"Je t'aime, Georges,"* he heard her whisper. *"Je t'aime, je t'aime."*

They spent the night in each other's arms, making love twice again, seeking both love and love's barricade against the world. She seemed more than he could ever have wished ... an opulent gift, and he felt an immense gratitude mixing with desire when he took her in his arms. Shuddering bodies blurred and made irrelevant the menace they felt coiling and stirring around them. Judgment and skill might be called for tomorrow, but tonight fear was banished by the enveloping abandon of sensuality.

They slept late the next day and didn't get to the hospital until early afternoon. Mulligan checked first to see if there had been any word from Ridgely. He found only the briefest of messages: "Astonishing. On my way." Remarkable brevity, he thought drily, and wondered if this was a universal virtue of espionage agents. A brief message, if intercepted, would likely reveal less.

When they reached the ICU they found that the boy's condition had deteriorated dramatically. He was near death. He lay in a coma, an ashen cyanosis coloring his lips and fingertips a cold and lifeless purple. The cough had become nearly continuous, but much more feeble, a useless torment as life ebbed away, and the effort to take a breath through it produced a rending gasp, a nauseating gurgle as the air was sucked in tormented jerks past the phlegm clogging his throat. Even from several feet away his exhaled breath was foul with the stench of pus and bacteria.

He was undergoing dialysis. A large-bore needle connected to a clear plastic catheter had been inserted into the radial artery near his left wrist and, with the assistance of a circular pump that squeezed it along in the tubing, blood was pushed into the hemodialysis machine. Once dialyzed and filtered free of the toxic materials normally removed by the kidneys, the blood was returned via another catheter leading to a vein in the same arm. Mulligan noted that the blood in the arterial catheter was nearly the same color as normal venous blood. The boy was scarcely getting any oxygen at all into his circulation.

"What are his blood gases?" he asked. Blood gases were a measure of pulmonary function.

Dr. Lussac looked haggard and exhausted, with deep shadows in half circles under his eyes. His voice was heavy with fatigue. "You can see for yourself," he said irritably, tossing his head in the direction of the arterial catherter. It was obvious he'd been up all night fighting a losing battle. He stood at the bedside, his arms folded across his chest, not taking his eyes from the child. "It's the pneumonia that's killing him, you know. He's too weak to cough; all that crap just sits there in his lungs. We've got him on the right antibiotics, I'm sure, ticarcillin and gentamicin. His sputum showed gram-negative rods, probably Klebsiella." Lussac stared mournfully at the sweating and struggling figure on the bed. "We're losing him."

Irene grasped Lussac's arm. "Don't let him die, Guy. Not now. Don't let him die!"

"What about a trach?" Mulligan asked. "You'll get better suctioning."

"Pardon?" asked Lussac, not understanding the slang.

131

"Sorry. A tracheostomy."

Lussac nodded his head ponderously. "That's next. It's the only thing left to do. I've got a surgeon on the way."

Mulligan stared attentively at the boy. They waited for the surgeon to arrive. All his energy seemed concentrated on the work of breathing. The bumps on his forehead seemed to have grown larger, covered with grained and ligneous skin, giving him a massive, misshapen cranium. A boy and not a boy; a man and not a man. The more Mulligan looked at him, the more he felt a sense of difference and distance, as though there yawned between them a gulf of unbridgeable proportions. He rememberd Claire Rosenberg's question: How many mutations does it take until you're not human any more?

Dr. Gaudy, the surgeon, arrived. He had the curt abruptness that characterizes surgeons, and, without saying much, taking in the situation at a glance, he began to lay out his instruments. While they watched him wash and glove his hands, Mulligan asked Lussac about the results of the blood and tissue-typing tests.

"Tissue typing? Oh, yes. That. I got the results this morning. Very interesting. Ivan and this one couldn't possibly have been identical twins. Definitely. But there seems to have been some consanguinity. They might be half brothers. They might have one parent in common, but that's all."

The mystery thickens, Mulligan thought.

The tracheostomy is one of the simplest, oldest and most straightforward of operations. Mulligan admired the surgeon's swift skill and dexterity. After tying his arms in loose restraints, the nurse bent the unresisting child's head back and put a small pillow under his neck, lifting and exposing the throat as though it were a ritual offering to the knife. She then swabbed the skin with iodine. Dr. Gaudy injected a local anesthetic on either side of the trachea. The boy twitched a little with the sting of the injection but made no movement of resistance. They waited a few minutes for the tissue swelling the injection produced to subside. Then the surgeon picked up his knife and made a vertical incision about an inch long, directly in the midline just beneath the thyroid cartilage. He did this smoothly and without hesitation. At this point he stopped cutting but reversed the scalpel and used the round end of its handle and a closed forceps to bluntly dissect tissue away from the surface of the trachea. Small arteries were carefully avoided and pushed aside. Lustrous white rings of cartilage emerged from the covering tissue as pearls might emerge from an opened oyster.

The surgeon used the knife again, cutting through one of the rings into the trachea. Instantly air hissed through the opening and the boy coughed so violently he had to be held down. Quickly Dr. Gaudy probed and widened the opening with his fingers. When it was big enough, he inserted the curved tracheostomy tube with a twisting downward motion and inflated the balloon at its tip. The natural airway was now completely closed. Air could enter or leave the lungs only through the tube. Respirator tubing was now attached, making the boy's respiratory apparatus a closed system, but one now completely controllable. No matter how much pressure was required to inflate his lungs, it could be delivered by the respirator. It was also possible to administer 100 percent oxygen, and this was done while the surgeon sutured the tube into place, attaching it firmly to the skin with silk sutures, so that even a vigorous cough wouldn't dislodge it.

"Now you can clean all that crap out of his lungs," Mulligan observed. And you'd better do it fast, he thought. Even on pure oxygen the boy looked cyanotic.

The lavage began. Another plastic catheter, one with several holes fenestrating its tip, was pushed through the tracheostomy tube and worked down into the lungs. The action again provoked a violent reflex. The muscles of his chest contracted in a prolonged spasm that made his ribs stand out like the rungs of a curved ladder; his neck and shoulders strained so fiercely against his restraints it seemed

133

they might shred themselves, and his legs uselessly flailed the bedcovers. A 5cc syringe of warmed saline was squirted into the catheter to moisten and loosen the sputum and then suction was quickly applied as the catheter was withdrawn.

A surprisingly large amount of yellow-green purulent sputum was suctioned out. The sight and smell of it made Mulligan feel ill. It was so thick that it clogged the suction tube and a new one had to be used. The procedure was repeated perhaps a dozen times, with less sputum and pus removed at each passage of the catheter, ventilating the boy with oxygen between each lavage, until Dr. Lussac was satisfied that all the obtainable sputum had been removed.

The result was immediate and profound. The child's cough subsided and his breathing eased. The pressures used by the respirator dropped substantially. Before their eyes his color changed, pink replacing purple in his lips and fingers, while his cheeks became a fiery, febrile red.

More importantly, the stupor faded. Mulligan could almost feel the brain returning to life as oxygen reached the boy's cerebral cortex. His eyes opened and immediately resumed their clicking snapshot pattern of surveying the room.

A hell of a situation to wake up to, Mulligan thought: unable to speak because of the trach tube, tied to the bed, catheters shunting your blood back and forth between your arm and some strange-looking machine, even your breathing controlled by another machine. Adjustment to this kind of situation was difficult enough even when everything could be explained and reassurance given; with no explanation or preparation, awakening from a stupor to this . . . Mulligan wouldn't be surprised if at the end they had a live but quite insane patient.

Irene attempted to comfort him. Stroking the child's forehead, her voice soothing and calm, she spoke to him in French, indicating the various pieces of medical equipment and explaining their use. It was obvious that the boy could understand only a few words of what she was saying, yet, like a master able to calm a frightened animal, her presence and manner seemed to reassure him.

Dr. Lussac was thrilled. "I think he'll survive now," he said to Mulligan. "The tracheostomy tube was the best thing. If we can keep his lungs cleaned out for just one or two more days, until the antibiotics have had a chance to work, I'm sure he'll make it."

At the sound of the English words the boy's head turned swiftly and his eyes, frantic and lively, sought out the speaker. He struggled to speak but could make no sound.

"*English!*" Mulligan shouted. "He understands English!" Rapidly he crossed to the bedside to stand beside Irene. "Say something in English."

"Do you speak English?" Irene asked.

The boy nodded as vigorously as he could. An expression suggesting relief came over his face.

"This is Dr. Lussac," Irene said, indicating the pediatrician. "He's in charge of your care here. You're in the Hôpital des Enfants, the children's hospital, in Paris. You've been very sick but you're going to get better now. And this is Dr. Mulligan from the United States."

At the sound of Mulligan's name the boy's eyes seemed to ignite, then blazed as a furious intellect surged outward through them, an inferno reaching out to singe and scorch. He strained upward again, trying to reach Mulligan with his hand, and his mouth moved in soundless incomprehensible speech.

CHAPTER EIGHT

His name was Yuri, just Yuri; he had no family name, a puzzling omission. Speech remained impossible. The tracheostomy tube blocked the passage of air through his vocal cords, so communication, though now established, remained fragmentary. But he was able to write brief answers to questions, and he had one of his own.

"Where is my brother Ivan?" It was the first question he wrote on the pad in a cramped, semi-Cyrillic script with letters etched laboriously on the paper. He looked at Irene with a quivering, tense expression, the restless eye movement stilled for once as longing and hope and fear mixed in an anxious expectancy.

Irene nodded her head as though she had anticipated the question. She took Yuri's hand and held it, stroking it almost absentmindedly for a long time before replying. Her low, mellow voice wavered with reluctance when she spoke. "He's dead, Yuri. He died four weeks ago." There was no way to soften the harsh truth.

For a moment Yuri remained motionless, as though stunned by an unexpected slap, immobilized by the instantaneous impulse to reject information too painful to absorb. Then his courage dissolved, and he began to cry. It was a distorted, silent crying. His eyes closed and rolled beneath thin veiled lids, and his forehead knit as though shrinking from talons clawing him from within. A violent tremor passed through him. His mouth opened and closed, contorted by a frantic attempt at speech. When he opened his eyes again to look at Irene they burst with sorrow and glistened with tears that spilled over to run in erratic rivulets down his hot, reddened cheeks.

Yuri reached again for the pad. "Then I am the last one."

The pen fell from his hand. He lay back on the pillow, limp and exhausted with grief. Humidified oxygen puffed from his respiratory tubing in misty white spurts.

Mulligan looked at Irene in astonishment. "The last one? The last one what? What does he mean? How many could there possibly be?"

Irene shook her head and raised her eyebrows; she didn't understand it any more than Mulligan did. Yet the boy's loneliness was unendurable. She gazed at the figure of the child/old man on the bed beside her and stroked his forehead tenderly, struggling to hold back her own tears. Mulligan felt his throat constrict. Had he been able to make sounds the boy would have been sobbing, but he remained silent, tears streaming down his face onto the pillow, trembling in a deep unreachable sorrow.

For the next hour Irene, Mulligan and Lussac stayed with him, saying little, each of them lost in his own thoughts, not daring to disturb the child's grief. Yuri lay in a restless half sleep, only semiconscious. But his eyes unceasingly clicked their untrusting vigil. From time to time an expression of agony and horror would pass over his face, and his body would shiver uncontrollably. At such moments his face seethed with emotions. His eyes were illumined, always,

137

even in stupor, by the colossal intelligence that lay behind them.

At last he fell into a deeper sleep. "Let's leave him alone for a while," Lussac advised.

Together they left the ICU and walked to Lussac's office. Irene sank into the deep leather chair, tilting her head slackly to the right and supporting it on a hand propped up at the elbow. She looked worn and tired. "I don't think I can take much more of this," she said.

"I still don't understand it," Mulligan said, speaking to Lussac, letting Irene rest. "The last one . . . what could he have meant by that?"

As always Lussac was pragmatic. "If he lives, he'll explain it. If he doesn't, it won't matter much anyway."

"And he referred to Ivan as his brother. I thought you said they couldn't be brothers," Mulligan accused.

"They *can't* be brothers." Lussac stood his ground. "There's no way we could have made a mistake in tissue typing. It's impossible. They *could* be half brothers, they *may* be half brothers, but that's all."

"He'll live," Irene said softly, staring vacantly straight ahead. "He'll live because there are cruelties yet to come. I don't think nature will be kind enough to let him die now."

"Do you want him to die?" Mulligan asked.

"No." She sighed deeply. "I suppose not. We need him. We need to study him, to find out whatever we can. But it would be kinder, wouldn't it?"

Ridgely arrived later the same day, at about four o'clock. Mulligan was paged to meet him at the main desk of the hospital.

"I was out in L.A. looking for you when I got your message," he said by way of explanation. Ridgely seemed even more brusque and intent than he had before—and large and imposing again. "Nice job they did on your lab." He inspected Mulligan carefully through slitted eyes, and his scowl reappeared. "Nice job they did on your face."

"Wasn't it, though?" Mulligan's hand reflexly went up to

touch the bandage on his cheek. "Nice people you play with. You didn't tell me I was going into get anything quite like this."

"I didn't know—honest. I really didn't. I didn't know what was so important about all this. But I do now."

"Maybe you'll let me know, then? Before we all get killed. You want to see the second kid? He's sick as a dog, in the intensive care unit."

"Sure. Can I?"

"This way. The guards know me by now." Mulligan described the second boy as they walked down the corridor, then asked, "You've heard what happened here, haven't you, at the same time my lab in L.A. was attacked?"

"What?"

"Someone, KGB I suppose, incinerated Ivan's corpse. Threw an incendiary bomb into the morgue at the Sûreté. Nothing left to study but ashes, and you can't get much useful biological information from ashes."

Ridgely stopped walking and stared at Mulligan. *"They what?"* Someone threw a fire bomb? Oh, Christ . . ."

"Why do you look so surprised? Didn't we agree there was something they didn't want us to find out?"

"It isn't that," Ridgely said and waved his hand vaguely in the air. "It isn't the fire bomb. It's something else that's just occurred to me—what this is really all about, what's really happened. Jesus Christ! Let's see this other one."

Yuri was asleep on the bed, an odd thin figure whose only movement was the slow tidal rise and fall of his chest synchronized to the rhythmic collapse and reinflation of the respirator bellows. His life seemed the more precarious for its dependence on the machine. The bulging, prominent forehead made his resemblance to Ivan immediately remarkable.

"They're brothers?" Ridgely asked, noting the similarity.

"Half brothers, maybe," Mulligan corrected. "We already checked on that. The disease itself, the progeria, makes them look pretty much the same."

"Astonishing," Ridgely murmured.

"More than astonishing," Mulligan said. "Inexplicable."

"Why? Why inexplicable? I thought you said a mutation could explain it."

Mulligan sighed. Dealing with the unenlightened was a constant frustration. He described his findings in Los Angeles and explained their implications as patiently as he could. "The problem," he concluded, "is that there are too many mutations at once, too many enzymes affected. A chromosomal mutation might explain it, but Dr. Sailland insists the chromosomes are normal. So it's inexplicable. These boys are a biological impossibility."

"Maybe how they did it can't be explained," Ridgely said as they walked away from the ICU, "but not that they did it."

"They? Who's they? What are you talking about?"

"The Russians. That's what hit me when you were telling me about the fire at the Sûreté. Look, I don't know anything about biology, but I know the Russians, how they work, how they think. I've been sparring with them for twenty years. And I got a lot more insight into this whole business when I was in Washington yesterday." Ridgely stopped walking, looked up and down the hall, waiting until a nurse had passed them by, then backed his bulk up against the gray stone wall of the corridor. *Sotto voce,* he said, "What I think is this: these children were the product of a deliberate mutation. The Russians made them on purpose."

"What? It can't be done."

"But that's the only way it makes sense," Ridgely insisted. "The only way. There's no other way to explain it. These are extraordinary things they're doing—extraordinary—even for paranoid Russians. They have to have a motive equal to the risk."

"Come on, don't be ridiculous," Mulligan said, but even as he spurned the idea he felt his initial surprise and denial begin to soften. It could be explained that way. Almost automatically his mind began to delve into the possibilities. "I'll give you this much," he admitted, "the odds against such a mutation happening twice, spontaneously, are astronomical."

"Suppose it's true. Suppose they did it. Then everything makes sense—why they tried to kidnap a cadaver, why they burned it later, why they broke up your lab. Look, I don't know how they . . . Jesus! That's it! That's what they don't want us to know. How they did it."

Mulligan had doubts not so easily dispelled. The politics might seem clear, but the biology was considerably less so. Gene-splicing experiments had been done only very recently, within the last several years. Ivan had been eight years old. Yuri was probably eight years old, too. The timing was wrong. But when had he published his paper? 1975, wasn't it? Ten years ago? Had someone in Russia read it and then tested the theory with recombinant DNA? Tested it on a human being? In the last year or two there had been a few such experiments performed on laboratory animals in the United States, but they'd all been failures. The spliced genes hadn't worked properly, or the mutation had proven lethal. Well, Yuri and Ivan, if they were experiments, were failures, too. They were dying of progeria.

"There's someone in Washington I'd like to check this all out with," Ridgely said, glancing at his watch and interrupting Mulligan's thoughts. "Can we meet later, say, for dinner? You and your friend Dr. Sailland? Right now I want to call Legras to make sure the security here is adequate. Eight o'clock, Chez Antoine? Do you know it?"

"Sure." Mulligan was still lost in thought. He didn't even try to imagine whom in Washington Ridgely would want to call. "Eight o'clock."

Ridgely called General Alexander as soon as he could secure a safe line at the American Embassy. "There's another one," he said.

"Another one?" Alexander sounded surprised, momentarily nonplussed. "Another one what?"

"Another little Russian boy with progeria. They're not sure yet he's as much of a genius as the first one, but it looks like it, and he's just as strong, from what Mulligan told me. Mulligan says the odds against such a thing happening spontaneously are fantastically huge. More, the two of them appear to have been half brothers."

"Mulligan? What's he doing in Paris?"

"He flew here on his own when he learned about the second boy. He told me his theory is true, by the way. He was able to prove it with the brain specimen from the first one."

There was a long silence at the other end of the line, so long Ridgely began to wonder if the line had been cut. "General?"

"I heard you." Alexander said hoarsely. His tone contained his hatred of the Russians, his anger at having been bested and a cold antagonism that would yield nothing to the enemy. "I heard what you said."

"You realize what this means, don't you?" Ridgely sensed the question was superfluous.

"Yes. It means they're *making* them, Goddamn it! That's all it can mean. The bastards are years ahead of us on this."

"That's right," Ridgely said quietly. "They're making them. That's the only possible motive for what they've done, the only way it all makes sense. Somehow these kids got loose and made it to Paris, and now the Russians are terrified we're going to find out how they did it."

"All right." Alexander had recovered quickly. "If they're years ahead of us, we'll just have to find out how it's done. Here's what we'll do. We'll bring everyone here, to Washington, to the NIH. We'll have better security here, better lab facilities. I'll arrange for the lab to be set up and get it cleared with the French government. Bring them here as soon as possible."

"Don't get too anxious," Ridgely warned. "It's going to be a while. He's pretty sick. They're not even sure he's going to live."

"Make sure! And make damn sure no KGB agents get anywhere near that kid!"

At the dinner table that evening Irene's voice was the only one of protest. Her opposition to the idea was as much ethical as scientific.

"Who would do this to a child?" she asked. "Who would do such experiments?" Her face was shadowed by disquiet and a sad reproach. "Bacteria, or fruit flies, or even rats . . . but people?" She shook her head in a slow, unaccepting denial. "No, no, not even in Russia."

"They didn't mean for the boys to have progeria," Mulligan protested, disliking the role of devil's advocate. "They couldn't have wanted that. That was the accident, the failure." Mulligan had thought a great deal about what Ridgely had suggested since the afternoon, and the more he mulled it over, the more plausible it seemed. "Think about it," he urged her. "We know the boy has some extra genetic material. He's got to have. We've already determined that much. That's the only way he could have so much of all those enzymes. And you insist the chromosomes are normal."

"They are normal." Irene nodded slowly, forced to agree yet disagreeing. "But that doesn't make it deliberate."

"No, it doesn't. Not by itself. But suppose there's some plasmid DNA . . ."

"What?" Ridgely interrupted. "A plasmid? What's that?"

"Extrachromosomal DNA. DNA not attached to a chromosome in the nucleus of a cell, but floating free in the cytoplasm."

"Plasmid children. I like the sound of that." Ridgely said it again, articulating the words slowly and carefully, relishing the phrase somewhat ghoulishly. "Plasmid children. It has a certain ring to it."

Mulligan grimaced in distaste and turned again to Irene. "The genes coding for the enzymes could be isolated and reproduced. Right? That much, at least, could be done."

"Eight years ago?" she asked. The timing didn't seem right to her, either.

"I know. They'd have been the first ones in the world to do it. But there are smart people in Russia, too." Mulligan

143

sipped his coffee and thought carefully before proceeding. "It would have to be an embryo, though. You'd have to figure out a way to get the genes into an embryo."

"Why an embryo?" Ridgely interrupted again.

"Because of what we found in Ivan's brain," Mulligan answered wearily,"—the huge number of axons and dendrites on the brain cells. A human being is born with at least two-thirds of his total number of brain cells already present—that's why an infant's head is so big compared to the rest of him. And brain cells can't change once they're developed. So all those axons and dendrites could only have developed in utero, in the embryo." He paused to sip more coffee. "That's why Ivan's brain proved my theory."

Irene remained silent, frowning. Reflected in her face was the effort required to surmount the revulsion of her initial reaction and to consider the idea with cold logic. Several times she raised her head to look quizzically at Mulligan, as though about to ask him a question, but then she looked away again as the answers occurred to her. He could see the idea gathering conviction in her mind as it had gathered conviction in his. The keystone of the argument was that the chromosomes were normal. He had always come back to that point. It was inescapable. If the chromosomes were in fact normal then there had to be extrachromosomal DNA. There had to be. And chromosomes didn't just fragment and leave bits and pieces of DNA floating around in cells. That just didn't happen. And even if it had happened once, it couldn't possibly have happened twice. So extra genetic material had to have been introduced into the embryo. But how? How?

Finally she capitulated. "It's too horrible to believe," she sighed, "but I suppose you're right." She sounded defeated. Discussion and protest were useless. Things would happen as they would happen. Free will was an illusion.

They finished dinner and went outside. Chez Antoine was on the rue St.-Jacques, half a block from the boulevard St.-Germain. The air that night was again cool and damp, with a thin mist settling and obscuring vision in shades of gray and brown. Irene remained depressed and withdrawn.

Ridgely walked with them to the corner. "I'll leave you two," he said. "Exciting, though, isn't it? Like I say, you never know what's going to happen next."

"I think I can live happily without this kind of excitement," Mulligan replied.

They were about half a kilometer south of the boulevard St.-Michel. Mulligan had a sudden incongruous urge to go to the Café des Deux Magots to eavesdrop on what the tourists were saying, to hear something light, innocent and inconsequential. It was nine o'clock. There was little automobile traffic on the Saint-Germain. A few taxis prowled, moving slowly, dark shapes with probing tentacular headlights. The noise they made on the street oscillated between a smooth whoosh and a harsher ripping sound as their tires passed over cobblestones that poked through bare spots in the thinly laid asphalt. Patches of sound and brave forays of song and laughter came from a distant doorway every time a nightclub's doors were opened to let revellers in and out. People passed by in small bunches—puffs of humanity—on the broad sidewalk.

The boulevard was patchily lit. Canopied by trees in the full leaf of spring, the Saint-Germain received no illumination from the rest of the city. Streetlights cast hazy yellow circles at regular intervals; the light spilling from shop windows and apartments created a crazy quilt of distorted rectangles. Couples strolling on the sidewalk passed from light to dark to light in a shifting uncertain pattern, and in shadowed doorways other couples exchanging a kiss could be seen as darker forms pressed against the gray stone facade of buildings.

Mulligan didn't notice the black Citroen approaching him slowly from behind. In fact, he never really saw it well at all. He heard a voice behind him, Ridgely's, screaming his name frantically, *"Mulligan! Mulligan! Down!"* and it was turning to the sound of the voice that saved his life. There

145

was a noise like that of a champagne bottle popping and then something struck his left arm between the shoulder and the elbow so forcefully that he was spun around. Whether the bullet knocked him down or he fell by instinct, he never knew, but his spin continued in a downward arc, knocking Irene down, too, and he hit the pavement hard. As he fell he could see Ridgely running down the street toward him, clumsily pulling at something under his left arm. Then the gun was in Ridgely's hand and it was fired with a crash and almost instantly there was the sound of shattering glass as the bullet hit the rear windshield of the Citroen. There was another report and another bullet whizzed over his head, striking the stone behind him, sending a shower of chips over him and Irene. The car zoomed on. As it went by Mulligan could see the figure of a man, half leaning out of the window and struggling to get back inside, the pistol still held in both hands and his face covered by a ski mask.

He was just beginning to feel the pain when Ridgely knelt beside him.

"Where did he get you?"

"My arm." Mulligan sat on the sidewalk staring dazedly at his arm. Something about getting shot made him feel stupid and careless, as though he should have been able to avoid it. He felt angry but oddly distant and euphoric. That's twice in two days, he thought. I'd better be more careful. Blood had already stained the sleeve of his jacket and he could feel it running down his arm to ooze through the band of his wristwatch and appear on his hand. Some large drops stained the gray of the sidewalk a deep burgundy. The arm hung slack and limp, not because it was paralyzed, but because to bend it, to contract the biceps, was excruciatingly painful. He awkwardly got to his knees, then noticed for the first time that Irene was down, too.

"Irene . . ." He was instantly frantic for her safety.

She was sitting on the sidewalk, her face drained of color, staring after the receding Citroen, her bare legs stretched clumsily in front of her. *"Le salaud,"* she muttered. She moaned when she saw Mulligan's arm. "George! *Mon Dieu! Tu es blessé!*"

"It's my arm," Mulligan grunted. "I don't think the bullet hit the bone, though. Help me take my jacket off, will you?"

She was as gentle as possible, but every movement hurt and he winced more than once as she slid his jacket off, sucking his breath in through gritted teeth. Blood was coming in little spurts from two holes in his arm, the entrance and exit wounds, and it was bright red and pulsing, arterial.

"I'll need a tourniquet. Take my tie off and tie it up near my shoulder."

She did as he asked, and when she had it tight enough the bleeding stopped. "I'll call an ambulance," she said, and ran to one of the nearby nightclubs to telephone.

Ridgely waited with him. "You guys really do play a little rough, don't you?" Mulligan accused.

Ridgely scarcely looked at him. He was standing near the wall with his back to it, a level gaze surveying the street, his hand near the shoulder holster under his left arm. "Sometimes, in fact, we play for keeps," he snapped. Ridgely's face was darkened as much by a menacing glare as by the dim, angled light of the streetlamps. He glanced down at Mulligan with a quick look of vindication. "This ices it, you know," he said. "They wouldn't do this just to keep you away from some little freak of nature." He resumed his surveillance of the street. In the distance, he heard approaching sirens. "They just wouldn't. But they would do this to keep secret something they've been working on."

The police arrived together with the ambulance. Ridgely had disappeared before their arrival. "Say nothing," he had warned. "They'll want to hold you in custody until they figure out what happened. For God's sake don't mention Russians or the KGB. I'll get hold of Legras and meet you in the emergency room."

In the emergency room the surgeon—a long-faced type whose lugubrious view of life was continually reaffirmed by the catastrophes that were his daily fare—clucked and sighed when he saw Mulligan's arm. *"Il y a trop de violence dans ce monde,"* he muttered as he inspected the wound. He looked at Mulligan's bandaged cheek but refrained from asking about it.

Despite the anesthetic, an attempted nerve block of the brachial plexus, thick bolts of pain shot through Mulligan's arm when the wound was probed. The bullet had passed clear through the biceps, creating a tunnel of torn flesh. The surgeon debrided the muscle of dead or dying tissue, then washed it copiously with saline. Bullets are hot and cauterize flesh on their way through, but when the tourniquet was released blood began to spurt again in tiny pulses. They could see that it was coming from a small, lacerated artery. Mulligan strove for a transcendent detachment, but he could feel and smell his body, which was drenched with the peculiar sweat of fear as the surgeon ligated the cut ends of the artery.

Irene smiled gamely as she watched. She was frightened and shaking, and her mascara was smudged from the crying she'd done earlier.

"You look like a raccoon," Mulligan said, wiping her cheek with his good hand.

They were just looking at the x-ray that showed the bone hadn't been hit when Ridgely returned with Legras. Ridgely had been right. The police wanted to arrest Mulligan, despite the fact that he was clearly the victim. Even Legras had difficulty mollifying the police captain, and it took half an hour of heated discussion and several telephone calls to higher authorities before the police record was expunged and they were allowed to leave.

"Where did you sleep last night?" Ridgely asked as they left the emergency room.

Mulligan nodded toward Irene. "Her place."

Ridgely glanced at Legras. "Can't go back there," he said. His grim mood had lightened. He patted Mulligan on the head, at once patronizing and consoling. "You'll obviously need more protection."

"Obviously."

"Then it's the Michelet-Odéon for you, my boy. We can guard you there."

Half an hour later Mulligan was checked into the hotel. They sat together in his room. The anesthetic was wearing off and his arm was beginning to throb painfully. Ridgely had magically made a bottle of bourbon appear and he poured a glass of it for each of them. Irene took hers and sipped it with a shiver.

"What about Dr. Sailland?" Mulligan asked. He didn't want them to forget about her. "She could have been a target, too."

Ridgely shook his head, then sipped his drink with evident pleasure. "No, she wasn't. You're the one they wanted."

"Why me?"

"Because you're the one who's going to find out how they did it—how they made those boys. Didn't you say that he seemed to recognize your name?"

"But he knew of Dr. Sailland, too," Mulligan protested.

"Her work is on aging," Ridgely said. "That's not their main interest. Your work is the genetics of intelligence. It's your theory that's been used to do all this. You're the one they want." Ridgely paused, remembering what General Alexander had said about following Mulligan's career by subscribing to the right journals. Somebody in Russia had been following Mulligan's career, too. "I hate to break it to you like this, but you're more important than you thought you were. Somebody in Russia admires you enough to want to kill you."

Mulligan swallowed a mouthful of the bourbon and welcomed the searing sensation as it went down. "I can do without the compliments. If I ever go into sociology I'll do my thesis on assassination as the highest form of flattery."

"I see that getting shot hasn't changed your personality," Ridgely said.

Mulligan had ample opportunity to consider things during the next week. He strayed little from his now well-guarded hotel room. Much of the time, though, he couldn't think very clearly. His wounded arm had swollen greatly by the next morning, and even though it was immobilized in a sling, the slightest movement sent agonizing reverberations back and forth from his shoulder to his elbow. For nearly a week the narcotics injections he required kept his mind fuzzy.

He telephoned to Claire Rosenberg in Los Angeles to inquire about Aaron.

"Recovering," Claire said in response to his question. "He'll be all right." Mulligan heard in her voice a distancing tone of repudiation and the suppressed vibrations fear produces. "What's this all about, anyway?"

"It might not be a good idea to tell you just now," Mulligan answered, deciding not to mention that he'd joined Aaron on the injured list. "Later, maybe. Just tell Aaron this is more involved than we thought."

He repeatedly questioned his own role in the affair. What should he do now? Supposing that Ivan and Yuri had been the product of deliberate genetic manipulation . . . did he have a duty to help find out how it had been done? He wasn't sure. He wasn't in the army or bound by any oath. But the injuries he'd received hadn't frightened him so much as made him angry, and he found now that anger, as much as his inveterate curiosity, drove him to want to attempt it.

Had it really been possible? He found himself more and more obsessed with the question. Had it really been possible? Had someone, some Russian biochemical genius, already applied the theory, already tried to create an improved version of humanity? Even in the United States no one had found a way to insert new genes into a human embryo. But that was no argument, he knew. Science lurched ahead unevenly, propelled by sporadic acts of genius, radical departures that vaulted from the known to the unknown.

It was new territory, unexplored, in which knowledge and wisdom might fail and ethics prove wanting. The implications were disturbing. Experimentation of this sort on human beings was simply unacceptable. It just wasn't done. It reminded him of the gratuitous cruelty of the Nazis, whose doctors had tied a pregnant woman's legs together during delivery to observe the mechanism of uterine rupture, and who had sutured a man's eyelids open and then turned his face to the sun to determine how long the retina could withstand direct sunlight before it burned. The Russians might be determined, harsh adversaries, but to experiment genetically on human beings implied a nadir of iniquity that he found difficult to acknowledge.

Irene, for the same reason, repeatedly questioned the idea.

"Think of another explanation, then." Mulligan would challenge her each time. "Think of a better one. You're the one who insists the chromosomes are normal."

She couldn't, and they both knew it. "It still demands proof, though" she insisted stubbornly.

During that week Irene shuttled back and forth between visits to Mulligan and Yuri. Her fears seemed diminished by the presence of the Sûreté bodyguards who accompanied her everywhere. In her daily reports on Yuri's condition Mulligan saw, with some concern, that her attachment to the child was growing. Regrettable but inevitable, he thought.

For the several days following the tracheostomy Yuri made little attempt at communication, as though he recognized that the first task was to recover, to not die. Dr. Lussac hovered and fretted at the bedside, crabbing constantly at the nurses, complaining all the time that he was a pediatrician and not used to treating old men.

Once Yuri's lungs could be cleared of inflammatory debris, though, his temperature steadily came down. His cheeks lost the rouge of fever and slid into a pallid glaze, becoming paradoxically less healthy looking as health returned. The cough remained, but it was less and less wracking. He needed to have his trachea suctioned only once or twice a day, and the color of the sputum changed gradually from a yellowish green to a clear white. His x-rays cleared. On the fourth day some urine appeared in his bladder catheter, only a little at first but still a herald of returning kidney function. The urine volume increased over the next few days, and the dialysis tubing was removed from his arm. His food and fluid intake was liberalized.

"You should see Yuri now," Irene said toward the end of the week. Her mood had mirrored the boy's progress toward recovery, brightening daily, and as she sat down on the edge of Mulligan's bed he thought again that her smile could still light up the dark corners of the world. "He's sitting up in bed a lot of the time now. Very alert. He notices everything, still with that funny clicking-camera look of his. He's been off the respirator for several days. Dr. Lussac says that the tracheostomy tube should be able to come out very soon."

"Then he'll be able to talk, won't he?" Mulligan said.

Mulligan's arm healed well. By the end of the week it was out of the sling, though to straighten it fully was still painful, and it throbbed constantly. He'd be able to use it, though—enough, anyway, to work in a laboratory.

Ridgely had disappeared again. The day Mulligan's arm came out of the sling he returned with what he assumed would be good news. "Your security clearance came through today," he announced cheerfully, as though he thought Mulligan should be both proud and relieved.

"My what?" Mulligan asked, neither proud nor relieved.

"Your security clearance. We do this all the time, whenever civilians get mixed up in things or when we need special expertise. You can't just assume that every American is loyal to his country."

"Interestingly enough," Mulligan sneered, pointing to his

arm, "the Russian who shot me had no problem at all making just exactly that assumption."

Ridgely flushed. "All the same, you can't trust everyone with classified information."

"What classified information?" Mulligan sensed the rebellious, anarchist impulse rising in his throat. "Since when is my research classified?"

Ridgely sat down, sprawling his bulk gratefully and gracelessly in a large leather chair. "Nothing you've done so far is classified," he said placatingly. "Don't get upset. Are we right in assuming that you're going to pursue this thing, that you want to find out what really happened and how it was done? We want you to. You're ideal for the job. You and Dr. Sailland. She's been checked out by the Deuxième, by the way, and she's okay."

"We assume? Who's we?"

"General Alexander and myself." Ridgely's eyes twinkled with private amusement. "That's the other thing I came to tell you today. We're going over to the American Embassy to meet him today. He came to Paris himself, to get it ironed out with the French government."

Mulligan suddenly remembered that he hadn't heard from Ridgely at all during the three days he'd been in L.A. Ridgely had said he'd been in Washington. He felt suddenly adrift again, with his sense of bearings inadequate to the mysterious, sinister forces surrounding him. Another nettlesome question suddenly sprang up: the question not only of how the Russian genius had done it, but why?

"Who's General Alexander?" he asked, feeling the lameness of the question and resenting the tone of dependent helplessness he heard in his own voice.

"Lieutenant General Joel Alexander. He's head of the army's office of technology assessment. Further investigation of Yuri will be done under his auspices. From now on anything you discover will be classified Top Secret by army intelligence. That all right with you?"

"I don't know. Not really. Do I have any choice?"

"No."

"Why bother to ask, then? The French have agreed to all this? They're willing to let us take over?" Ridgely's easy assumption of American primacy would irritate Irene, he thought, somewhat irrelevantly.

"Sure." Ridgely grinned and his bulbous nose stood out the more sharply. "They're only too happy to get rid of it after all that's happened. We have better research facilities, anyway. It's all been arranged."

"How did the army get into this?"

"I'll let General Alexander answer that."

What else is going on that I haven't been told about? Mulligan wondered. The lines of compulsion seemed to be drawing tight, leaving little room for maneuver. How long did they have, anyway? Yuri was recovering for the moment, but how much longer did he have to live?

"All right," he said to Ridgely. "Let's go meet this General Alexander. But we'd better bring Irene, too. Yuri probably won't go anywhere without her."

"We've anticipated that," Ridgely assented. "That's why we asked the Deuxième to check out her security status."

"I'm thrilled to learn she's not a communist spy," Mulligan said sarcastically. "You can't imagine how my sleep has been troubled by that possibility."

CHAPTER NINE

They met Irene at the hospital. Her mood was dark and dejected. She'd told Yuri just that morning that she didn't have the cure for the progeria he'd hoped she'd have.

"He cried, George, for hours" she said. "Just as Ivan did. I felt awful. I felt I'd crushed him, crushed his last hope. He's so alone, George, so lost and alone." She sighed deeply.

"What about the CPK?" Mulligan asked. "Did you tell him about that?"

She nodded slowly. "The one ray of hope. He grabbed at it." She looked at Mulligan through smoldering eyes. A grim determination chiseled at the fine features of her face. "We start studying chemistry tomorrow. He has a lot to learn."

Ridgely stood diplomatically aside when Mulligan told her what they wanted. She bristled instantly. "Go where? To meet whom? What for?"

"I don't like it either," Mulligan admitted. He held her

155

slim shoulders gently in his hands and waited for her irritation to subside. "I don't like it either, but there's something happening here that you and I have been missing, that we haven't been told about, and I think we're about to find out what it is."

The American Embassy is an enormous neoclassical building of tan and sooted stone just off the Place de la Concorde. It is a heavy structure, an imposing symbol of the wealth and power of the nation it represents. Two marine guards in dress uniform, tall expressionless men frozen menacingly in the at-ease position with fixed bayonets, flank the entrance gate. Mulligan consciously had to resist a sensation of being reduced to insignificance. They do this on purpose, he told himself. Don't be intimidated. The atmosphere inside was scarcely more congenial. Marble walls and floor, bare except for an occasional photograph of the Capitol or the president, echoed their footsteps in the hall.

"What sort of man is this general of yours?" Mulligan asked Ridgely as they approached their rendezvous. "Does he know anything about genetics or biochemistry?"

"Don't sell him short," Ridgely advised. "He knows more than I do, anyway. He's the one who saw right away the implications of this case and its overall significance."

What overall significance is that? Mulligan wondered.

General Alexander was waiting for them in one of the smaller conference rooms. He sat at the end of a long table. Mulligan assessed him quickly, suspiciously. Alexander was dressed in civilian clothes, but his close-cropped hair and rigid bearing stamped him as unmistakably military. His expression revealed little, though an unwavering, clear gaze indicated a ruthless intensity of purpose. This is not a man with whom to discuss ethical philosophy, Mulligan thought, and, glancing at Irene, he could sense her instant dislike.

There was a forced cordiality in Alexander's manner as Ridgely made the introductions. "I've heard a good deal about you, Dr. Mulligan," he said, half sitting on the edge of the table. "It may surprise you, but I'm very well acquainted with your work. And with yours, as well, Dr. Sailland." He nodded politely to Irene, then stood and began to pace mechanically around the room, ignoring the fact that his audience had to twist uncomfortably in their seats to see him. "This whole business is really quite extraordinary, isn't it? History seems to have thrust you two to center stage for the moment." He paused to let the effect of his words sink in.

"Isn't that a little melodramatic?" Mulligan asked.

"Is it? You got shot, didn't you?"

"Touché," Mulligan admitted.

In one corner of the room was a coffee percolator and Alexander walked over to it. "Coffee?" he asked over his shoulder. "This is probably the only place in Paris you can get real American coffee in a real American Styrofoam cup. No one? All right." He took a cup for himself and returned to the edge of the table. "How's the boy now?"

"The boy? Yuri?"

"Is that his name? Yuri? No one told me. How is he now?"

"Much better," Irene said, cautiously, defensively. Alexander might be an opponent challenging her protective interest. "Nearly well. Dr. Lussac told me today that he's going to remove the tracheostomy tube soon, perhaps in another few days."

"Then he'll be able to talk, won't he?" Alexander leaned forward in eager anticipation, his eyes alert. "He'll be able to tell us all about what happened back there in Russia. How much do you think he knows?"

"We haven't asked him much yet," Irene replied slowly, with a suspicious reserve, still hesitant to acknowledge Alexander's authority to ask her questions and uncertain about her responsibility to answer them. "We want him to be stronger first. Anyway, there's a language problem. The ony language we have in common is English, and he'll need to study it more before we can talk easily. So I don't know

157

how much he knows. His brother, Ivan, the one who died four weeks ago, told us nothing—either he didn't know or wouldn't say."

"But we're all agreed, aren't we," Alexander asked, leaning forward still further, his eyes darting back and forth between Irene and Mulligan, "that these boys were the product of a deliberate mutation?"

"As repulsive as the thought is, yes," Mulligan answered. "What troubles us, Dr. Sailland and me, is *why?* Why would anyone want to do that? What could be the motive for such a thing? And how did the army, how did you get involved in this?"

"That's easy," Alexander said. He stood up and walked to the other side of the table, then sat down to face them. "There's one answer to both questions. You may not believe it right away, but they're doing it to create better soldiers, mutant soldiers."

"*What?*" Irene and Mulligan exclaimed. "*C'est absurde,*" Irene added contemptuously.

"No, it's not absurd. And I'll tell you why it's not absurd," Alexander said. He looked at Mulligan. "It's really all an extension of your theory, Dr. Mulligan, or, at least, one aspect of it. That's why you became a target for assassination after they knew the second boy had reached Paris alive. It's all based on your idea that simple enzymatic changes in the embryo might have enormously profound effects." In his practiced and persuasive way, as he had done with Ridgely a week earlier, Alexander listed the military advantages of simple mutations. He concluded with a thin-lipped smile that was at once sinister and beatific. "A simple genetic change and, presto! we have a soldier who can carry a hundred pounds of ammunition, or a pilot whose reaction times make him invincible, or even," he finished significantly, "an eight-year-old boy who can make it on foot alone from Leningrad to Paris."

Mulligan felt an empty, falling sensation as he listened to

Alexander. He knew that he must have had a stupid, vacant look on his face, yet he couldn't help it. His stomach turned nauseatingly, pivoted by the same awe and horror with which one might witness a human sacrifice. Alexander was right. He was sure of it, instinctively, conclusively. Yet on the heels of that conviction came a hot, blistering outrage that his theory had been perverted even before it had been proven.

Irene voiced her own disgust. "No one would do that. I can't believe it."

"That's what they said about poison gas and napalm, too," Alexander said quietly. "But they would do that, *madame*. I assure you they would."

"It's too ugly," she said with a dry tone of disbelief. "It's too awful. Yuri knows that he's dying, that he has progeria. That's why he ran to Paris. He hopes I can save him." She looked steadily at Alexander, daring him to try to prevent her. "I am going to try."

"And I sincerely hope you'll succeed," Alexander said quickly. He sought no argument with her. "Have you any ideas?"

"Yes," Mulligan said, answering for her, although his arm throbbed miserably. "We think the progeria is caused by an excess of CPK. His energy metabolism is thrown off. If we can find an enzyme inhibitor to block it, maybe we can slow down the disease. It's a place to start, anyway. The question is, can we do it before he dies?" he concluded gloomily.

"We'll find out, won't we?" Alexander said brusquely. He turned to Irene. "You don't mind coming to the United States for a while, do you?"

Irene shrugged, then looked at him with a cold stare. "Not really. So long as you don't interfere." She looked questioningly at Mulligan. "What do you think?"

"You're ideal for this," Alexander urged Mulligan. "Need I say your country needs you?"

Mulligan looked pained. "You needn't. I'm so ideal they

159

try to kill me." A new thought occurred to him. "I wonder why they didn't kill me in L.A. when it would have been easy."

Ridgely spoke for the first time. Until this moment he'd been watching and listening to the conversation. "I've thought about that, too," he said. "It must be because the second kid hadn't turned up yet. There must be something you can't do with a dead one." He glanced apologetically at Irene. "Sorry to be so cold about it, but I think that's it."

The answer flashed into Mulligan's mind as he listened to Ridgely. "It has to do with purifying the DNA. Or even doing chromosome studies. We have to proceed on the assumption that what Irene found is true, that the chromosomes are normal. So there's a plasmid. There has to be. The answer's on the plasmid. So, I'll have to separate the plasmid from the chromosomal DNA, purify it, maybe slice it up with restriction enzymes, use portions of it to make antibodies . . ." Ideas poured into his mind as he spoke. "That must have been what went wrong, too," he added suddenly.

"What's that?" Alexander interrupted, attentive to every word. "What was it that went wrong?"

"It occurred to me just now," Mulligan continued. "The plasmid . . . that's what went wrong. You'd want new genes to be on chromosomes, so that their activity and multiplication could be coordinated with the rest of the cell's activities. A plasmid can't be controlled. That's what went wrong."

"Interesting," said Alexander. He brought a small notebook out of his inside jacket pocket and jotted down a few words. "Do you think you could find out more about that?"

"Maybe. The problem is that if he dies I won't be able any more to get white cells to work with. The blood coagulates. I'd have to grind up solid tissue to get anything to dissolve, and the problem with that is that the process breaks chromosomes, too, into fragments. Then I can't tell which fragment is the plasmid."

Ridgely smiled benignly, still enjoying the contest with the shadows. "So the unknown Russian genius is coaching the KGB well, isn't he?" he pointed out to Mulligan. "He's probably anticipating every move you'll make."

Alexander had followed Mulligan's explanation carefully. "Let me get this straight," he said with the intense, grim expression of a veteran of prolonged combat, "If the boy dies we'll never know how they did it?"

Mulligan nodded. "Yes. Normally we'd have no problem. We'd simply take some white cells and grow them in tissue culture. Then we'd have all the plasmid and chromosomal DNA we could need. But Yuri's white cells die in tissue culture."

Alexander's face was darkened by a bleak, impotent rage. "Is he? Is he going to die soon?"

Mulligan shrugged, then instantly regretted the unconscious gesture as a shaft of pain went through his arm. "I don't know."

"Time is relative," Irene said slowly, staring straight in front of her into space. "Once Yuri learns biochemistry he'll be able to do in a few days what would usually take months." She turned to look soberly at Mulligan. "You didn't have the same experience with Ivan that I had. Wait until you see what Yuri can do."

"Just what can an IQ of five hundred do?" Alexander asked. A faint note of anxiety penetrated his curiosity.

"You'll see," she said. "You'll see. You'll be amazed."

They were starting to leave the conference room when General Alexander asked Ridgely to stay behind. "Wait a minute, will you?" he asked. "There's something I need to discuss with you privately."

Later, when she and Mulligan were alone at his hotel, Irene voiced her misgivings. "I didn't like him," she said unequivocally. "That general reminds me of what my mother said the Germans looked like when they occupied France. He looked as if he'd do anything, anything at all, to get what he wants. What did he want to talk to Ridgely about? What sort of plot are they hatching? And the whole idea of making mutant soldiers is repulsive. I'm not sure you should do this, George." She looked at Mulligan for the first time with an expression that held something less than complete trust.

"And if I refuse, what then?" Mulligan countered, disturbed by her doubts but overriding them. "Do you really think the KGB will believe I've had qualms about it and have quit the project? Will they call off the assassination squad? Not a chance. But if I quit they'll take the guards away and then where will I be? Alexander would just find someone else to do it, anyway."

Before replying, Irene looked at him searchingly for several seconds, her face downcast with disapproval. "That's not the real reason, George. Be honest. You want to know how it was done, don't you?"

Mulligan found he couldn't look her in the eye. "Yes," he said, admitting the obsession both to himself and to her. "God help me, I do. I want to find out how they did it." He took Irene's hands in his and forced himself to look at her. "How did we get into this, anyway?"

Yuri's education began in earnest the next day. English came first. Mulligan gave him an English dictionary, one of the little dictionaries used in high schools, the kind containing the fifteen or twenty thousand words most often used in conversation.

"We're going to America, Yuri," Irene explained in answer to his look of inquiry. "As soon as you're better. So you'll need to improve your English. That's the language we'll use to study biochemistry."

Yuri's progress was astonishing. His mind seemed to reach for and grip the words the way a magnet grips iron filings. He'd stare fixedly at a page for ten minutes or so,

162

absorbing the vocabulary, imprinting the words in his memory, and then would close his eyes as though testing himself. A cheerless smile would cross his face.

Mulligan found that watching Yuri studying made him apprehensive in a way he couldn't fully understand. The child seemed to be a disembodied intellect, to have no personality at all. Only with Irene did he reveal anything resembling human emotions. With her he seemed able to express the fears that drove him. He kept himself tight, contained. His eyes clicked remorselessly through the dictionary and, later, through the novels that he absorbed at the rate of several per day. Later still, when Mulligan brought in a video recorder and played tapes of old American movies so that Yuri could learn the sounds of the language, the boy watched them with disinterest, never laughing at the comedy nor appearing excited by the adventures.

Irene shrugged off Mulligan's concerns when he mentioned them. "Ivan was like that, too," she said. "He didn't react to things the way you thought he should. You got used to it after a while."

"As though he were another species?" Mulligan suggested.

She appeared startled by the thought. "No . . . no, not another species. Different, separated, alien . . . but not another species. Don't forget what a morass of confusion he is . . . and must be . . . Physiologically a man in early old age. Emotionally a child. Intellectually a giant. He probably thinks we're all idiots, you know. And still sick, too, exhausted, frightened, aware that a terrible disease is rushing him along to his death—how would you expect him to act?"

Like a schizophrenic, Mulligan thought.

Several days later Dr. Lussac at last pronounced Yuri well enough to have the tracheostomy tube removed. The procedure is simplicity itself. The sutures tying the tube to the skin are cut, and the balloon at its tip is deflated. Then it is simply pulled out. Withdrawal of the tube doesn't hurt, but its movement in the trachea induces a violent spasm of coughing. When the hole is bandaged air can't come through it any more and is then forced to go where it normally goes, through the vocal cords. The power of speech is restored.

When the tube was removed, and after his cough had subsided, Yuri sat up slowly, stretching and testing his muscles. He'd been confined for more than two weeks. Sitting on the edge of the bed made him seem more than ever an emaciated old man, with short thin legs sticking out as though they belonged to someone else, muscles made stringy by wear and disease. With his whole body visible, no longer covered by blankets, the disproportion between the size of his head and the size of his body was even more striking, the vast, oversized forehead bulging over the wizened face, dwarfing the wiry child's body beneath.

Suddenly he leaned his head back and screamed "Ivaaan!" He drew the name out, letting go in a long shriek the tormenting loss that had been bottled up inside him. It was a cry of grief, of devastated bereavement, and it seemed to have enough anguish to pierce through the boundary of life and death and reach his brother on the other side.

The cry provoked another spasm of coughing, and with each cough the muscles between his ribs contracted, creating hollow grooves in his chest, as though he were being squeezed by a giant, invisible hand. Slowly the spasm subsided. Yuri stared at the doctors around him—Lussac, Sailland, and Mulligan—his gaze shifting from one to the other in his peculiar snapshot sequence of vision.

"Dr. Sailland," he said, and reached a hand out to her. His hand, Mulligan noted for the first time, had already been deformed by arthritis, the fingers curled and stiffened, the knuckles gnarled and large. His voice was not high pitched like a boy's but low, whispered, a old man's voice, weak and lacking resonance. The rolled "r's" and sibilant "sh" sounds of Russian heavily accented his speech. Breathing hard, still coughing a little, he was able to say only a few

words at a time. "Dr. Sailland, we must begin . . . immediately . . . you must help . . . I need to study chemistry,
biology, physics . . . urgently. Medvedev made terrible
errors."

"Medvedev?"

"Yevgeny Medvedev. He was head of the project."

"The project?" Mulligan asked, looking at Irene. He
looked back at Yuri. "How much do you know about it?"

"We were told very little," Yuri said, shaking his head
sadly. "So much I don't know . . . Only at the very end . . .
when Ivan and I . . . broke into the library and later . . . into
Medvedev's office . . . did we begin to understand."

Over the next several days they were able to extract the
whole story.

CHAPTER TEN

In the winter the wind from the north acquires an additional glacial edge as it passes over Lake Ladoga and sweeps down over the river Neva. Yuri's first memories were of the wind and the cold and of being bundled up in bulky winter clothing to be taken outside. This was when he was only eight months old, and so his memories, although vivid, were patchy and inconsistent, with people and events fading and reappearing in odd permutations. He recalled the round, red faces of the nursemaids and their warm hands and chattering voices as they struggled to put on his sweater and parka and black imitation-fur Cossack hat, patiently laughing and putting his mittens back on again each time he took them off and threw them to the floor. Once outside, the cold was so intense that it pinched and scraped any bare skin like dry, frozen sandpaper, and the sense of freezing was heightened, especially just after a storm, by the unbroken whiteness of a winter world blanketed by ice and snow.

The nurses were kind and considerate but never loving or warmly affectionate. Yuri had no memory of having ever been hugged or cuddled. When his nose ran with the cold, they produced huge handkerchiefs from the deep pockets of their coats and wiped it gently. Later he would remark, with just a faint suggestion of surprise and hurt, that the boys never called the nurses "mother." So far as they knew they had no mother; at least no one answering to that name ever came to see them. The nurses were called by name, Anna or Katerina or Alexandra, but they were never called "mother." There were several shifts of them every day, and they came and went with a regularity that gave order to time. None of them ever tended the children for more than a year.

Inside the institute it was warm, of course, but even so, a glance through the frosted windows at the blowing ice crystals might make one shiver with cold. Living inside the institute was like living in a large apartment that occupied the entire second floor of the building. There were a number of bedrooms, a large one the children shared in common and smaller ones for the nurses. The living area and playroom, as well as the kitchen and dining room, were shared by everyone. The furnishings were of the heavy, ponderous kind favored by people in cold climates—large deep chairs and couches and unpainted wooden tables. Some of the rooms had light blue carpeting, although the walls were a lackluster beige and, except for portraits of Lenin and Pavlov, devoid of any art or decoration. In this apartment it was the children themselves who were the objects of interest and inquiry.

Downstairs, on the ground floor, were the library and offices and laboratories. The children were instructed never, under any circumstances, to go there. It was forbidden territory. Yuri and his brothers played in the common areas on the second floor. There were four of them, four brothers, and as far back as his memory could take him they were always together. Every waking moment was shared, every experience communal. They ate the same food, wore the same clothes, engaged in the same activities at the same time.

Although not identical, they resembled each other greatly, and they were nearly the same age. Four brothers—no sisters. Later, during the brief clandestine moments when he read through Medvedev's notebook, Yuri would learn that this had been the first hint that all would not go as planned, that in biological experiments some unexpected unpleasantness could almost be counted on. The mutation had been lethal to the female embryo; the aborted fetuses had all been girls. But that knowledge came later. Being of the same sex reinforced their identification with each other, a submersion of individual ego in the manner of twins whose sense of self is always at least partly diffused and shared with the other. Yuri, Ivan, Andreyev, Gorgi—the four boys thought of themselves in many ways as four aspects of the same person.

They were always under observation, like specimens in a collection or animals in a zoo. Much of the adult activity around them involved measuring and monitoring their growth. The boys had no contact with other children, and so no direct comparison, but even so, they acquired a sense, profoundly disconcerting, that they were different, very special or very odd—they could never be sure which. Even during their earliest "play" activities—recognizing colors and sounds, rolling or catching a ball, matching geometric objects to holes of the same shape—there was always someone with a clipboard and stopwatch timing them, peering down intently and making notes or giving instructions such as, "Here, Yuri, let's see how quickly you can put this puzzle together." These were their teachers and, like the nurses, they were kind and considerate but never affectionate.

And always, a shadow hovering in the background, quietly conferring with the teachers and the nurses, was Medvedev, Yevgeny Medvedev. Yuri quivered with rage and hatred when he spoke of Medvedev, though it wasn't that Medvedev had ever been brutal or cruel. In fact, in the early years he rarely spoke to them directly, so that he appeared as a presence rather than as a person. Yuri had a clearly remembered image of Medvedev sitting quietly in a corner, leaning forward with his elbows on his knees, watching them hour after hour, pale blue eyes peering from above impassive features that veiled his thoughts. Medvedev was like the director of a drama, who establishes the sets and the manner in which the play is acted but is never seen onstage himself. The children all learned, though, that the lines of authority led to him.

Nature might be rearranged, but she would work the wonder at her own pace. The simple tasks of infancy went on for years, much longer than expected. A normal child, on the average, learns to walk at twelve months and utters his first words at one and a half years. Not so the four brothers. They remained clumsy crawlers until they were well over four years of age, and their hand-eye coordination, in catching a thrown ball, for instance, was greatly substandard until age six. Their first words weren't spoken until they were five years of age.

Their teachers' disappointment was great. They'd been led to expect genius bursting like great fireworks in a night sky. Medvedev constantly had to encourage them.

"It will take more time," Yuri recalled his saying one day. "More time! If the theory is correct, they have a more complex brain. It will take longer to grow and mature." He gave one of the teachers a heartening clap on the shoulder, and his voice was loud and confident. "Let's not give up yet! It takes more time to draw a dodecahedron than a square, eh? Be patient!"

"It's five years," the teacher grumbled, stubbornly uninspired by Medvedev's forced enthusiasm. "They don't talk yet. Something went wrong."

"Be patient," Medvedev urged. "We have only these four children. That's all I could arrange. We must do our work with these."

Only later did Yuri understand what was meant by that.

169

The difference, though, the crucial difference, was that once a certain level of ability was reached, when the brain finally said, "I am ready for this now," the skill emerged fully developed, like Athena springing full grown from the head of Zeus. Once ready, the expanding intellect was like an explosive force moving irresistibly outward from its germinating center. The children didn't talk until the age of five, but they never said things like "da-da" or "na-na." The plateau reached, they went from no speech at all to speaking in complete sentences. Gorgi said blandly one morning, as if it were the most natural thing in the world, "I think I'll have breakfast now." The teachers' spirits revived quickly after that, and a broad grin of self-congratulation began to alter the flat planes of Medvedev's face. Within six months they had progressed to complex sentences. Yuri could remember Ivan saying at age five, "Andreyev, who usually doesn't like such things, and normally wouldn't want to, today would prefer painting to sorting blocks."

They didn't learn to read, however, until they were seven years old, the usual separation of verbal and written language, different centers in the brain maturing at different rates. Until then they hadn't even been able to learn the alphabet. And then suddenly one day, again without warning, Gorgi picked up a magazine one of the teachers had brought, a trade journal in psychology, and began reading it as casually as if he had been doing such things for years.

"What are you doing?" Ivan asked him.

"Reading," Gorgi replied, not taking his eyes from the magazine. "An article on cognitive development in a socialist society."

"Really?" Ivan asked. "Let's see."

All four of them sat together in a semicircle on the floor and read the article. Ivan asked for a dictionary so they could look up the few words whose meanings couldn't be divined from the context. In a moment of transition so quiet as to be almost surreptitious they had spanned a length of intellectual and linguistic development that would take an ordinary child a decade or more.

Medvedev's expression changed to one of unending wonder and delight.

Once they had learned to read, it became clear that the boys had nearly perfect recall. Gorgi not only understood the article on cognitive development, but months later, even, could spout it back nearly verbatim. They had only to glance at a page to remember it. As knowledge accumulated, memory became a vast storehouse whose contents could be tapped at will, effortlessly and instantly, a stone engraving on which words and ideas were indelibly inscribed.

But it was in the realm of mathematics, in the domain of pure reason and the logical manipulation of symbols, that their greatest genius lay. This ability, too, lay dormant at first, quietly gathering strength until it ignited. Then intellect glowed with an incandescence that inspired awe. They learned in several months what took years for normal children to master. In arithmetical functions they were more like calculators than anything else, as though they had an ability to picture huge numbers mentally and imagine their rearrangements. You could ask Yuri, for example, "How much is 41,285 divided by 361?" and he would close his eyes for an instant and then reply, "114.36288." They went through Euclidean geometry as though it were a game invented solely for their delight and laughingly solved for themselves the Pythagorean theorem. Algebra and trigonometry were delightful toys whose moving parts were x's and y's, quadratic equations, sines and cosines.

Shortly after they demonstrated their abilities in mathematics, when they were just six years old, a man named General Kermonov appeared. The boys shrunk from him instinctively. He was a huge, terrifying man, a head taller than Medvedev. A thin white line of scar tissue extended from the middle of his forehead diagonally across a partially closed right eye. He watched them quietly during an algebra lesson for an hour but then spoke in the angry outburst of a man who felt he'd been deceived. "They're not at all what you said they'd be," he snarled at Medvedev. "What do I need a human calculator for?" He stormed off in disgust.

Once the extent of their genius became apparent, the attitude of their teachers, and especially of Medvedev, began to change again. Indistinct, tenuous at first, a tiny note of trepidation crept into their voices. They became wary of the children, cautious about them. "There's nothing supernatural here," Medvedev reassured the teachers, but it was Medvedev himself who told the boys again and again that they must never read anything not specifically given to them. Yuri experienced a feeling of empty disuse, sensing only a hungry craving for knowledge during the long boring hours when they were given nothing to read. The boys began to resent the limitations imposed upon them. Often there was little to do except to play interminable games of blindfold chess. Information about the outside world was strictly limited. They were never allowed to watch television, or listen to a radio except to hear a concert.

Whenever new nurses arrived they seemed startled and dismayed by the appearance of the brothers and hesitated to touch them until they'd become used to them.

"Why do I frighten you?" Yuri asked a new nurse called Katerina, sensing her shrink from him as he approached. "Am I ugly?" He asked the question indifferently, merely curious.

Although she forced herself to look steadily at him, he saw her shiver and step back a little. Then her gaze wavered and, blushing, she looked down. "Not ugly, Yuri," she said, "but very odd. Your head is very large and your forehead has lots of bumps on it. Your chin is very small. And your eyes move about in a very peculiar way."

"But I need a big head," he protested. "I'm so much smarter than the rest of you." Saying that, Yuri became aware for the first time of his nascent contempt for people who thought him repugnant but who couldn't do the simplest arithmetic without a pocket calculator.

All of their time was spent at the institute. Until the athletic training began they were never allowed beyond the high brick wall that separated the institute from the street, although Medvedev permitted them to play in the cobblestone yard that surrounded the building. They almost never saw other children. On the rare occasion when they caught a glimpse of another child through the large wrought-iron gate, the sight only deepened the isolation to which they felt increasingly condemned. Other children were happy, laughing and shouting, eager—as the four brothers never were.

Medvedev made it clear he didn't want them playing where they could be seen by passersby. "Don't let them near the gate," he often warned the nurses. "There will be too much talk. Gossip could ruin everything."

As they grew older Medvedev himself spent more and more time with them. When they clamored to go out, to go into the vast metropolis that they could see through the second-story windows, he would always say, "Later, later, when you're ready. Then we'll take the world by storm!" They didn't understand what he meant, and their pleas were unavailing. Still, in response both to their evident need and to his desire to explore their potential, he increased cautiously the scope of their education. The problem for him was that they learned so fast and so thoroughly that each new bit of knowledge served only to whet their appetites for more. Their curiosity was insatiable. He permitted them to study world geography and meteorology, careful always to keep the instructional materials ideologically neutral. They learned some Russian history and began English. Much of their patchy knowledge of the world came as a secondary gain through the English reading materials, since language had to say something.

The medical monitoring that had beleaguered their infancy never ceased. They were constantly being prodded and measured and it seemed as though the doctors never tired of thinking of new blood tests.

"Not again," Yuri would complain. He hated the needles more than the others did. "Why every week?"

"Just a little more," Medvedev would reply, standing beside the doctor while the venipuncture was performed.

"You have plenty more where that came from. You're making new blood all the time."

They were never told what all the tests were for, but later Medvedev's journal revealed that they were looking for hormone or enzyme changes.

They had monthly electroencephalograms. After they learned to read they took IQ tests at least every three months, until their teachers realized they couldn't devise a valid test. When their athletic abilities developed they all had muscle biopsies; small pieces of lateral thigh muscle were removed for study under the electron microscope.

"Why do you suppose they watch us so carefully?" Andreyev asked the others one day. "Why do they measure and record everything we do?" More and more the children grew to an alien self-awareness, a sense of themselves as freaks, objects of inquiry removed from the human family.

Medvedev waited impatiently for their development to include the muscle part of the experiment. The brothers learned to walk with reliable stability only at age five, but by then Medvedev still hadn't given up hope. When they were seven he judged their muscles were ready, and decided to test them.

On a quiet Sunday in September, 1984, the boys were piled into a new Volga sedan and taken to a small soccer stadium just outside Leningrad. It was their first automobile ride, their first real excursion beyond the walls of the institute, and they thrilled to the sights of the great city. Everything enchanted them; the world expanded a thousandfold. They had never seen a tree before, nor a river, except in pictures, and so the strips of park lining the stone-encased Neva seemed a wilderness. "Look at that!" Ivan shouted, pointing to an old trolley clanging its way on rails down the Nevsky Prospekt. They were awed into silence by the enormous facade of the Winter Palace as they passed by. The world outside the institute became real, filled with sounds and sights and movements, no longer something glimpsed only distantly and silently through a dirty window. Cars honked. A bus in front of them fouled the air with diesel exhaust. Store windows seemed filled with a thousand mysterious and fascinating things. Boisterous youths jostled each other on the sidewalks. Young couples walked slowly, the boy's arm around the girl's shoulder, heads bent low in earnest conversation, while slightly older couples pushed baby carriages. To the boys ordinary life was as overwhelming as a carnival.

They seemed stunned by the sheer vastness of the city, mile on mile of heavy stone buildings and broad sidewalks and majestic avenues of what had once been an imperial capital. Leningrad, despite its size, is a city where people walk, especially on Sundays, and the four boys studied the thousands of faces intently, each one unspokenly verifying that none of the people looked quite like them. At a stoplight they paused next to another car containing two boys nearly their own age, and the two groups silently stared at each other. It was the first really good look they had ever had at other children, and as they stared, their enthusiasm dampened. Normal children really were much different, with smaller heads and wider faces and expressions less peaked and birdlike. Despite their excitement at seeing the city, they had a sinking feeling of exclusion.

Medvedev later confided in his journal that he'd taken the boys out of the institute only with some hesitation, concerned that having seen something of the world they'd revolt against their confinement and lose the docile cooperativeness of the child. Still, the chance had to be taken. They were seven years old and it was time to test them. Their development had been slow, and he wasn't sure what aspect of muscle function would be affected by the gene for creatine phosphokinase. It might be strength or speed or endurance, or all three. The neurotransmitter-enzyme part of the experiment had worked—in a staggered, uneven fashion, to be sure, but the boys were brilliant beyond his wildest dreams. Now the extent of success in the other part of the experiment would be determined.

VARIANT

It was a fall day, cool and clear. A light wind blew from the west, bringing with it the salty scent of the Baltic. The stadium was empty. A tiered oval of vacant seats looked down on a grassy field belted by a four-hundred-meter track. The boys' spirits lifted as they hopped up and down in the center of the field, enjoying the springiness of their running shoes. Loose-fitting athletic shorts allowed them a freedom of movement whose potential they were just beginning to realize. Medvedev let them warm up on the grass.

He blew a whistle and the boys clustered around him. "What I want you to do," he instructed, "is just to run around this track. That's all. Just run. As fast and as far as you can until you get tired and have to stop. Start when I blow the whistle again."

Medvedev walked to the sidelines, where he stood with his stopwatch in hand. Uncertainty tinged his excitement with anxiety. At the last minute he remembered that he hadn't consulted an athletics coach. He didn't know what to expect. The boys were small for seven-year-olds, and he wasn't exactly sure of how fast or far a seven-year-old could run. But he assumed that running fifteen hundred meters, if they could do it at all, would take them at least eight or nine minutes.

"Go!" He blew the whistle and started the stopwatch.

The first hundred meters, Yuri remembered, was an astonishing revelation. The discovery of what his body could do gave him an exhilarating, almost overwhelming sense of freedom. It was an explosion of energies too long restrained, a secret too long concealed. Up and down, up and down, he felt his legs drive and push against the ground in an unrestricted free flow of muscle and sinew. A hoarse cry of sheer animal exultation burst from his throat, and he found himself wanting to run faster and faster. There was no effort, no fatigue . . . up and down, up and down, drive and push, he could feel his heel drive into the ground, feel his weight roll forward on his foot to push off again, the smooth, coordinated movement stretching out to cover more and more ground with each stride. Yuri later said that this was the single happiest moment in his life.

The other boys felt it, too. "Come on," Gorgi yelled, "let's race!"

They finished the fifteen hundred meters in six minutes flat and kept going for five kilometers more. They would have continued farther still but Medvedev stopped them, afraid that they might hurt themselves by doing too much for the first time. He wasn't sure he could believe what he had seen and he looked repeatedly at his stopwatch. A wide toothy grin spread across his broad face and stayed there.

"Are you all right?" he asked. "Nothing hurts?"

The boys were breathing heavily but otherwise seemed only invigorated by the experience. Their cheeks glowed with the sweat and flush of effort and their eyes danced with excitement. They had never looked healthier. "Let's do more!" they clamored.

Medvedev wouldn't allow it. "That's enough for the first time," he said, shaking his head. "We'll do this again soon."

"Promise? Do you promise?"

Medvedev nodded. "Next week. There are some people who ought to see this. You fellows are really quite extraordinary runners," he murmured in mild understatement, still grinning approval. "Quite extraordinary."

The next week they repeated the performance. The difference was that this time there was a small audience of somber men dressed in officers' uniforms of the Red Army. They said nothing to the boys but watched stolidly, attentive and appraising. As the boys came around the track on each lap, they could see the expressions of the men change from saturnine doubt to wide-eyed incredulity, then to gesticulating jubilation. They slapped each other on the back, shouting and pointing at their stopwatches, like team coaches sharing a victory. The boys ran five kilometers in half an hour. The officers shook hands ceremoniously with Medvedev. One of them lost his self-restraint and ran boisterously toward the boys, as if to sweep them up in his arms, only to stop short when he saw them up close, stumbling in recoil with an expression of horror on his face.

"What's this?" he shouted to Medvedev. "Why do they look like this?"

"Don't let appearances fool you, Comrade Colonel!" Medvedev shouted back. "You're witnessing history!"

After that the boys were taken to the stadium several times a week. An athletics coach supervised their training and advised them on calisthenics and running. Regular exercise soon revealed another development. Ivan was the first to notice it. "I'm getting stronger," he said. "I can lift things I never could lift before." Whether it was an effect of training or merely something that would have happened anyway they didn't know, but soon they began to exhibit enormous strength and were able to lift a hundred pounds with ease. Each day they grew stronger.

A change came over their lives in other ways. Now men in uniform were often at the institute, implacably austere men who frightened the boys but who were obviously accustomed to authority. General Kermonov reappeared and became a frequent visitor. Everyone, the nurses, the teachers, even Medvedev seemed to defer to the officers. They were interested in testing the boys' reaction times and grunted their satisfaction when, after some practice, the boys demonstrated that they could, on signal, move their hands from one handle to another in 0.22 seconds. And they seemed to be getting faster. Some of the officers were also interested in their mathematical abilities and asked them to calculate mentally, after giving them the formula, such things as at what angle of elevation a howitzer should be fired to propel a shell six kilometers into a twenty-kilometer headwind.

It was three months later, in December, that things began to go wrong. Now the boys learned that they were different from other people in other, more terrible ways. At first there was only an overheard stray comment or two:

"What's the matter with Ivan? He looks so old!" or "Gorgi is losing his hair. Imagine! A seven-year-old going bald!" The boys themselves noticed changes. It was harder to get up in the morning. They felt stiff and sore after a hard workout. They tired more readily. Bruises lasted longer. Fine wrinkles appeared on their foreheads and under their eyes, spreading and deepening within weeks to cover their entire faces with the delicate indelible imprint of time and wear. Hair that didn't fall out was turning gray. If maturation had been excruciatingly slow, senescence was horrendously quick.

CHAPTER ELEVEN

Andreyev was the first to get sick. One day in early February he complained of pain in his stomach, a burning pain, he said, as if it was on fire. And the next day his stool was coal black and unusually foul smelling. Doctor Mialek was summoned and arrived quickly.

"He's must have an ulcer," the doctor said after examining Andreyev carefully. "His stomach is bleeding."

"How could he have a bleeding ulcer?" Medvedev complained. He'd hovered anxiously over the doctor's shoulder while Andreyev was being examined. "He's only seven years old. Seven-year-olds don't get ulcers."

"That's just it," Dr. Mialek grumbled, stroking his chin with a thoughtful and disturbed look. "He's seven and not seven. I want to do some further checking. These boys look much older than their age. Much older. I want to look up something in my old pediatrics text. Something I can't quite remember. A rare congenital disease called progeria. If these

children have it, then they're really, physiologically, anyway, more like sixty or seventy than six or seven."

After Dr. Mialek left Medvedev grew peevish and irrita-
ble. He stalked about the institute glowering balefully at the
boys as though he held them responsible for their frailties.
His head jutted forward from his shoulders in a simian posture, and he seemed constantly to be on the verge of a
vengeful eruption. Success, seemingly so complete just a
short while ago, was rapidly slipping away. He ordered an
immediate new round of medical tests, not looking for hor-
mones or enzymes this time, but the kinds of tests done on
the elderly to chronicle their decline. A treadmill examina-
tion revealed the presence of coronary artery disease in Ivan
and Gorgi. Pulmonary function tests and arterial blood
gases showed a weakening of Yuri's breathing capacity and
oxygen transport. X-rays of the spine revealed compression
of the vertebrae, arthritis and displacement of the discs in all
of them. Creatinine clearance studies showed that kidney
function was only half what it should have been. Every
measurable organ had dramatically decayed.

Their aging, the inexorable pressure of time on flesh, had
vastly accelerated and achieved terror by its compression.
"Why is this happening? What's wrong with us?" Their
questions grew more and more frightened. They now felt as
trapped by the closing jaws of a merciless destiny as they
were forced indoors by the icy grip of winter. More than
ever they felt like caged laboratory animals, curiosities to be
peered at and prodded. An impenetrable barrier, the noisome taint of death and decay, began to build around them,
and their teachers and nurses reacted with an instinctive
withdrawal. They looked at the boys with ill-concealed
expressions combining pity and revulsion. Yuri remembered
long nights of crying in his bed, shedding the lonely tears of
abandonment. For support the brothers had only each other
and the knowledge of a shared fate. What was happening to
one was, clearly, happening to all.

A week later Doctor Mialek came back and examined

them again. This time he knew what he was looking for and was more certain. "Definitely progeria," he pronounced. He had brought a book, and the boys overheard him talking to Medvedev. "Look at these pictures in the text. See the way the face is narrowed, pinched up in front, the tiny jaw, the eyes set so close together? The narrow shoulders and the light bones? Balding and graying at age seven? These children fit the description perfectly."

"Can anything be done?"

Mialek shook his head negatively, disconsolately. "You can't treat genetic diseases."

Their fate was sealed. It was mid-February. Through the windows ice crystals could be seen blowing in the steady driving wind from the north. The temperature outside rarely rose above twenty degrees; and the chill outside mirrored the despair within, as though winter had reached inside to lay an icy hand around everyone's heart. Instruction in English and mathematics was abandoned more or less spontaneously. A dispirited lackluster malaise seeped through the institute. Everyone simply waited for the end.

Gorgi was the first to die. They were playing a game of blindfold chess when he suddenly sat back with a quizzical look on his face, the symptom at first only dimly perceived. Then uncertainty passed into recognition. The color drained from his cheeks as the pain became clearer, more distinct, and his right hand reached to his chest and pressed against it. A wild frantic look came into his eyes and his forehead was instantly bathed in sweat. With a groan he pushed his chair back and attempted to rise but fell heavily to the floor.

He struggled to a kneeling position on one knee, bent over in a tormented posture, clutching his chest and breathing heavily as the others rushed to his side.

"Gorgi!"

He looked up at them, pleading silently through his agony, unable to speak.

"Katerina!" Yuri cried. "Katerina! Come quickly! Gorgi

is sick!" Suddenly they were no more than frightened little children, genius abolished in a twinkling by terror.

Katerina came at a run and bent over Gorgi. He was gasping for air, his face white and drawn, scratching at his chest as if trying to tear something out of it. "Help me," she instructed the others sternly. "Let's get him to his bed."

Dr. Mialek arrived within half an hour. The electrocardiogram told the story. Gorgi had had a heart attack.

"He's going into shock," the doctor informed Medvedev. "Cardiogenic shock. It's almost always lethal. If he's to have any chance at all, he's got to be transferred to a hospital immediately."

"No!" Medvedev commanded, adamant, fear crystallizing his impulse for secrecy. "No hospital! He can't be seen in a public place. How would I explain it?"

It wouldn't have made any difference. Gorgi's blood pressure fell quickly as the heart muscle died. Dr. Mialek gave him a shot of morphine to ease the pain, but within a few minutes he had lost consciousness, anyway. The others, Yuri, Ivan, and Andreyev, stood helplessly at the bedside, an integral part of each of them withering away as they watched their brother die. His hands and feet grew cold, suffused with a murky, dusky purple. He seemed to get smaller as he died, as though something of substance departed as life ebbed from his body. A few moments before the end he wrenched himself into a sitting position, forced upward by a last shred of vitality, staring wildly through panic-glazed eyes. "My brothers!" he shouted. "Where are my brothers?" Then he collapsed.

"They'll all go like that," the doctor said.

Andreyev was next. In many ways his death was even more horrible than Gorgi's, though it was a variation on the theme of atherosclerosis. One week after Gorgi's death, while walking into the playroom, Andreyev fell abruptly and clumsily to the floor, unable to move his right side. He was unable to speak, although he seemed to understand what was said around him. For four days afterward he lay in his bed, his right arm and leg limp and flaccid, lifeless, his face distorted, pulled to the left side by the unbalanced muscles. He was barely recognizable. When he tried to talk, his mouth gyrated in a grotesque mockery of speech. He struggled to say something, anything, to reestablish communication; but the effort was unavailing and he remained as isolated and mute as a stone. His helplessness was pitiful. At one point Doctor Mialek raised Andreyev's right arm over his face and let go, to see if there was any instinctive movement of self-protection. The hand crashed down onto his nose and made it bleed. Ivan and Yuri stared at each other in horror. Their brother Andreyev had become a pathetic, grotesque figure, one half of his body useless, a lobe of his magnificent brain obliterated. Sporadic tears of self-pity rolled down Andreyev's cheeks. When he developed pneumonia Medvedev mercifully decided to let it go untreated and Andreyev finally died.

Yuri and Ivan saw their future laid out before them in bold brushstrokes.

"What's wrong with us?" Ivan asked for the hundredth time. "Why does this happen?"

"I don't know," Yuri replied, unwilling to give up completely, "but I'm going to find out. The doctor said something about a disease called progeria. Why don't we see if we can break into the library?" Desperation generated boldness, and he intinctively saw knowledge as the key to any hope of survival.

They had never been allowed into the library. After he'd gained an awareness of how intelligent he was, Yuri realized that the policy was an outgrowth of the awe in which the boys were held. Libraries meant knowledge; knowledge meant power; power implied danger. The full reach of their intellect was unknown, but it was intimidating nonetheless, and it seemed somehow hazardous to allow such an instrument an unrestricted expression of its abilities. In retrospect, Yuri was able to recognize the heavy shadow of fear that had darkened Medvedev's brow and sullied his triumph when the boys had performed some particularly clever mathematical feat. More than anyone else Medvedev was able to intuit that to equip fully such a mind might have unforeseen, disastrous consequences. Ignorance kept people docile, malleable, manageable.

Security, though, was lax. They were, after all, little boys who did as they were told. The library was on the first floor of the building and the boys had been simply, if repeatedly, told never to go there. It wasn't locked. It never occurred to anyone that Ivan and Yuri would pinch themselves to stay awake until the early hours of the morning in order to steal a few furtive hours with the books.

They looked first in a medical dictionary. Progeria—the dictionary defined it as a congenital disorder characterized by abnormally rapid aging, cause unknown, thought to be genetic, very rare. There was no further information; nothing else was known.

Pushed by desperation, never knowing when their brothers' fate might overtake them, Ivan and Yuri drove themselves to near-collapse, allowing themselves only a few hours sleep a night. They skimmed through texts and journals in chemistry, biochemistry, genetics, medicine, physiology, imprinting huge masses of information. They were unprepared for such a task, and their reading lacked cohesion and direction. They absorbed mountains of useless, irrelevant facts, searching always for a remedy to the lethal flaw that had impaled them on the spear of a malicious fate.

At the end of a week, exhausted and disheartened, they had learned a great deal but knew little more that was useful than they had known before. What they needed to learn didn't seem to be known by anyone. The knowledge simply didn't exist. And they were running out of time.

Medvedev, too, looked more and more harried. He spent little time now with Yuri and Ivan but kept to himself in his office on the ground floor. One night the boys crept past the windowed door to his office and saw him inside, half buried behind a mass of journals. He was writing in a notebook that lay open on the desk and seemed despondent, bent over in defeated weariness. They guessed that he, too, was searching for the answer to their dilemma.

"Let's go into his office," Yuri suggested in a whisper the next night. "Let's see what he's reading. Let's see what he's written in that notebook."

The office was locked. It was two o'clock in the morning on March 14, 1985. They stood outside Medvedev's office and wondered what to do.

"What if we get caught?"

"So what? What have we to lose?"

"Nothing. We're dying anyway. Let's break in."

Yuri abruptly shoved his elbow through the glass pane of the door and reached through the hole to turn the doorknob.

They crossed swiftly and silently to the desk and crouched, perched at the edge of wild flight. They waited for what seemed hours, motionless, sure their pounding hearts could be heard for miles around, and then hesitantly turned on the lamp. The hall outside the office remained quiet.

The looseleaf notebook lay open on the desk, its unlined white pages covered in a script they recognized as Medvedev's. Ivan gently put the lamp on the floor to diffuse its glare, and in the soft and shadowed light he and Yuri turned the pages of the notebook, bending over it in trembling and eager apprehension. The notebook was Medvedev's personal chronicle, not an official scientific notebook, but one containing his private thoughts and reactions to the experiment. The last entries were the most compelling.

January 1, 1985. Eighth year of the experiment. Eighth chapter of this record of my thoughts. Perhaps of interest one day to historians of science. I am almost amused at my own vanity, the more so since success is only partial. Still, despite its shortcomings, I remain convinced that this is the most significant advance in experimental genetics since Mendel crossbred the white and the purple sweet-peas. What would the American, Mulligan, give to learn that I have confirmed his theory? But Nature is more devious than I imagined. She has many twists. True enough that the children are intelligent beyond my wildest dreams, stronger and faster than I would have dared anticipate . . . but they age rapidly, almost as though consumed, ravaged by the very force that lifts them to such heights.

I should perhaps have resisted the temptation to try the experiment all at once on humans. I should have tried simpler species first, animals with a shorter generation time, mice or rats, perhaps, or dogs. But only men had the real prize . . . the human brain!

January 10. Andreyev has an ulcer. Or so Mialek says. He suspects they have a disease called progeria. This is new, disturbing. The children have been flawed from the beginning. I have noted, of course, their most peculiar appearance, though I never recognized in it the signs of a congenital illness. Such are the advantages of a medical education! Mialek comes and in an instant identifies the problem!

What is to be done? I apply Lenin's famous question here in a scientific context. Should I attempt any correction? How to do it? Where did I go wrong? Where is the flaw?

January 14. I am torn with indecision, riven by uncertainty. What to do? In the end, though, my inclination is to allow the experiment to run its course. Its natural history must be unaltered. Only in this way can valid information be obtained so that I'll be able to do it better next time. In any event I do not believe it can be salvaged.

February 16. Grotesque. We went to the stadium today, despite the cold, though for the last time, I think. Although they are aging rapidly their muscular prowess continues to grow. They are quicker and stronger than ever. What bizarre dissociation . . . the muscles and neuromuscular synapse remain in a state of growth while the rest of the body decays. Their strength is becoming phenomenal—Yuri, although he weighs only 35 kilos, can easily lift 125. He runs 100 meters in 8.3 seconds.

February 20. The children know what is happening. Fear creeps into their expressions and corrupts their souls. Will this decay lead to madness as well? They have never seen death. What knowledge can they have of it? But the smell of it is in the air. They've known for a long time that they aren't normal. But now they know that something is horribly, dreadfully wrong.

February 25. Triumph crumbles and slips from my grasp. The tragedy I feared most has occurred. Gorgi died today of a heart attack. I knew of their atherosclerosis but I had no idea it was so far advanced. Mialek says this is the way progeria victims usually die. He will try to have the autopsy report for me within forty-eight hours. I await it with anxiety and dread. Will it give any clue to what went wrong? Is the situation hopeless? The genes for seven enzymes were spliced into them, the six neurotransmitters and the CPK. What causes the aging? Is it some imbalance of enzymatic product? Mulligan's techniques might give an answer to such questions, but I am doubtful that I can duplicate his methods in a short time. Can success be recaptured?

February 27. They all know now they are dying. Their fear has become a thing one can almost touch. Ivan asked me today for permission to enter the library. This is what I have always denied them, and I remain hesitant even now to permit it. Curious that I, who created them, created this incomparable intelligence, should fear it so. The decision to restrict their education should be looked at again. To have this resource and not use it! What folly!

Still, I remain fearful, though it is perhaps more dark intuition than fear. What thoughts would they have that I could not comprehend? What thoughts do they have even now? Do they know how intelligent they really are? What would they do with a real education? What might they create? Could I, could anyone understand it? They've been allowed primarily English and mathematics, the one to test their memory, the other to test their reasoning. Of other disciplines they remain largely ignorant . . . this produces strange effects. Yet in this way it is contained. I cannot overcome my reluctance to let the genie out of the bottle.

March 1. No help at all from the medical profession. Mialek says the pathologist found premature atherosclerosis, rotten arteries and nothing more. This adds nothing to what I already knew. They have sent brain tissue for electron microscopy and ultrastructural studies, but that will take weeks to complete.

March 2. Addendum to the pathology report. The pathologist stated that in preparing slices of the brain for microscopic study he found what seemed to be a density of neurons greater than any he had ever encountered. If he could learn of this Mulligan would feel vindicated again. After all, his were the seminal ideas. Ironic that he may never learn his theory was correct . . . such are the vagaries of international science and state secrets.

Yet it all went wrong. My heart sinks in despair.

March 4. The second victim succumbs. Andreyev has been felled by a stroke and lies mute on his bed. Death broods over him.

March 7. Kermonov was here today. For the last time, he said. The Army is no longer interested. The experiment needs "perfection." He asked what use could the Army have for a child who cannot walk until age five and dies of old age at eight? Demeaning myself, I pleaded with him to reconsider. His sarcasm is intolerable! The fools! The damnable short-sighted fools! The military deserve their reputation for having all the imagination of donkeys. Did they think it would be perfect the first try? All they want is a soldier who can carry fifty kilos and walk one hundred kilometers a day. Or a pilot with faster reactions. They can't even understand that the brain is the real weapon.

And those idiots have no insight at all into the wider significance of the achievement . . . that in the most profound sense man might now direct his own destiny. That now, at last, the divine has been rivalled!

But I have committed my career to this . . . I must learn what I can from this failure and modify the experiment the next time. Army or no Army. But where will I acquire the appropriations I need? How will I proceed?

March 8. Andreyev died today. Ivan and Yuri are in a state of panic. It is sometimes hard for me to remember that they are only little children. Could they save themselves if I allowed them to learn biochemistry? Dare I tell them how I created them? Would knowledge of how it was done help them to undo it? I fear it is already too late, that they are already locked irretrievably into the iron destiny of their genes.

March 10. I am nearly sleepless, scarcely resting a moment, scouring the world's literature on aging. I must not let myself be defeated! Where was the mistake? The greatest scientific achievement in history lies at my fingertips and still I cannot grasp it. There is little known of aging, almost none of it useful. The only ray of hope is in the work of Irene Sailland in Paris. She relates aging phenomena to intracellular enzyme imbalances. What I would give to be able to consult her at this point! And Mulligan!

March 13. Ivan and Yuri whisper between themselves. We don't even try to give them their usual classes any more. We wait. They have become quietly sullen, like sacrificial victims before the moment of martyrdom.

This was the last entry in the journal. Yuri and Ivan looked up from the notebook. Each saw the tears and despair in the other's eyes.

"A genetic experiment," Yuri whispered dully. It was difficult to accept. He looked down at his body, as if he suddenly found it a foreign and distasteful thing and had difficulty accepting it as his own, as if he expected something bizarre and uncanny to happen. "An experiment," he whispered again. "Genetic."

"Look at this," said Ivan. He held up the journal with the abstract of the article by Irene Sailland, and they read it together. Aging, her theory stated, was ultimately caused by imbalances or inadequacies in the enzyme systems needed for cellular maintenance and repair. Could she help them? Could she stop it?

"It's our only chance," Ivan stated with finality. "We've got to get to Paris."

"How? We're not even allowed out of this building."

"I don't know. But to stay here and do nothing means just waiting to die."

"By morning," Yuri pointed out, indicating the broken glass on the floor, "Medvedev will know that we broke into his office. What do you think he'll do?"

The question forced them to a realization that they'd already gone beyond a point of no return.

"Lock us up, probably." Ivan's expression was grim. The light from the lamp on the floor cast peculiar, long, inverted shadows over his face. "He's never wanted anyone to know about us. Now we know why."

Yuri and Ivan looked at each other for a long time without speaking, relying on each other for courage. Reality offered only the most arduous choices.

Indecision was momentary only. They quickly formulated a plan of action. Paris lay twenty-five hundred miles to the south and west of Leningrad. For resources they had their intelligence and an endurance limited apparently only by its caloric requirements—these, and a sense of desperation. The difficulties did not seem insurmountable . . . to some degree they were what General Kermonov had sought. They could carry an uncommonly heavy weight without tiring, and that meant they could load on their backs substantial quantities of blankets, food and water. If they moved mostly by night, they could simultaneously keep warm by exertion and diminish their chances of detection and recapture. How keen would the search for them be? Would anyone imagine that their goal was Paris?

It was March 14th. The first step was to get out of the institute itself. The Institute of Advanced Biochemistry lay in a great bend of the river Neva, on its southern shore, several blocks from the Nevsky Prospekt. Once the winter residence of a Russian archduke, it was an enormous, squat, two-story building of red brick, set well back from the street. The only way in or out was through the massive front gate set in the wall, a gate always padlocked and guarded by a soldier.

At three o'clock in the morning, dressed in three layers of clothing under heavy parkas, they crept silently to the front door. Extra pairs of shoes and more clothing were stuffed into blanket rolls strapped across their shoulders. The front door of the institute was unlocked from the inside. They opened it and crept out.

It was a clear, cloudless night, crackling cold, and their exhaled breath frosted as it hit the air. A crescent moon cast a pale light over the gray cobblestone of the courtyard and red brick of the wall. Beyond the gate the great city was silent, its streets frigid and empty. They crossed the courtyard to the gate, cold elusive shadows sliding across the cold stone.

The soldier was sleepily warming his hands over a small heater in his guardhouse.

"Comrade!" Yuri called softly.

The soldier looked around.

"Over here."

The soldier peered through the gate. He could make out two small children, their appearance oddly disquieting, but he couldn't see clearly in the half light. One child was lying on the ground while the other tried to get his attention. "What are you doing there?"

"My friend has hurt himself. Could you help me get him back inside?"

The soldier unlocked and opened the gate. It was the last mistake he would ever make. Moving faster than anyone he had ever seen, far more quickly than his own reaction time, the child grabbed his arm and, with equally unexpected force, spun him around and threw him to the ground. There was a loud crack as his head struck the unyielding stone, and he didn't move any more.

"I have killed him," Yuri said, looking in alarm at Ivan. He felt no remorse, but the murder might intensify the search for them. "I didn't intend that."

"No matter," Ivan said, equally indifferent. "We're committed, anyway. Let's go."

Their journey to freedom began, as journeys to freedom so often begin, with an act of homicide.

They began to run, trotting at a pace that would consume about eight miles an hour yet one they could continue for hour after hour without tiring. They kept to the shadows, crouching in doorways to avoid the police patrols. Ivan had stolen a map of Leningrad from the purse of one of their nurses, and they moved erratically but persistently to the south and west. By dawn they were out of the city.

Their luck held. Early in the afternoon of the first day they were sixty miles out of the city when they were able to steal the rucksacks of some road repair workers. Each man had had a liter bottle of water in his pack, and Yuri and Ivan took three each. They stole knives and matches as well. And in the cabin of a truck they found the greatest treasure of all, a road map of Eastern and Western Europe.

They had little problem evading detection. The greatest difficulty was finding enough food and water. It could be done, but it required more time than they had thought, and their pace slowed. By keeping to secondary roads they could travel through agricultural areas. An early spring thaw was just beginning and water could be obtained from irrigation pipes, ponds and ditches. Food was stolen whenever the opportunity arose, from workmen's lunches or barns or farmhouses. The knives were useful for killing small animals, chickens and dogs, mostly eaten raw.

They managed to stay together until they came to the Polish-German border. There, clambering over the rocks of a river embankment, Yuri slipped, crying out in pain as he fell.

"What's wrong?" Ivan shouted, frightened, knowing instantly that disaster had struck.

"My ankle! I think it's broken." Yuri tried to rise but fell back again. Pain shot through his leg. Ivan carried him to the shelter of some nearby woods.

It was five in the morning. In the distance, across a field, they could see a barn where they might hide. Ivan helped Yuri hop across the field, and together they crept into the barn and hid in the loft, just as the first workers came in, bleary-eyed and yawning, to begin the day's chores.

"You go on," Yuri whispered. "I'll follow in a few weeks when this heals."

"Nonsense," Ivan replied. "I'll stay with you. You'll never make it alone with a broken ankle."

"Yes, I will," Yuri insisted. "I'll be able to hop or crawl around enough to get food and water and this is a good warm place to hide. We don't know how much longer we have to live. If you wait for me we both might die here. What good is that? If you go on you have a better chance."

The logic was compelling. Ivan waited another two days, stealing as much food as he could and storing it within Yuri's easy reach. But then he left to continue the journey by himself.

That was why Ivan got to Paris four weeks before Yuri, and why, to protect his brother, he said nothing about where he had come from.

CHAPTER TWELVE

PARIS, *June 14, 1985*

Yuri's story wasn't related all at once or even in chronological order. It emerged piecemeal, in response to questions put to him mostly by Mulligan and Irene Sailland, although Ridgely interrogated him closely about the military men. General Alexander hadn't wanted to be away from Washington for long, but he telephoned Mulligan every evening to hear the latest installment of the tale. The general was disappointed. "I was hoping he'd know how it was done," he growled, "but I guess that would be too much to ask for." Even over the telephone Mulligan could hear Alexander's belligerent voice smoldering with the resentment he felt that the Russians had leaped ahead of the Americans this time. "Eight years . . . that's a lot of catching up."

"Maybe not so much," Mulligan said to mollify Alexander's chagrin, although he felt little sympathy for it. "So far as we know those were the only four boys. Only one experiment, really. At least it confirms our suspicions that it was a deliberate mutation. No doubt at all now. We know that much for certain. And that they grafted the genes for seven enzymes into him. Beyond that . . . we'll have to find out for ourselves."

There was a long pause on the other end of the line, and then Alexander asked, "You said before that it was the plasmid that went wrong. Do you think this Medvedev knows about that? Do you think he knows why the progeria happened?"

Mulligan had wondered about that, too, as he'd listened to Yuri's story, and the answer had seemed clear. "Not unless he lies even in his own journal. Yuri remembered the words exactly. No, Medvedev didn't know. He doesn't know."

"Why not?" Alexander asked.

Mulligan snorted a short harsh laugh. "You think it's so easy? In biology you're dealing with thousands of variables, some of which you don't even know exist. Add to that Murphy's Law, that if something can possibly go wrong, it will . . . Medvedev didn't even seem to know that there's a plasmid, that his grafted genes didn't stick to the chromosomes the way he must have intended. The answer's on the plasmid somewhere—I'm sure of that."

Alexander began to sound hopeful. "So you might find out before he does not only how it was done but what went wrong, why it didn't work the way it was supposed to?"

So you can improve it? Mulligan thought ruefully, so we can beat the Russians at this game? He felt the muscles of his back tighten as though recoiling before a cold object touching his skin. The thought of what the Russians were doing filled him with a bottomless dread. He was amazed and repelled that Alexander appeared not to sense this at all. But all he said was, "I don't know. I don't know if I can or not. But I know Medvedev can't . . . he's helpless now. To isolate the plasmid, or even to do chromosome studies, he'll need white cells, and he can't get those from a dead child.

He must know by now that the autopsy studies he's done on the first two didn't give him any answers. He's probably going slightly crazy about it." Mulligan paused as a question that had been bothering him recurred, and he posed it now to Alexander. "What I don't understand is why Medvedev didn't describe the method in his journal. Especially if it was written out of vanity for some future historian of science. You'd think he'd want everyone to know how clever he was."

"Not in Russia." Alexander's reply came swiftly; he saw no contradiction. "Not in Russia. That's not the way they do things. Everyone keeps secrets there because everyone's always a little bit afraid of everyone else. No one ever knows when his personal papers will be read by someone . . . uninvited. If Medvedev doesn't write it down, no one else can learn about it and that gives him an advantage he'd be reluctant to lose."

The paranoia of totalitarianism, Mulligan thought. How odd. Glad I don't live there. Still, the explanation answered his question. "Is everything ready in Bethesda?" he asked, changing the subject. He'd given the general a descriptive list of the lab facilities he and Irene would need.

"Within a few days it will be. You'll have everything you need by the time you get here."

"It can't be very soon. Only when Dr. Lussac says Yuri can travel."

Yuri recovered with excruciating slowness, and his recovery was incomplete. There was no doubt that he'd been permanently weakened by his ordeal. Normally children bounce back from an illness virtually overnight, the way a drought-stricken flower blossoms when given water. Not so old men; not so Yuri. Mulligan had seen it happen many times before during his medical residency—a severe illness, a heart attack, say, or major surgery, some impolite reminder of mortality, rudely shoving a vigorous middle-aged man or woman into the infirmities and indignities of old age. Yuri emerged from his illness with an aura of withered brittleness, like dried leaves.

The broken ankle had never healed properly. He walked with a pronounced limp, unable to put his full weight on his right foot, leaning so far to the left that he seemed constantly on the verge of toppling over. It was an astonishing testament to both courage and desperation that he'd been able to run a thousand miles on it. He tired easily, sagging in limp weariness after an hour or two of study or conversation. Deprivation and exposure had stripped him of every ounce of fat and much of his muscle, but he ate poorly and regained weight only slowly. His face remained gaunt, sculpted as though by a woodcarver's gouge, and his skin was the color and texture of thin onionskin paper through which a network of pink capillaries could be seen spreading outward from his nose.

Dr. Lussac, wrapped in the imperial authority of the attending physician caring for his patient, refused to allow Yuri to leave the hospital until he was more thoroughly and safely recovered. "You wouldn't want a relapse now, would you?" he asked. "His health is precarious enough as it is." He remained impervious to entreaties about the necessity to get to Washington as quickly as possible. His only concession was that he agreed to move Yuri to a private room so that his education could proceed. Lussac didn't mention it specifically, but the idea that Yuri was an old man whose death couldn't possibly be far off loomed ominously in everyone's mind and blighted their optimism.

They couldn't leave for Washington until June twenty-first, Lussac said. That left one week to wait. Irene tried again, and failed again, to get the white cells to grow in tissue culture. It was disheartening, but there was the small consolation that if they couldn't get the cells to grow, Medvedev couldn't have either. His efforts to determine what went wrong would have been stymied.

Mulligan spent most of his time either at the Michelet-

Odéon or at the hospital. He began to hate the confinement of being under guard. It was assumed that they were all under round-the-clock surveillance, but the KGB was subtle enough to be invisible and made no further attempt to kidnap or assassinate anyone.

"Lots of people like being protected this way," Ridgely loftily opined, mocking a little when Mulligan complained. "It makes them feel important." There was a guard from the Sûreté outside the door, another downstairs in the lobby and one stationed outside the front door, the only way in or out of the building.

Irene refused to sleep with him under these circumstances. "I can't do it," she said. "I can't make love to you knowing there's a policeman outside the door listening to every sound."

There's more to it than that, Mulligan thought sadly, fearing he was losing her. He sensed her withdrawal from him, her disapproval of his determination to find out how the mutation had been done. She suspected that he'd become General Alexander's willing confederate, and the suspicion created in her a layer of reserve that formed a barrier between them.

The presence of the guards produced in him, as well, a heavy deadening sensation of enclosure and oppression, of entrapment in an encircling net. He felt as though caught on a vaporous and shifting battleground, uncertain where combat was to be joined, uncertain who was friend and who was foe. Somewhere out there, beyond his reach, men who had already tried to kill him once were conspiring, fabricating plans. That thought reminded him that his work had suddenly and arbitrarily been declared classified. He found he resented that, too, resented ceding questions of primacy and importance to General Alexander. He'd use Alexander as much as Alexander was using him, he thought—exploit the exploiters, learn what he wanted to learn and await the unfolding of events.

After Irene explained that they thought the best chance to halt his decay lay in suppressing the CPK enzyme, Yuri studied avidly, constrained only by the limits of his energies. With some instruction in biochemistry, she said, he ought to be able to develop the inhibitor himself. Ordinarily such a task could take months, or even years, but she had boundless confidence that he could to it much faster than anyone else, perhaps even within days.

As his health returned, Yuri's attitude, except for his obvious devotion to Irene, became more distant and haughty. He was, after all, so much more intelligent than Mulligan, who had to use pencil and paper to solve quadratic equations, or than Ridgely, who couldn't learn new vocabulary simply by hearing the words once. He didn't become exactly scornful or supercilious. It was just that he often regarded them with an expression of impatient disdain and surprise, as though he found it miraculous that they could think at all. Usually he had the air of a teacher waiting impatiently at the head of the class for a child to think of the right answer to a question just asked. Irene didn't seem to mind this much, but Mulligan continued to find it unnerving.

He learned inorganic chemistry with casual ease, absorbing in several days, despite his lingering fatigue, what a normal student might take a year to learn. Mulligan was fascinated just watching him. Yuri studied at the desk they'd set up for him in his room. He was a tiny gnome-like figure, absolutely motionless except for the staccato jerks of his large, owl eyes as they moved across and down the pages of the textbook. His stillness accentuated the image of a powerful, grasping intellect reaching out to gather knowledge the way a vacuum cleaner sucks up dust. Every minute or two his hand would raise slowly, fingers hanging limply from a wrist drawn upward as though by a marionette string, to turn the page. Until exhaustion overwhelmed him, his eyes remained clear and focussed. He rarely asked a question.

There was apparently nothing he didn't understand. Mulligan and Irene found that their main function was to act as an instant dictionary.

Within several days, by the seventeenth of June, Yuri had advanced to organic chemistry. Here for the first time he revealed an aspect of his personality, though it was cerebral, dry and laconic. He seemed amused by the athletic and cooperative carbon atom. "It's wonderful," he commented with a thin smile, as though he regarded carbon as a somewhat comical plaything.

But he immediately perceived its possibilities and more subtle implications. "The covalent bond is fundamental, isn't it?" he said to Mulligan one afternoon.

"It's strong, if that's what you mean. The carbon atoms share two pairs of electrons instead of one."

Yuri shook his head negatively. Thin strands of graying hair fell over his forehead. "That's not what I meant," he said. His voice still had the dry quality of rubbed and dusty leather and seemed as though it were coming from a great distance, but he spoke confidently. "That's not it. It's fundamental because it can be broken. That's what allows for substitutions. It gives the molecule flexibility. That's why the benzene ring is so central. It has three covalent bonds in a ring structure."

"I think he *sees* the molecules in his mind," Irene said later, commenting on Yuri's achievements. The speed of his education had been encouraging, and her dejection had been lifted by a growing hope. As he progressed she'd become more alive, energetic and enthused, and her face lit with radiant smiles of satisfaction at each giant stride. "Not the way we do, not as diagrams on a page, or even as models. I think he can almost feel the clouds of electrons as pulses of circular energy swarming around a nucleus. He can actually picture molecules in his mind, visualize their collisions and transformations. It allows him to predict what's going to happen when two of them interact. That's why he'll be able to develop the inhibitor so quickly. You'll see."

Yuri guessed five pages ahead of the textbook that protein chains would be formed by linking one amino acid to another. It was sort of obvious, he said, from the way the nitrogen was stuck off in one corner of the molecule, practically inviting the carbon to attach to it.

The next morning Yuri was engrossed in the chapter on enzyme activities when he looked up at Mulligan in sudden consternation. "There's something missing here," he said.

"What's that?"

"There's an easier way to do this. Look here. In the text it says that enzyme activities vary according to the temperature of the reaction as well as to the concentration of the ingredients."

"So?"

"So there ought to be a way of expressing that mathematically."

Mulligan sat back and looked at Yuri. This was something he hadn't expected. "Go on."

Yuri rose from his chair and went to the blackboard they had put in his room. He stood there for a moment, turning a piece of chalk over in his hands. In his bathrobe and slippers, with his large head and protruding eyes, he looked more eccentric than ever, almost a caricature of the proverbial mad scientist. He drew a graph on the blackboard. On the abscissa he wrote "speed of reaction" and on the ordinate he wrote "temperature." He then drew a straight line at a forty-five-degree angle bisecting the graph. "Each point on that line," he said definitively, "represents a given reaction speed at a given temperature. The line itself, the angle at which it climbs, represents the rate of change of the speed of the reaction relative to the rate of change of the temperature." He then drew a parabola alongside the straight line and sketched in several more straight lines, each one touching the parabola at a different point. "Each of these lines represents the rate of change at that one single point on the curve. Another graph like this would represent the rate of change relative to the concentration of the ingredients.

There ought to be a way of combining the two graphs and expressing them in symbols. That would allow you to predict what would happen across a whole range of temperatures and concentrations."

"There is," Mulligan said. "It's called calculus."

Irene didn't seem surprised. "Why shouldn't he invent calculus?" she asked, smiling broadly in proud satisfaction. "Newton did. Descartes did. Leibnitz did. Yuri is almost certainly more intelligent than they were."

Once it became clear just what Yuri was able to accomplish, Mulligan understood why Medvedev had boasted in his journal that his was the greatest achievement in genetics since Mendel's—and also why Medvedev had hesitated, why he had shrunk from fully educating the children, why he had been afraid of them. Yuri was intimidating. Mulligan sensed instinctively the enormous distance separating himself from Yuri, much greater than, say, the distance in the other direction, the one separating him from the village idiot. "Do you know what he makes me feel like?" he told Irene. "Remember when you were a little kid, maybe five or six, and your parents did something that you couldn't understand at all, like a multiplication problem, or speaking a foreign language? It seemed so much beyond you, beyond your reach, almost divine. Yuri makes me feel like that. He sees things that you and I will never see, never even imagine."

"That's what you'd expect, isn't it?"

During the week they had to wait Mulligan chafed with impatience, anxious to get to the laboratory in Bethesda as soon as possible. The more he conjectured the more his doubts were dissolved by overwhelming waves of curiosity. The question before him was straightforward and simple, no longer *what* but *how*. How had the Russians done it? They had spliced new genes into a human embryo . . . of that there could no longer be any tenable doubt . . . but how? He turned the question over and over in his mind so often that it began to acquire a taunting, resonant echo and loomed before him like a blank, featureless wall, an enormous obstacle he could neither surmount nor circumvent. How had Medvedev done it? No matter how much he thought about it the question refused to yield to the sort of mental permutations that usually resulted in a rewarding insight. Would he be able to figure it out in time? He could see no choice but to proceed in the usual way, pushing laboriously from the known to the unknown, using methods he'd long ago mastered.

By the end of the week his torn cheek had healed well enough for the bandage to come off. He noted, somewhat ruefully, that he'd be left with a scar of the sort that Prussian officers of another age had worn with pride. The wounded arm still ached, though it was out of the sling. The pain kept him optimistic. If they tried so hard to kill me, he thought, that must mean that somebody, Medvedev himself probably, is confident that I can solve it.

He researched the vast library of the Institut de Biologie Moderne. Could any clues be found in Medvedev's published papers? There were none. Strangely, or perhaps not so strangely, Medvedev had suddenly stopped publishing research papers in 1977. Until then he'd been prolific. But he'd left no footprints in the scientific literature, no traces of the line of experiments that had culminated in the birth of the four mutant boys. His published work was concerned only with his experiments regarding the biochemistry of intelligence. Only in his reference to Mulligan's own papers was there recognition that he'd even heard of the possibility of genetic modification.

The library also contained a 1980 catalog of the members of the Academy of Science of the USSR. Mulligan looked up Yevgeny Medvedev, somewhat embarrassed by the growing sense of rivalry and antagonism he was beginning to feel for this colleague he'd never met. There was a small, blurred picture alongside a biographical sketch. Medvedev's face had the broad planes of a Slavic peasant with firm, thick features that conveyed an impression of truculent Russian pugnacity. He didn't seem to have a neck. Iron-gray hair, cut short and straight, made him look older than his forty years. The biographical sketch was brief: Medvedev had been born in Minsk in 1944 and received his training in biochemistry in Moscow, although he'd spent three years in Cambridge, England, on a fellowship in the late 1960s. A testimony to his brilliance was the fact that he'd been appointed to head the Institute of Advanced Biochemistry in Leningrad at the age of thirty-two.

Ridgely approached the problem from a different perspective entirely. "Suppose we sent a man to Leningrad?" he asked Mulligan one afternoon. "What would you want him to find out? What kind of information should he look for?"

The question took Mulligan by surprise. It hadn't occurred to him that there was more than one way to acquire the information. He'd thought only of discovering it for himself. Ridgely was thinking of stealing it. "I suppose I'd want him to snoop around the institute," he answered after some consideration, "to look for more of Medvedev's records. I still can't really believe that any research scientist would perform an experiment like that without leaving a written record of what he'd done."

"Forget that," Ridgely said without hesitation. "You couldn't get near the place now. Not after all that's happened. I was thinking more about talking to people who might have worked there."

"Talking to people?" Mulligan smiled to himself. This was something else that hadn't occurred to him, and he began to see the usefulness of spies. "One thing about that . . . no, two things. One, the first thing, is that we do know he needed a lot of support. No matter how much of a genius Medvedev is, he couldn't do this alone. There was the pediatrician, Mialek, for example. There were teachers. And squads of nurses. Any one of them might know something.

"The other thing to remember," Mulligan continued, "is that this experiment took place eight years ago. From what Yuri said there are no other mutant children, at least not at the Leningrad institute. There were only four of them. That means the experiment was a one-shot deal. The people who worked on it might not even work there any more."

Ridgely grinned broadly. An opening had been perceived.

The next day, the fifteenth of May, Ridgely came to the hospital with another man. "This is Mr. Krasny," he said, introducing him with a deliberate, evasive nonchalance. "He's going to go to Leningrad to find out some of the things we were talking about yesterday."

Mulligan studied Krasny as they shook hands. He had the kind of nondescript pan-European look that might be mistaken for any Causasian nationality. A man of medium height, with a mild, square face and brown hair beginning to thin and gray at the temples, he projected an air, not of preoccupation, but of vague disinterest and unconcern. One might easily assume he was rather slow witted, not worthy of a second glance. He was the sort of man who might blend magically into a crowd and vanish in an instant, whose description people might later have trouble giving the police.

"And just how will you do that, Mr. Krasny?" Mulligan asked pointedly. "I've always been told that the Soviet Union is closed up tighter than a drum."

Krasny laughed, a warm laugh of genuine pleasure, and Mulligan began to like him. "Not so tight," he said. He spoke English with a thick not-quite-French accent. "Every society has its flaws, its cracks in the armor. Sometimes the weakness is inherent in the strength, Dr. Mulligan."

"Wonderful comment, that." Mulligan smiled appreciatively. "Philosophically profound, no doubt, and delightfully obscure."

Krasny laughed again.

"He'd like to ask Yuri some questions," Ridgely interrupted.

"Of course."

Mulligan watched the interview. Krasny spoke to Yuri in evidently flawless Russian. "It's his native language,"

Ridgely whispered to him in answer to his look of inquiry. "His parents were White Russians who came to Paris in the 1920s. He's done a number of these missions for us . . . gets in and out of Russian quickly . . . the real secret of success . . . travels under a French passport."

"What did he mean, 'The flaw is inherent in the strength'? Or can't you say?"

"Only if you promise not to tell the KGB." Ridgely's broad red face reflected the pleasure he anticipated in putting one over on the Russians. "The plan is to try to find someone who worked at the institute eight years ago, some nurse or other staff person . . ."

"I thought you said you couldn't get near the place."

"You couldn't. Not now. But we're talking about eight years ago. Maybe eight years ago, before they realized quite what they had, security wasn't so tight. There are always leaks. Maybe Medvedev got drunk one night and told everyone what he was doing. You never know. What we want is someone who doesn't work there any more."

"And if you find that someone . . . ?"

"That's where the flaw is inherent in the strength. The great strength of Soviet society is its authoritarian character. Everyone does what he's told to do. Everyone is afraid of authority. Suppose you find a nurse who used to work there and convince her that you're a plainclothes KGB officer or a Party investigator looking into certain anti-Party activities that took place at the institute . . ."

"You wouldn't have much trouble getting them to tell you everything they knew," Mulligan completed the thought for him.

"Exactly. The flaw is inherent in the strength," Ridgely said, enjoying the irony. "We've used this ploy a lot. It almost always works."

The interview lasted half an hour. Yuri was suspicious at first, withdrawing into a grim silence when he heard Krasny speaking Russian, but he cooperated after Irene assured him that no one would send him back. Then he seemed to enjoy speaking the language again. Krasny asked lots of questions and made notes of the replies on a pad, names mostly.

Mulligan accompanied Ridgely and Krasny as they left the hospital. Before they parted Krasny turned to Mulligan one last time, and he didn't seem at all slow witted or unconcerned. "Let me make sure I've got this straight," he said. "That child is a mutant, a genetic experiment, and the idea is to find out how the mutation was done." He seemed to find it difficult to believe.

"You'll need to be more precise," Mulligan corrected. "You have to know just what to ask for. He was created by the introduction into his body, while he was still an embryo, though I can't tell you exactly when, of seven additional genes, genes that coded for one muscle and six neurotransmitter enzymes. What we need to find out is exactly how those genes were introduced into the embryo. Right now we haven't a clue."

"Well, we'll see what I can find," Krasny said. He shrugged fatalistically and made a dour face. The gesture conveyed an impression that he hadn't much hope for the success of the mission. "I've got some names here to work with. Maybe we'll get lucky. Maybe some of these people haven't been told not to say anything. We'll know in a few days."

The morning of the twentieth, the day before they were to leave for the United States, Irene and Mulligan arrived at the hospital to find a small crowd of nurses and security guards outside Yuri's room. Dr. Lussac paced the hall nervously. "It's Yuri," he said, rubbing his hands together, clearly not knowing what to do. "He's gone mad."

"We can't let him hurt himself!" Irene gasped in alarm and clutched Mulligan's arm. "We can't, George!"

Mulligan slowly opened the door. He and Irene entered the room cautiously. It was a shambles, looking like the debris left from a cyclone or an explosion. The bed was overturned in the corner, its metal frame twisted and bent, the mattress torn. The dresser had been picked up and hurled against the wall with such force that it had broken into chunks and splinters of shattered wood. Some object had struck the wall hard enough to gouge out a fist-sized hole of plaster.

Yuri huddled in a corner looking small and frightened, clutching his arms to his chest, bobbing up and down in a slow wave-like motion. He was chanting *"Nyet, nyet,"* rhythmically synchronous with some inaudible music. His eyes were glazed and distant. Suddenly he jumped up and began shouting in Russian, flinging his arms wildly in the air as though warding off a cloud of invisible mosquitoes.

He seemed quite insane.

"Yuri!" Irene rushed forward but stopped halfway across the room, halted by the frightening lack of recognition in his eyes. When he heard his name Yuri looked up and stared at Irene blankly for a moment, his face a livid mask dominated by black circles under his eyes. His mouth hung half open and a weird moaning sound replaced the rhythmic chant. Then he began to slap his forehead with his left palm, like an autistic child striking himself repeatedly. The blow made a noise like a flat piece of wood striking water.

Mulligan stepped across the room and grasped Yuri's wrist in mid-blow. "Stop it," he commanded. He had forgotten how strong the boy was, and the next moment found himself sitting on the floor against the far wall rubbing the sore spot on his chest where Yuri had pushed him.

"Yuri," Irene called again. Her voice was high and clear, the tone of a mother raising her voice in firm but loving reprimand. "Yuri. Stop that."

Yuri stopped hitting himself and stared at her for what seemed a very long time. The moaning ceased. His breathing slowed. Anguish and madness left him slowly, like a fire sinking to embers that might at any moment flare up again. He raised a hand to her timorously, shaking uncontrollably, recognizing now the psychosis that had possessed him. Then he sat again on the chair and bent forward, clutching his thin arms around his chest once more, sobbing.

Irene crossed the room and knelt by the chair, folding her arms around him like protective wings, talking to him softly and quietly. "It's all right, Yuri," she said. "It will be all right."

He was little more than a whimpering child, alone, now agonizingly aware of the decay that was beginning to obscure the clarity of his mind and terrified, too, that some part of him had sought the alluring but insufficient refuge of madness.

"Tomorrow," she comforted. "Tomorrow we'll go to America and you'll find the inhibitor. We'll stop the disease. You'll see. It will be all right."

Mulligan hadn't the heart to contradict her.

CHAPTER THIRTEEN

They flew to Washington the next day. Mulligan, reminded of their vulnerability by the frequent stabs of pain he still felt in his left arm, asked Ridgely how they'd shake off the KGB.

"Easy," Ridgely said. They were on the highway to DeGaulle Airport. Ridgely instinctively turned around, craning his neck to survey the escort car behind them. "We just disappear into the U.S." He smiled grimly. "It's a big country, you know. Lots of places to hide. How can they know where we want to go?"

They did it by flying from Paris to New York on a commercial airline, then going directly to a private plane waiting for them on the runway at Kennedy. "No way for them to follow us now," Ridgely said. "We could be anywhere."

During the long flight Irene sat next to Yuri, soothing and reassuring him. Leaving the security of the hospital in Paris had made him intensely anxious. He feared notice and

212

recapture and struggled awkwardly to appear inconspicuous. There were moments when he had again a wild, frantic look. Mulligan sensed that only a wafer-thin barrier separated him from psychosis, that only Irene's presence tied him to reality.

Yuri had been clothed in American-style boy's clothing. He wore sneakers and blue jeans, a T-shirt that said "Chicago" on it and a baseball cap. The bill on the cap, pulled low over his forehead, hid his baldness and oversized forehead and partially concealed his face, so that if you didn't look too closely he could pass for a slightly strange-looking six-year-old boy. It was just as well, Mulligan thought, that he had no sense of embarrassment. With Mulligan and Ridgely, Yuri was always critical, suspiciously asking lots of questions, but with Irene he lapsed easily into the comforting dependence of a child.

The day was bright and humid when they finally disembarked and walked across the hot runway cement to a waiting automobile. Their route to Bethesda skirted the city. Yuri dozed most of the way, curled up next to Irene. At times he twitched fitfully, jerking upward with a sharp cry, his eyes darting frantically about until Irene could console and quiet him. Mulligan wondered what the content of the dreams was that frightened him so. Once he thought he heard Yuri whisper the name "Medvedev" and noticed the boy's lips curl back in a snarl.

Bethesda is a not-too-distant suburb of the capital, similar in most respects to a hundred other such American suburbs, green and pleasant at this time of year. The apartment building Ridgely took them to was a four-story structure, square and brick-faced in imitation colonial style, set back from the street by a hedge and broad lawn. It wasn't far from the campus-like collection of laboratory and hospital facilities that constituted the National Institutes of Health.

Ridgely had evidently assumed that they would all stay together, Yuri and Irene and Mulligan, presuming that the circumstances that bound them together would compel them to live in the same quarters. It was a large apartment, new and clean, furnished in pseudo-Danish modern furniture, which, although comfortable and functional, renders tasteless and unoriginal so many American hotel rooms. Two couches faced each other across a small coffee table. A small balcony off the living room overlooked Bethesda, and over the treetops the taller buildings of the NIH could just be perceived. There were three large bedrooms, two bathrooms and a kitchen. "You won't have to do any cooking, cleaning or shopping," Ridgely said, looking at Mulligan meaningfully. "A maid will come every day to take care of all that. You'll have a car and driver at your disposal. The only thing you have to do is to work in the laboratory." In other words, don't waste any time, and don't fail.

"Such solicitude," Mulligan murmured, patting Ridgely on his large shoulder. "Such pampering. I hope I don't get too used to it."

There was a knock on the door. Ridgely opened it and nodded in recognition when he saw that it was General Alexander. "I sort of thought you'd want to see him for yourself," he said. "Come in, General."

General Alexander walked into the room slowly, with an air of circumspection, silently indicating rank by leaving to Ridgely the task of closing the door. He was dressed in uniform, and, like all uniforms, it made him look larger and more important than he had seemed in civilian clothes. The three stars on his collar seemed to add three inches to his height. Mulligan looked at him warily, once more consciously warding off intimidation.

Alexander removed his cap, and, holding it in his hands, sat on the edge of the couch opposite the one on which Yuri and Irene were sitting. His gaze was sharp and trenchant. He looked at Yuri in the critical, disbelieving way one looks at some rare and ugly animal in a zoo, making mental notes. "Well, Yuri," he said, "it's nice to meet you at last. I'm happy you're finally well enough to join us here. Welcome to Washington." The words were friendly but his tone was coldly formal, and he didn't hold out his hand to shake Yuri's. Yuri squiggled closer to Irene on the couch, retreating further under her sheltering arm. His large, protruding eyes gave him the appearance of a baby owl staring out from under its mother's wing.

"I've heard a great deal about you," Alexander continued, ostensibly addressing his remarks to Yuri but including Irene and Mulligan in his audience. Ridgely stood behind him at the door, quietly attentive. "Rather an extraordinary story, being one of four brothers raised in the institute. Do you mind if I ask you a few more questions about it?"

"He's already said everything he knows," Irene said, glaring at Alexander with obvious hostility. She reached her arm further around Yuri. "We're very tired. Couldn't we do this some other time?"

"Just for a minute or two," Alexander said, ignoring her. "Just one or two questions. Tell me, Yuri, again please, what was the name of the Soviet general who came to see you so often?"

"Kermonov." Yuri spoke reluctantly, as though the name were being dragged from him like a confession to a petty crime. "Vladimir Kermonov." Yuri pronounced the names in the Russian manner.

Alexander nodded to himself. "My counterpart in the Soviet army," he murmured to no one in particular. "Fortunately for us, not a very insightful man." Then he leaned forward and stared at Yuri, his eyes glistening intensely. "Is it true? You actually ran from Leningrad to Paris in nine weeks?" His voice resonated with incredulity and suspicious accusation.

"My brother did it in five weeks," Yuri said proudly. He still spoke English with a heavy Russian accent, but his grammar was perfect. "I was delayed for four weeks by my broken ankle."

Alexander smiled to himself, apparently satisfied now that some private doubt had been answered. "May we try something else? A little game of catch." A thoughtful CIA agent had put a bowl of fruit on the coffee table, and Alexander took an orange from it. He tossed the orange gently into the air as he stood up, testing its size and weight. "Catch this when I throw it to you, please."

Now it was Yuri's turn to smile, a smile that mixed sardonic humor and a bitter scorn. If the general wanted to play a stupid game, Yuri would indulge him. "Your friend General Kermonov liked to play catch, too." He moved away from Irene a little but did not stand.

"Not my friend," Alexander corrected curtly. "Catch." He threw the orange at Yuri, not the gentle toss you would expect from someone standing only three feet from you, but hard, with a quick snap of his wrist and elbow, like a second baseman making a fast flip of the ball to first. It was much too fast to catch, and the speed of his movement made Irene gasp. Mulligan sat forward with a start.

Yuri caught it. He caught it easily, not even appearing hurried. Mulligan thought he had seen the whole thing in slow motion and blinked unbelievingly. It was almost as though Yuri had the ability to project a slowness on things, that his own speed made everything else slow down. Yuri laughed. It was a sound of thorny self-mockery and came from between lips drawn back to reveal yellowing and displaced teeth. It was the first time Mulligan had heard such a laugh from Yuri, and it sent a shiver of apprehension down his back.

Even Alexander was amazed; he stared at Yuri for a long time, expressionless, and then a wide grin spread over his face. "Extraordinary," he whispered. "Extraordinary. I'll tell you what, Yuri," he said, now less cold and formal, "put the orange down and let's shake hands."

Yuri smiled again but said nothing and did as he was asked. This time he stood and faced Alexander. The disparity in size made him appear puny, a small, starved child. His light-boned arms stuck out of his T-shirt like thin sticks. His hand was small, so small that he had difficulty getting a grip all around the general's palm, and brown age spots

216

marred the finely wrinkled skin. Ridges of veins crossed the tendons that stood out as his fingers curled.

"Give me as strong a grip as you can," Alexander instructed.

Yuri's hand tightened. He didn't contort his face with effort, but the muscles of his forearm contracted, defining themselves as ropy linear bands. His skin, as well as Alexander's, blanched where the force was applied. Alexander looked startled for a moment; then his brow furrowed in concentrated effort as he squeezed back to defend himself. He bent slightly forward to add his weight to it, and sweat appeared on his forehead. "Enough!" he shouted.

Yuri jumped back. "You said to grip as hard as I could," he said, frightened and apologetic.

Alexander rubbed his right hand with his left and shook it out at the wrist. "Maybe you shouldn't do everything I ask," he said ruefully. "You're a lot stronger than you look."

"I'm getting stronger all the time," Yuri stated matter-of-factly, as though he'd long since grown accustomed to bizarre developments from his body. He bared his teeth and barked a laugh again in the same harsh tone of self-mockery. "My biggest problem is that I'm dying. The experiment failed, remember?"

"Yuri!" Irene spoke sharply, with stern disapproval. "You mustn't say that! Don't ever give up hope." She stood up and faced Alexander. "Are you quite finished, General?" she challenged, her cheeks flushed with defiance. "We'd like to unpack and eat. Then we need to rest. Tomorrow the real work starts."

Alexander had seen all he needed to see and was smoothly indulgent. "No objections here. Until tomorrow, then." He turned to Mulligan. "Would you accompany me to my car, please?"

It was not a question. Mulligan had to suppress his initial impulse to refuse. Ridgely accompanied them to the elevator. Mulligan kept silent until they were inside it.

"Impressed?" he then asked, knowing what Alexander's response must be. "Why didn't you ask him to memorize Hamlet by tomorrow morning? Then you'd really see what he can do."

Alexander was slowly shaking his head side to side in the manner of someone who can't believe what he has just seen and is going over his memory of it to make sure he hasn't been deceived. "This is just the beginning . . ." he said to Mulligan, his voice barely above a whisper. His eyes blazed with excited anticipation, and his right hand curled into a fist that thudded softly into his left. "Just the beginning. You've seen what that kid can do," he said gruffly as the elevator door opened on the ground floor. "I can't stress enough how important this is."

They walked out of the apartment building together. General Alexander radiated the grimness of a soldier already at war, as though he could hear the enemy armies gathering beyond the next ridge, could smell already the smoke and blood of battle. The general's driver snapped to attention and saluted. They forced on Mulligan the thought that he was working now in a moral atmosphere far removed from his own. There would be no ambivalence or hesitation, no attempt at considered judgment. Alexander wanted an improved man to combat the Soviets and wouldn't settle for less. Intense, single-minded, he'd drive straight to his objective, brushing aside or crushing any opposition.

The general lifted his eyes, squinting into the sun under the visor of his cap, and pointed to the apartment where Yuri and Irene were unpacking. "What about them?"

"What do you mean?"

"What will they do?"

"Work on the CPK inhibitor. Irene thinks Yuri can develop one in just a few days. To block the enzyme, slow it down, maybe slow the aging process. We'll see. It'll be a good test of how smart he really is. It would normally take at least six months to produce such a compound."

"Suppose he can. Will it slow down the aging?" Alexander asked.

Mulligan shook his head disconsolately, his optimism seared by the remorseless reality of Yuri's condition. Unconsciously he rubbed a finger over the scar on his cheek. "I don't think so. Even if she and Yuri manage to inhibit the enzyme, I can't see how that would make any real difference. It's too late. There's too much tissue damage already. How old is he, really? Seventy? Eighty? You can see for yourself what Yuri looks like. He's dying. It's obvious. I know it. Yuri knows it. Irene knows it, too, though she doesn't want to admit it right now."

"How much longer would you give him?"

"Doctors who make predictions end up looking like idiots," Mulligan said sourly. "I presume you wouldn't want me to look like an idiot." He paused and scraped his foot on the sidewalk, then looked sideways at Alexander. "Not long, though."

"The lab's ready and waiting. Everything you said you needed." Alexander withdrew slightly from the intensity of Mulligan's gaze, and for the first time a note of doubt crept into his voice. "I don't know," he said slowly. "I don't know if we're going to win this one or not." He stood up straight and looked at Mulligan expectantly, as though hoping for an affirmative contradiction. "Well, at least you have a plan."

"I *always* have experiments in mind, General," Mulligan rejoined. "That's what I do for a living, remember? It's only a question of having enough money and time."

"Money's no problem." Alexander waved his hand in the kind of vague gesture of dismissal that only those with access to vast funds enjoy. "Time I can't buy for you, though—don't waste any."

Mulligan shrugged and realized suddenly that he'd acquired a touch of the European fatalism he'd detected in Irene and Krasny. "It takes the time it takes," he said.

Yuri retired immediately to bed after dinner. Mulligan looked inquiringly at Irene. "How many bedrooms do we use?" he asked. "One or two? No guards in the hall here."

She looked at him for a long time before replying. Indecision held her face softly motionless, but the small muscles around her mouth subtly altered its expression as conflicting emotions passed through her. "One," she said at last, smiling, stepping close to Mulligan and wrapping her arms around his neck. "Just one bedroom."

But he sensed again the reserve, the nubbin of distrust, diminishing her passion when they made love. Afterward, she lay quietly with her head leaning against his shoulder. Mulligan broke the long silence of her unease. "You're thinking about Yuri again, aren't you?" he accused gently.

"Yes," she answered without lifting her head, without looking at him. "I'm frightened, George. I feel that something awful is going to happen—something even more awful than his death."

Mulligan's impulse was to comfort her, to offer any hope, even a false one. "There's always the chance, you know, that if we can find out how the Russians did it we'll have some better clues about how to undo it as well."

She raised herself on one elbow to look at him. "Do you really think so?"

He couldn't bring himself to lie utterly. "A chance of it, anyway. Besides, it's the only thing I can do to help him, isn't it?"

She fell asleep with her head on his shoulder, and he lay awake for a long time, staring into the darkness, feeling the warmth of her exhaled breath on his chest, hoping that she was wrong, that nothing more terrible than death could happen.

Yuri nearly succumbed to psychosis again the next morning when Mulligan took him to the blood bank at the National Cancer Institute to use their cell separator to harvest white cells. Yuri took one look at the large, swishing machine and drew away from Mulligan, hostile suspicion corroding the trust in his face.

"It's the only way, Yuri," Mulligan explained. "White cells are already separated from each other. They have chromosomes and the plasmid. Normally we'd just take a small sample of blood and grow all the white cells we need in a tissue culture. But we can't do that with you. You know that. Your cells die in culture. So the only way I can get enough material to work with is to harvest the white cells from your blood—and hope I'll have enough."

Yuri hovered between cooperation and rebellion, slinking into a defensive crouch, and a spasmodic twitch began to jerk at his head and shoulders, as though he was either anticipating violent action or resisting the impulse to it. "Will it hurt?"

"Just the needle-sticks."

"We need to, Yuri," Irene implored, the more persuasive for speaking reluctantly, glancing again at Mulligan with her piercing look of reproach. She knelt on one knee to bring her head level with Yuri's and looked into his aged, distorted face with more affection then Mulligan would have believed possible. "We have to find out how Medvedev did it."

The procedure didn't take long. Yuri lay on a chaise lounge with his arms outstretched on boards. Irene sat beside him and held his hand. The technician, a trim, young black woman, glanced at Irene and Mulligan with a look of pity and sympathy, silently commiserating with the lovely young people who had had such an awful child. Then she deftly inserted eighteen-gauge needles into the antecubital vein in each arm. Yuri's blood passed through plastic tubing in a slow, continuous stream from one vein, into the cell separator, where centrifugation separated the cells by weight, then back minus the white cells into the other arm. In two hours Mulligan had secured the white cells from about four units of blood.

When they finally arrived at the NIH Mulligan saw immediately that Alexander had kept his promise. They'd have everything they could possibly need. The laboratory was a large room, perhaps thirty by fifty feet, divided agreeably into four circular work islands instead of linear benches. The wall facing the door was half window, making the room bright and cheerful with sunlight. The equipment was comprehensive and new. The glassware and instruments sparkled their crystalline, pristine indifference to the purposes to which they were put. Each work island had its own constant-temperature bath for controlling enzymatic reactions, electrode panels for agarose-gel electrophoresis, spectrophotometer, and variable-speed centrifuge. Ehrlenmeyer flasks, test tubes and beakers, as well as a complete array of standard chemical reagents were stored in a glass-panelled wall cabinet. Several computers sat quietly in the corners.

"No wonder you Americans win all the Nobel prizes," Irene complained. "You have all the equipment. It's not fair."

"The equipment has nothing to do with it," Mulligan growled. "We win the prize because we know that if we find something really good we can get stinky rich."

Irene laughed, but Yuri remained dour and sullen. He prowled the laboratory, familiarizing himself with the equipment, anxious to get started. His education in biochemistry had progressed to a point at which he was able to mentally imagine protein enzymes, molecules consisting of long chains of amino acids folded and twisted on themselves like coiled snakes. Sections of the chains were cross linked by disulfide bonds, creating enormously complex three-dimensional structures that existed solely to create the active site of the molecule, the part of it that served as a catalyst to speed other chemical reactions. CPK, creatine phosphokinase, was such an enzyme; its purpose was to attach high-energy phosphate radicals to creatine. Creatine phosphate was the ultimate energy source for muscle cells. Without it, quite literally, nothing moved.

What Irene and Yuri needed to do was to design a molecule that would stick to and inactivate the active site of the enzyme. Proper use of a biochemistry laboratory required a manual dexterity that came only with long practice, no matter how smart you were. Yuri had no time for that. He and

Irene had worked out in advance the method they would use. Yuri would think of the experiments, visually imagine the transformations of the molecules and outline the sequence of steps to be taken, while Irene performed the actual manipulations. She didn't seem to mind the demotion in rank to technician.

They set to work immediately. Mulligan paid little attentin to Yuri and Irene. His own next step was to extract the DNA from the white cells. He'd barely have enough. The white cells would have to be disrupted gently, smoothly, without fragmenting any of the cell's internal structures or breaking the chromosomes. Mulligan accomplished this by pouring the cell suspension into a large beaker of distilled water. The water, hugely hypotonic relative to the interior of a cell, was drawn inside by osmosis, stretching the membrane past its breaking point. The cell's contents spilled into an aqueous solution when the membrane ruptured.

Now everything was merely dissolved in water, and certain chemical properties of DNA could be used to advantage. Mulligan worked slowly and carefully, obedient to the demanding rituals of chemistry, aware that this might be the only specimen he could get. Precise and measured, step by practiced step, he used an ethanol extraction procedure to separate the DNA from the rest of the cell's contents.

It was a time-consuming and demanding process. He worked all afternoon and all night, oblivious to time and hunger and fatigue, driven by the excitement of coming ever closer to his goal. By early the next morning he'd finished. Irene and Yuri had fallen asleep hours before and sat on their stools with their heads down on the benchtop, folded arms serving as pillows. Mulligan stood and stretched, feeling an ache in his back. He hadn't spent the entire night in a laboratory for many years. Morning sunlight was streaming through the broad window and Mulligan held his beaker to the light.

The result of the night's labor was a solution of pure human DNA, Yuri's DNA, the DNA Medvedev had somehow changed. In ethanol solution it created a yellowish translucent haze, glittering slightly from reflected light when he shook the beaker, the way lake water glitters when the muddy bottom is stirred. Deoxyribonucleic acid . . . familiarity with it never lessened his sense of wonder. This was the miracle, the self-replicating molecule, the very stuff of life. Its intricate chemical cryptography contained all the information necessary to form another human being.

If anything in life were sacred, he thought, this was it. A sense of veneration rose like a wave within him. Genetic material spanned time, approached eternity, bound past and present and future in an enormous evolutionary chain linking ancestry to posterity. To change it seemed sacrilege, an invitation to divine wrath. Yet that was what Medvedev had done. Mulligan smiled at himself and his thoughts, aware that such ideas were superstitious, antithetical to the cool rationality of twentieth-century science, and he didn't believe them for a minute. Still, his equanimity was unsettled as he looked at the glittering beaker in his hand.

He poured the solution into a flask and corked it tightly. The next step, separating the plasmid from the chromosomal DNA, would have to wait for another time. He was too tired to proceed.

He woke Irene and Yuri. "Good morning." Irene smiled sleepily when he shook her shoulder. "Don't look at me. I'm sure I look a mess."

Her smile lifted him momentarily into an odd, incongruous optimism. "You look fine to me," he said, kissing her on the cheek. "Come on. Let's get some real sleep."

Yuri had exhausted himself again and dozed in the car on the way back to the apartment. Mulligan asked Irene how much progress they'd made.

"Astonishing," she murmured quietly so as not to wake Yuri, but indicating him with a nod. "Amazing. He never guesses at anything, never estimates. He knows. He knows just what's going to happen when the chemicals are mixed, just how much product we'll have, exactly what its molecular structure will be. At this rate we'll have the inhibitor in a few more days." She stroked Yuri's head in satisfaction, feline and sleepy. "I told you he could do it."

Mulligan gazed contemplatively at Yuri. He was leaning against Irene in the back seat. The network of tiny pink capillaries spreading out from his nose seemed like threads running through a thin, paper currency. He was shrunken in sleep, a tiny misshapen old man, a child blighted from birth by the flawed manipulation. Mulligan still found the boy's genius hard to believe. What a tragedy, he thought. What a farce.

He was awakened at noon by a telephone call from Ridgely. "Sorry to wake you," Ridgely apologized, perfunctory and insincere, "but I've got important news."

"Oh?" Mulligan shook his head to clear it. He guessed what had prompted Ridgely's call. "Something from our man in Leningrad?"

"Right. Krasny got back already, faster than I thought he would. He telephoned this morning from Paris."

"Let's hear it. Anything useful?"

"I'm not sure. I'm not sure how much this will help you. Security there was very tight, as we thought it would be. He was able to find only one informant, an obstetrical nurse who worked at the institute eight years ago, when the experiment was just getting started. Apparently there was a great flurry of activity at that time, some sort of scandal." Ridgely paused and Mulligan heard the click of his cigarette lighter and a cough. "Medvedev nearly lost his job, she said. Unauthorized experiments, she thought, though she was never really sure. There was a great deal of speculation and gossip, but then anyone who knew anything about it was either fired or transferred away from the institute. Four women, four young girls really, had babies there within three weeks of each other. Four of them. All boys. But the most significant thing was that the women had all been made pregnant by in vitro methods."

"In vitro methods?" Mulligan asked emptily, momentarily puzzled, then almost laughed aloud as the obviousness of it became clear to him. Of course. It would be infinitely easier to modify an embryo if it were outside the mother's body. Mulligan made annoyed little clicking sounds with his tongue against his teeth as he realized the boldness of Medvedev's experiment. Medvedev was a double genius. Not only had he isolated the genes he wanted before anyone else in the world could do it, he'd also performed one of the very first in vitro fertilizations. Somehow, the marriage of those techniques had produced the four boys.

But that still didn't explain exactly how it had been done.

Mulligan's admiration was broken by a vision of Medvedev approaching the girls, the broad flat face perhaps earnest and sincere, perhaps just touched with a leer. "How would you like to have a baby, my dear, a very special and unusual baby . . . extraordinary in so many ways . . . like no baby ever seen before?"

CHAPTER FOURTEEN

Mulligan met with General Alexander at the general's office later that afternoon. The tedious passage through the Pentagon's security precautions left him with that peculiar nettlesome outrage that having one's loyalty repeatedly questioned can engender. Alexander was disgruntled, too, when he heard what Mulligan wanted. "I don't like it," he snapped, balking at the idea of including anyone else in the project. "The more people that know about this, the more chances there are for security leaks."

"What security leaks?" Mulligan asked, thinking Alexander fatuous. "We're trying to discover something the Russians already know, remember? How can there be security leaks?"

"I don't mean leaks to *their* side," Alexander said, glaring at Mulligan. It was easy to imagine him stomping around a field headquarters tent with a huge cigar sticking out of his mouth, terrifying subordinates. His square jaw jutted forward. "I mean leaks to *our* side. To the public. What if it gets out? You think the public is ready for this sort of thing?"

"Oh, sure they are," Mulligan replied airily, the muscles of his mouth drawing back in the slim exiguous smile of patronizing contempt. He enjoyed the chance to vent his irritation at the general's expense. "We all love science fiction, don't we? Everyone knows about mutants."

"Very funny," Alexander grunted, sitting back heavily in his chair. "Don't be so damned cute." He swivelled the chair and stared out the window for what seemed a long time, gloomily considering Mulligan's proposal.

With some satisfaction Mulligan imagined him struggling to control a long-suffering exasperation at having to deal with a lot of wise-ass civilian scientists who not only didn't understand but positively rejected the proper military view of things. The spartan simplicity of the general's office reinforced his impression that Alexander's was an unwavering determination. He couldn't fail to notice the wall map behind the desk, the one depicting the Soviet Union as an enormous, engulfing red menace. That's how he sees the world, Mulligan thought, as a diametric antagonism, a fight to the death between us and them. In such a scheme ethics would likely prove unresistant to the corrosion of hatred.

"Weapons research is tricky stuff," Alexander said finally, swivelling back to face Mulligan again. "There are things the public has trouble getting used to, and the press is, well, the press . . . uncontrollable, unscrupulous."

Mulligan refused to back down. "We're talking about *people*," he reminded the general, "not weapons."

"No, we're not," Alexander barked. He jabbed a thick forefinger at Mulligan and punched out his words. "We're talking about weapons, weapons and people, people as weapons. And you damned well know it. We've already had that discussion."

Mulligan shrugged. This wasn't the right time to argue the point. "Have it your way, then—for the moment, anyway. That's not the most important thing right now. The fact is that I need to consult an obstetrician. Whatever he did, Medvedev's method involved an in vitro fertilization. Understanding it requires more obstetrics than I've ever learned. So it's either consulting an obstetrician or wasting a month while I go to the library and learn it on my own."

Alexander took a deep breath and sighed, an incongruous gesture of resignation. "All right, all right. Tell me again what you want. A crash course in in vitro fertilization?"

"More or less." Mulligan had thought carefully about the information Ridgely had given him and knew exactly what he needed. "I need to see what's done, how it's done, if it's possible to introduce new genes at any stage of the procedure, and if so, how you'd go about it. Look," said Mulligan, "I'm really close now, really close. I've got the DNA from Yuri's white cells that I needed . . . "

"Oh?" Alexander interrupted, lifting his eyebrows. "So it doesn't matter anymore if Yuri dies?"

"Yes and no," he answered slowly, chewing thoughtfully on his lower lip and regarding Alexander through narrowing eyes. "If I can learn what I need from this batch of material, well, yes, you're right, it wouldn't matter. But if I can't, I'll need more."

"Let's hope you won't, then." Alexander had already written Yuri off.

Mulligan's mood darkened as he felt his dislike for Alexander increase. "As I was saying," he continued, "I'm really close now. But I don't know any obstetrics. I don't know any more about in vitro fertilization than anyone else who reads Time magazine does. Somehow, as part of an in vitro fertilization, Medvedev managed to introduce seven new genes into an embryo. But how? What was the technique? That's the one question remaining. Isolating the genes from human DNA and splicing them together into one chain is something I can do myself. That's just biochemistry. It's done in test tubes and flasks and on electrophoretic panels.

229

But everything changes when you start to work with living things. How do you get extra genes inside an embryo without killing the embryo?"

"And seeing the procedure and talking to an obstetrician will give you some ideas?"

Mulligan sat back and folded his arms across his chest, resting his case. "I can't be certain of it, but that's what I hope."

Alexander leaned forward on one elbow and rested his chin in his hand. A dreamy speculation replaced his vehement look. "And we already know what went wrong, don't we?"

"Still thinking of going them one better, aren't you?" Mulligan asked, "making a more perfect mutant?"

"Yes, exactly," he said, his opinion cast in iron and unassailable. "I've tried to tell you how important this is. They're doing this, so we have to do it, too. Only we have to do it better."

For what seemed several minutes the two men stared at each other. Mulligan said nothing. Should I quit now, he asked himself, before I get in any deeper? *Can* I quit now? Even if Alexander just let him walk away, refusal to do anything further would mean that he would never know the answer, never know how Medvedev had done it. I've got to see this through, he thought, and hope that in the end I'll be forgiven. Maybe what I find will keep Yuri alive, after all.

The sense of confrontation faded when Alexander broke the silence. "I'll have to call around," he said, "to find out where the nearest place is. There's probably an infertility clinic somewhere in D.C. Or maybe somebody a little farther away, Richmond perhaps, or Baltimore. You won't say anything about Yuri, of course, will you?"

"I'll say as little as possible," Mulligan replied sourly, annoyed at being treated like a little boy who has to promise his mother he won't stray out of the yard if she leaves him alone to play. "But at some point I'm going to have to ask if it's possible to make genetic alterations."

"Then I'll have to find someone who knows how to keep his mouth shut," Alexander muttered to himself. He looked at his watch. "It's three-thirty now. Too late to do anything else today except maybe set something up for tomorrow. I'll get back to you later."

Mulligan returned to the laboratory in Bethesda. It was five o'clock by the time he got there. He felt worn and drained, depleted, not with the clean muscle fatigue of exertion, but with the soiled enervation of prolonged tension and uncertainty. He distrusted the cunning Ridgely, and he didn't like Alexander, not a bit. And he found, too, that he was beginning to dislike himself. Maybe only a few more days, he told himself, and we'll be done with it.

Yuri and Irene had spent the afternoon immersed in their search for the enzyme inhibitor and didn't notice Mulligan when he entered the laboratory. Brent Ridgely sat in a corner, a quiet onlooker perched on a lab stool in the posture of Rodin's Thinker. Mulligan sat on a stool near him and they watched quietly. Speed and precision are difficult goals to accomplish simultaneously in biochemistry, and Yuri and Irene were completely engrossed in the work.

They made a bizarre team. Yuri issued instructions and Irene carried them out, as though she'd been enslaved by a specimen of an alien conquering race. Her face was taut and shiny with concentration. She performed the manipulations with deft, long-fingered hands, and her only concession to femininity was the way she absentlymindedly brushed back her hair when it fell across her face. Yuri sat to the left and slightly behind her, a small gnome-like figure looking as though transported from the dark pages of medieval necromancy. His eyes were dreamily half closed and his head tilted to one side as he sat leaning back on a stool with his hands clasped around one upraised knee. He gave directions in a voice thinned and dried by senescence. "Heat the solution to exactly forty-two degrees for ten minutes," he'd say. "Then cool it so the crystals precipitate, then decant the supernatant, and redissolve the crystals in ether, then add the decarboxylase . . ." The instructions were precise and detailed, leaving no room for the slightest deviation.

Mulligan's fascination verged on reverence as he watched the display of genius. He found that he could follow what Yuri was doing, but each new step was one he hadn't been able to anticipate.

Irene evidently had moments of puzzlement, too. "Why are you doing that?" she asked Yuri at one point, speaking for the first time in the half hour that had passed since Mulligan entered the laboratory. "Isn't that going to make the compound too highly polar."

"No, it isn't," Yuri answered impatiently, irritated at having his thoughts interrupted. "It has to be polar to pass through the skin."

"Why pass through the skin?"

"That's how I'm going to give it."

Irene looked at him with a quizzical expression and started to ask something else, but then she shook her head and said nothing.

Ridgely leaned toward Mulligan and nudged him with a thick elbow. "What's that for?" he whispered. "What's he want it to pass through skin for?"

Mulligan knit his eyebrows and shook his head slowly, curious about it himself. Why would Yuri choose this particular route of administration? "I don't know," he said, looking past Ridgely to Yuri. "It didn't even occur to me the molecule could be small enough to be absorbed through the skin. Maybe something to do with the dosage, or how long the drug effect will last." He turned to Ridgely. "It's hard to tell what he's thinking, you know. He really *is* a lot smarter than we are."

Irene heard Mulligan's voice and looked around. She waved in greeting and smiled. "Hello, George. We're making fabulous progress here. We may even have it done by tomorrow." She seemed excited and satisfied, her optimism, however illusory, restored.

232

"Wonderful," he called back. "Nothing like having a genius on your side. What do you think, Yuri?"

Yuri pivoted slowly, and for a moment it seemed as though he hadn't heard the question. His eyes clicked back and forth across the width of the room before finally coming to rest on Mulligan with an expression that was haughty and distant and with no recognition in it. Mulligan felt as though he were a curiosity being inspected through a magnifying glass. "The inhibitor has already been synthesized here," Yuri said slowly, tapping himself with a curled middle finger on his bumpy forehead. "It's only a matter of making it come out here." He tapped the test tube that Irene held in front of him.

Later in the evening, when the three of them had returned to their apartment, Mulligan debated briefly with himself whether or not to tell Yuri about the in vitro fertilization. What would be the effect of such information? Would it cast him further adrift on a sea of psychotic terror? In the end, though, he decided that Yuri would want and had a right to know. As they sat at the dinner table Mulligan described what had been done. An ovum had been taken from his mother's body, fertilized and altered somehow, then reimplanted in her womb for the nine months gestation.

Irene reacted first. "We might have thought of that," she said bitterly, shaking her head in self-criticism. "Of course it would be easier to modify an embryo outside the body." A curious mixture of sadness and revulsion came into her eyes. "It makes my skin crawl. It's perverted. It's like watching the rape of nature."

Yuri at first stared moodily straight ahead as Mulligan talked, absorbing the new revelation quietly. The sallow, yellow-gray skin of his cheeks sagged heavily, though his jaw was clenched. An expression of disgust, as though he had just noticed a nauseating odor, came over him. He pushed his chair back from the table and bent forward over the floor, wrapping his thin arms tightly around his chest.

For a moment Mulligan thought he was going to be sick; but then he began rocking slowly forward and back, a small autistic metronome. The solipsistic movement seemed an attempt to heal the rift that separated him from the rest of humanity, to comfort him, to fill the hollow place inside.

He had a nightmare that night. Mulligan and Irene rushed from their bedroom to find Yuri screaming, shaking, cowering in retreat before some image of desolation that had sprung unbidden to his mind. Irene gathered him in her arms and sang French lullabies, not knowing what else to do, while the child cried and clung to her. The tiny misshapen Russian superman, oscillating between genius and madness, dying of decay at age eight, was comforted like a baby by his adopted French mother. Mulligan, silently watching them, struggled in a haze of foreboding to overcome his sense of disbelief.

Later, Irene snuggled close to Mulligan in their own bed, not in passion, but to seek solace in the closeness of their bodies. "Hold me, George," she whispered. "Hold me, please." They lay in troubled sleep through the rest of the night, listening for more of Yuri's terrified cries, though none came.

General Alexander telephoned early the next morning. "You've got an appointment today," he informed Mulligan, "at the Lansdowne Clinic in Baltimore. Eleven o'clock. It's perfect. Lansdowne was an obstetrician in the army for six years before he resigned his commission to set up an infertility clinic. I talked to him a few minutes ago. He's okay. He won't ask you any questions and he won't tell anyone anything he learns from you."

A CIA chauffeur drove Mulligan to Baltimore. The Lansdowne Clinic was one of those clean, pleasantly low-key but rigorously efficient, for-profit medical establishments that dotted the suburban American landscape. Dr. Lansdowne himself was a balding man in his thirties, tall and thin, with a slow, patient manner nicely suited to his langorous southern accent. His brown eyes looked at Mulligan directly from behind thick rimless glasses. He said nothing about having spoken to General Alexander and asked no questions about Mulligan's motives.

"I'm new at this," Mulligan admitted frankly, after they'd introduced themselves. "I need to learn as much as I can about in vitro fertilizations as quickly as possible. Let me ask you something first: how long has this been a practical procedure?"

"Five or six years, I guess," Lansdowne replied, raising his eyebrows slightly at the question. "Baby Louise was the first, remember? In England? That was 1980 or so, I think."

"Could it have been done earlier? In 1976?"

"Possibly." Lansdowne took off his glasses and inspected a smudge on the lens, then wiped it clean with his handkerchief as he considered the question. "It was sort of an idea whose time had come." He put the glasses back on. "Lots of people were working on it. But if someone achieved it in 1976 he'd almost certainly have been the first in the world to do it. I suppose it could have been done. So far as I know, though, Steptoe in England was the first, and I'm sure that was later than 1976. Listen," he concluded, leading Mulligan to the dressing room for surgical staff, "you're in luck. We've got a case starting in a few minutes. Why don't you watch one first? Maybe that will answer some of your questions."

"This case is sort of typical," Lansdowne explained as they changed into the green pajamas that were de rigueur for surgical suites. "This woman's thirty-four, married six years, can't conceive. The reason turned out to be the most common one, scarred fallopian tubes, you know, from gonorrhea in her younger years, when she was single and," he coughed slightly, "somewhat less discreet. Sperm can't get up an obstructed fallopian tube, obviously, and the ovum can't get down, so the procedure we'll do today is a sort of detour, going outside the body to get around the blocked channel."

235

The operating room was a high-ceilinged brightly lit rectangle, its walls covered in washable white tile squares and with a floor of white vinyl. The atmosphere inside seemed to dissolve immediate reality with an odd, timeless sense of dislocation and incongruity. The scrub nurses, three of them, swished softly in their green gowns as they moved, their caps and masks cloaking individuality in a sterile anonymity. In the center of the room was the operating table. At its head stood the anesthesiologist with his bulky paraphernalia of gas bottles, respirator and IV tubing. The patient was already on her back on the table when they entered, drowsy and floppy from the preanesthetic sedative she'd been given. One arm was outstretched on a support to expose the veins into which the IV flowed. Most of her body was covered with heavy green sheets, except for her head, which was separated from view by a low screen across her neck, and her lower abdomen and groin, which the nurses, like busy acolytes at an altar of human sacrifice, were shaving and scrubbing with Betadine. Depending what side of the screen you stood on, she appeared either disembodied or decapitated.

Lansdowne approached the head of the table and leaned over her slightly, careful not to touch anything. "It's Dr. Lansdowne, Evelyn," he said, quietly, reassuringly, knowing he couldn't be recognized. "We'll be getting started momentarily, when you're asleep. Everything's fine. The procedure takes only a few minutes. Don't be afraid. It always goes smoothly, and you'll have practically no pain afterwards."

"Thank you, doctor," Evelyn whispered in the meek acceptance and trust that are the only possible emotions for those about to undergo surgery.

The anesthesiologist injected some Valium into the IV and Evelyn fell asleep almost immediately. Easily, infinitely practiced, looking almost bored, he then put the long-bladed laryngoscope, a metal spatula the size and shape of a tongue blade but with a light on the end and a handle to pull on, into her mouth upside down. Lifting the lower jaw and tongue upward and outward to expose the trachea, he inserted the endotracheal tube, sliding it through the vocal cords into the lungs. The dehumanization of the patient was completed by attaching the endotracheal tube to the respirator that administered the oxygen and gas mixture of general anesthesia. The surgeon could now proceed objectively.

The operation began. It would be an abdominal and pelvic laparoscopy. Lansdowne picked up the laparoscope and checked it. It was a small, flat-ended tube, slightly smaller in diameter than a garden hose and about two feet long. Inside the tube, other than a light source, were the fiberoptic bundles that permitted the surgeon both to look through the instrument and to bend it around corners. Should one wish to do so, the entire inside of the abdomen could be easily visualized. Lansdowne made a small midline incision about an inch long and three inches up from the pubic symphysis. "We already know from the ultrasound studies that it's the right ovary that's ovulating," he explained to Mulligan as he ligated a few small bleeding vessels, then cut deeper with blunt and sharp dissection until the peritoneum was pierced and the abdomen entered. He pushed his forefinger into the wound and swept it around in a slow circle, feeling for any adhesions or other scar tissue that might impede passage of the laparoscope.

He peered intently through the instrument as he inserted it into the abdomen, turning the knobs at his end to guide its passage deeper into the pelvis. "Ah," he said, "there it is. Take a look." He held his head away from the eyepiece and offered it to Mulligan. Mulligan peered through it. By turning the controls up and down or side to side he found he could see almost the entire contents of the right side of the pelvis.

Coils of small intestine, undulating rhythmically, dotted with blobs of fat, could be seen just above the uterus, a smooth, glistening, grayish dome about the size of a large orange. From the side of the uterus the fallopian tube emerged, a short, curving structure the diameter of a pencil, attached to the uterus by a broad sheet of golden brown ligament. Wrapped around the fallopian tube, strangling and distorting it, was the scar tissue that prevented normal conception. Following the tube laterally Mulligan could see its open end, where fimbriae floated like the wafting tendrils of sea anemone in a slow current. Just lateral to that was the ovary, almond-sized and shaped, its brownish-red surface dully reflecting the light.

The surface of the ovary was distorted by what looked like a swollen, tense blister about the size of a fingernail. Lansdowne took back the laparoscope. "Did you see the follicle?" he asked. "Okay. Now comes the fun part." He took a long needle, about three inches long with a glass syringe at the end, and poked it through the abdomen just lateral to his incision. "What we do now," he explained as he worked, "is to aspirate the contents of the follicle, ovum included, into a syringe. Since it's done under direct observation you really can't miss." With one hand steadying the laparoscope, he maneuvered the needle with the other. When he was ready he lifted his head and nodded to one of the nurses. "Okay, Marie." She took the syringe in both hands. Lansdowne pushed the needle another quarter inch down, saying, "Now," as he did so. Marie pulled back the plunger of the syringe and it filled quickly with a spurt of perhaps 5cc of a yellowish fluid.

Lansdowne looked up and pulled the needle out. "That's it," he said. He nodded toward the syringe. "You can't see it, of course, but the ovum's in there. Simple, isn't it?"

Too simple, Mulligan thought, and so far it hasn't explained anything. "What's next?" he asked.

"The ovum is washed a little in saline before fertilization," replied Lansdowne, "—to separate it from mucous and to make things easier for the sperm. Marie does that while I close the lady up."

She'd already been extubated and the anesthetic would wear off in another few minutes. The needle hole required

nothing more elaborate than a band-aid, while two dissolv-
ing sutures closed the peritoneum and three silk sutures the
skin. The entire procedure had taken less than twenty
minutes.

Lansdowne motioned to Mulligan to follow him, and
they walked into the adjoining room. "We call this the fertilization room," he said, "for lack of a better name." It was
just as sterile as the operating room, and they still wore their
caps and masks and gloves. Mulligan could see an incubator
with plastic tubing running to oxygen tanks. A small table
with Petri dishes and pipettes and bottles of sterile saline
stood near it. His attention was drawn, though, to a large
two-headed microscope on a table in the center of the room,
its lens hovering over a broad flat Petri dish into which
Marie was squirting the contents of the syringe.

"There goes the ovum," Lansdowne said, continuing his
running commentary. "We have to inspect it to see that it's
healthy. Then we can add the sperm. Come have a look."

They bent over the microscope, each of them looking
through one of its heads. Lansdowne maneuvered the Petri
dish until he saw the ovum and then focussed on it. In the
microscope it was ovoid rather than circular. Its internal
structures, magnified a thousand times, shimmered and
vibrated in the flow of cytoplasm. "Looks fine," Lansdowne muttered to himself.

The sperm had been obtained in the usual way. Evelyn's
self-conscious and embarrassed husband had been sent down
the hall, fortified and inspired by recent issues of Penthouse
magazine, to masturbate in a room reserved for that purpose. The ejaculate with its five hundred million sperm now
rested in a covered beaker kept in a constant-temperature
bath at thirty-eight degrees centigrade. Lansdowne took a
small syringe full of it and added it to the surface of the
growth medium in the Petri dish.

"Not as satisfying as sex," he commented drily, "but it
seems to work just as well." He tapped the side of the dish.
"This growth medium contains all the sugars and amino

acids and vitamins necessary to sustain the embryo for several days. We add some antibiotics to help keep it clean. In the incubator we circulate pure oxygen over the surface to be sure it gets enough, but eventually, as the embryo gets bigger, the oxygen available by diffusion isn't enough. Then it either dies or gets implanted in a uterus to develop a placenta. But for several days it can be kept alive in the dish. Want to see the fertilization?"

Mulligan peered through the microscope again. The sperm were thousands of miniscule coiled tadpoles, darting here and there in a brave aimless chaotic display of masculine energy. They were tiny compared to the ovum, perhaps fifty times smaller. The sperm was a package of pure chromosomes and stored energy, while the ovum, like any egg, contained nourishment as well.

To fertilize the ovum, to penetrate its outer membrane, a sperm had to hit it just right, at just the right angle. After several minutes one succeeded. The sperm struck and penetrated, inserting its head through the cell wall. The tail immediately wiggled even more vigorously, as though inspired by its triumph, driving the sperm ever more deeply into the ovum. It looked a little like a snake wriggling into a hole. As this occurred, nearly instantaneously, the ovum changed, its outer membrane expanding outward, visibly thickening, becoming totally impenetrable to other sperm. Mulligan watched them bounce helplessly off its surface, the losers in the race, until, their energy expended, they stopped wiggling and died. The sperm that had penetrated the ovum wiggled its way to the nucleus, where it seemed to melt and disappear, merging its chromosomes with those of the ovum.

The act of regeneration was complete. The human genome had been restored. A new life was beginning.

"I'm going to ask you a question you might find a little odd," Mulligan said after they'd returned to the dressing room. "Suppose you wanted to add some new genes to that embryo, a piece of DNA containing seven genes . . . could you do it?"

Lansdowne was stripping off his green pajama shirt but stopped and stared wonderingly at Mulligan. "I won't ask you why you want to know that . . ." he began.

"Please don't—thank you."

"Anyway, you couldn't," Lansdowne continued. He threw the pajamas into a clothes hamper and started to put on his own shirt again. "Not any way that I can think of. You can see that for yourself. The membrane around the ovum actually defends it against anything but a sperm— that's what a sperm is for, you know, for penetrating into an ovum. It's a highly specialized structure. Unorganized pieces of DNA couldn't just be passively absorbed into an ovum."

Mulligan recalled Aaron Rosenberg's technique of microstaining cells. "What about mechanically injecting the DNA into a fertilized ovum by using some sort of micropipette?"

Lansdowne shook his head. "You'd kill it if you did that. An embryo's pretty delicate, you know, when it's only one cell."

Mulligan felt his mood sink as Lansdowne talked. He was enormously disappointed. He'd hoped the answer would suggest itself when he watched the procedure, but it hadn't. The secret remained shrouded in ignorance and mystery. He felt a familiar surge of competitive antagonism. You're a clever bastard, Medvedev, he thought, more clever than I'd imagined, but I'm not finished yet.

When he left the clinic to return to Bethesda Mulligan found, to his surprise, that Ridgely was waiting for him in the back seat of a long black limousine. The large man seemed even more attentive and alert than usual, as though anxious and apprehensive about something he didn't want to talk about. "Learn anything useful?" he asked hopefully, as he moved over to make room for Mulligan. "Got it figured out yet?"

"No. Not yet." Mulligan struggled awkwardly to get settled in to the back seat without putting any strain on his left arm. He found he couldn't conceal the wave of discouragement that suddenly swept over him. "I'm not sure now I ever will."

Ridgely regarded him somberly for a moment without replying. "That's too bad," he finally said, his tone conveying, not regret, but a sense that Mulligan's words had helped him come to an uncomfortable decision. "That's too bad," he repeated.

They drove back to the laboratory in Bethesda in silence. Mulligan stared gloomily out the window of the car. The green beauty of the Maryland countryside in spring did nothing to lift his spirits. He sensed that there was something that Ridgely hadn't told him, and the suspicion made him sullenly hostile, resentful of the webs of conspiracy that seemed to emanate from the agent. He remembered the bouncy spirit of adventure with which he'd started out just a month before and wondered just exactly when it had evaporated.

When they arrived in Bethesda, Ridgely remained in the car. "There's something else I have to do," he said. "I'll see you tomorrow." Mulligan merely nodded.

Irene's optimism had been bolstered by a productive day. "We've got it!" she announced happily as Mulligan walked into the lab.

Mulligan was too preoccupied to understand right away what she meant. "Got what?" he asked moodily.

"The CPK inhibitor, of course!" She glowed with success and pride. "I knew he could do it! I told you, didn't I, that Yuri could develop an inhibitor in just a few days."

Yuri was seated at one of the lab islands and hadn't noticed Mulligan come in. In front of him on the benchtop was a small, pyramid-shaped, tightly corked Ehrlenmeyer flask, half filled with a colorless liquid. Mulligan walked over and stood next to him and watched quietly for a moment. Yuri was rapidly scribbling mathematical notations on a pad of paper, working too rapidly for Mulligan to follow the calculation.

"What's that?" Mulligan asked, tapping Yuri on the shoulder and pointing to the flask. "That the inhibitor?"

Yuri looked around. For the first time his leaden despondency seemed a little lighter. "This is it," he said. His eyes shone brightly and a smile of stained, crooked teeth lit his face in hopeful expectation. "I've designed it to irreversibly inhibit CPK on a molecule-for-molecule basis. I'm trying to calculate a dosage."

"You better be careful about that," Irene said behind them. "It drains muscles of their energy. Too much and you'd become as flaccid as overcooked spaghetti."

"Better try it first on an animal, then," Mulligan said. "There must be some rats or something around here we could use to experiment."

What they found was a cat, one that had been used for an experiment in cancer chemotherapy and was scheduled for sacrifice. Mulligan placed it on one of the benchtops, receiving several furrows down his forearms for his trouble. The animal lay on its back in a V-shaped restraining device, screeching and clawing, its legs held apart by straps to expose its underbelly, where fur wouldn't prevent the fluid from contacting the skin.

"A half cc should be enough," Yuri said, carefully drawing up the solution into a syringe.

"So little?" Irene asked.

"It's enough," Yuri repeated confidently. He stepped back from the benchtop and stared thoughtfully for a moment at the spitting and furious animal, hesitating momentarily, then sprayed the contents of the syringe onto the animal's stomach.

For a minute or two nothing happened. The cat continued to claw at the air, spitting out its outrage and fury. But then its movements slowed. The spitting became less furious, the clawing less frantic. The cat seemed to relax, almost as though it had accepted the indignity. But it quickly became apparent that it wasn't a calm at all, it was paralysis. A narrow beam of unyielding hatred glistened upward from its slitted eyes. Slowly, over five minutes, its movements weakened and muscles lost their ability to regenerate energy. The cat's legs hung limply, joints flopping into awkward postures determined only by gravity and the restraints. Its head and tongue lolled slackly to the right, and its breathing became so shallow as to be scarcely perceptible until it stopped altogether. But the hatred remained in the eyes for the several seconds that consciousness persisted after respiration ceased.

"It's dead," Yuri said simply, unmoved by the setback. "I gave it too much."

Mulligan uncorked the pyramidal Erhlenmeyer flask and sniffed. There was no odor. "Some poison," he commented. "Odorless, transcutaneous, deadly."

Yuri smiled grotesquely. "Yes, it is, isn't it?"

Irene was frightened. The elation of a few minutes before had been punctured by what had just occurred. She stared at the body of the cat and the color drained from her cheeks. "It's too strong," she said, biting her fingernails nervously. "It's too deadly." Her face tensed with worry and dismay. "Oh, Yuri!" she cried out suddenly. "How can we ever learn how much is safe to use?" Tears formed in her eyes.

Yuri, though, remained unconcerned. The grotesque smile stayed on his face and became almost angelic. He was sustained by some private consolation he either couldn't or wouldn't share. His calm seemed that of a soldier accepting a suicidal mission, resigned to death but animated yet by duty, every moment and movement brushed by eternity.

That evening, though, he complained of pain in his chest, a heavy sensation, as though someone had put a large, warm stone under the breastbone. He lay on his bed, motionless except for a labored breathing. Beads of sweat formed on his forehead for a few minutes until the pain subsided.

"It's angina," Mulligan said. He didn't need an electrocardiogram to diagnose the symptom. "It's a warning." He telephoned to Ridgely, who arranged for some nitroglycerin and Inderal to be sent over from a pharmacy.

After a while Yuri fell asleep. The pain didn't recur, although Mulligan and Irene spent another nearly sleepless night watching over him. Irene seemed totally crushed. "We came so close," she whispered to Mulligan. "So close."

"He's too far gone," Mulligan said, unwilling to let sentimentality distort his perceptions. "He's too old."

Yuri awoke the next morning as though nothing had happened. He made no mention of the angina he'd had. "We'll go to the library today," he announced to Irene. He wanted to find out how many cells he had in his body and begin to approximate a dosage of the inhibitor. He seemed unhurried, as if he were waiting for or preoccupied with something.

Mulligan returned to the laboratory. He'd always liked working alone, and was somewhat romantically inspired by the idea of solitary assaults on the unknown. The flask containing the DNA solution, when he took it out to begin work, seemed to project a silent challenge. It would test his conceit that matter would invariably yield its secrets to intelligence and will. He swirled the fluid in the flask; and as he looked at the shimmering opalescence, he thought, I'd better get this right the first time. Yuri doesn't look as though he'll last much longer. He knew—instinctively, and with the firm finality of instinct—that the flask contained the answer to the last, the final question. He had only to be clever enough to find it. Medvedev had done something to the fertilized ovum before reimplanting it in the mother's uterus, and that something had added the seven genes. Mulligan had the annoying sense of being on the edge of discovery yet finding the answer still elusive, like trying to catch an animal that's just a little quicker than you are.

The first step would be to separate the plasmids from the chromosomes in the solution by subjecting them to ultra-high speed centrifugation. If the plasmid theory was correct, the solution should contain two sizes of DNA molecules. Since a normal chromosome contains about two thousand genes, the chromosomal DNA would comprise huge, heavy molecules, enormously long, strung-out chains of nucleic acid. The plasmid DNA, on the other hand, containing only seven genes, would be only a small fraction of that size. In the centrifuge the chromosomes would sink to the bottom, pushed by centrifugal force to the periphery of the circle, while the plasmid particles, much lighter, would stay near the top.

He pipetted some of the DNA solution into a well at one end of a sucrose-agarose gel strip, a strip of transparent plastic six inches long and one inch wide onto which a 2mm-thick layer of the gel had been baked. The gel provided a constant-density gradient through which the molecules migrated while spinning, separating them even further and keeping them apart after the centrifuge was stopped. He prepared four strips for the centrifuge, using up nearly all his DNA solution to do so. He'd get only one chance. At the end of ten minutes of centrifugation, Mulligan expected to find that his strip of agarose gel contained two lines across it, a thick one at the bottom, containing the chromosomal DNA, and a thin one very near the top, containing the much smaller molecules of the plasmid. His intention was then to slice out and redissolve the plasmid DNA and subject it to chemical analysis, snipping off the genes one by one using restriction endonucleases. Somewhere in the process, he hoped, the answer he sought would make itself apparent.

He waited impatiently for the centrifuge to do its work, making himself a little dizzy by watching its blur while it whirled around at 20,000 rpm. Ten minutes would be enough. As he waited his mind wandered, reviewing the cascade of events of the past several weeks, the arrival of mutant boys in Paris, the confirmation of his theory of intelligence, the attacks by secret agents, the insidious marriage of molecular genetics and in vitro fertilization techniques . . . his reminiscence had the illusory and ephemeral quality of a dream, of unreality. Images faded and dissolved, reappeared in sequences that distorted the actual chronology. The photograph of Medvedev floated into his mind; the broad Slavic planes of the face seemed to grin, challenging and mocking him. Mulligan tried to banish from his mind the dampening realization that if his plan didn't work, or if there was no plasmid, he had nowhere to go, no more ideas.

At the end of ten minutes he took the strips out of the centrifuge and examined them carefully, holding them against a white paper-background so the lines could be seen more clearly. There were two lines, all right, but immediately he noticed that something was wrong. At the bottom of each gel strip, as expected, was the thick line of chromosomal DNA. That was as it should be. But the thin line of plasmid DNA, which he had expected to be near the very top of the strip, was located instead near the middle of it. The molecule of plasmid DNA was evidently much bigger and heavier than he had thought it would be. Seven genes alone wouldn't migrate so far through the agarose gel. He stared at the thin line in surprise for a moment, uncertain if the finding was real or not. Later on he realized he was lucky to have noticed it, since failure to have done so would have meant failure to solve the mystery.

Something else was there, he realized. Some *other* DNA was attached to the seven genes. And more, the thought came as an illuminating flash, it was this other DNA that gave the seven genes the ability to penetrate a fertilized ovum. What kind of DNA can penetrate mammalian cells?

Sometimes finding an answer depends merely on asking the question the right way. What kind of DNA can penetrate mammalian cells? Stated that way, the answer became obvious, gleaming from the dark morass of ignorance the way a lost penny, finally found, shines brightly enough to arouse wonder that it hadn't been seen before.

A virus. Viral DNA can penetrate mammalian cells.

Medvedev had spliced the seven genes to a viral chromosome and used the virus to infect the fertilized ovum. That was how it had been done. Even without proof, even without duplicating the accomplishment, Mulligan was certain that this was the answer.

It must have been a retrovirus, too. Mulligan stood rapt with admiration at the genius and originality of Medvedev's idea. A retrovirus—an insidious disruption of inheritance, a prime example of the resilient perversity of nature—was the kind of virus that did more than penetrate human cells. Retroviruses attached to human chromosomes, became an integral part of them, merged their own genes with the genome of the host cell. Attached to chromosomes, retroviruses duplicated when the cells duplicated, died when they died, synchronous and consonant with the rest of the cell's life.

Medvedev's conception was a stroke of brilliance, of daring, a masterpiece of genius of the sort that could sweep an entire scientific discipline ahead decades in one leap. Mulligan thought suddenly of the chimera, the legendary beast of Greek mythology, that was a combination of two species, like a unicorn or a winged lion. The children were not quite a true chimera, he thought, but close enough, a fanciful genetic beast brought to life.

Now, too, he could refine his conception of the error. The error lay in trying to attach too many genes to the virus all at once, so that the virus itself had been altered. It would still penetrate an embryo, but it would no longer attach to chromosomes. The virus, with its baggage of the seven genes, had remained as a plasmid in the cellular cytoplasm, multiplying uncontrollably, producing huge and unwanted amounts of the enzymes. The progeria had resulted.

Mulligan took a deep breath and let it out slowly, with a sense of certainty and relief. The bottom of the mystery had been plunged. There were no more unexplained riddles. Yuri and Ivan and their brothers had started life in Petri dishes as an in vitro fertilization, with the embryo deliberately infected with a retrovirus to which had been spliced the genes for the neurotransmitter and muscle enzymes.

CHAPTER FIFTEEN

Mulligan sat for a long time staring at the gel strip and sorting his thoughts. The dark lines of precipitated nucleic acid in the translucent, pale agarose gel were evidence that admitted no other explanation. Strangely, though, he felt no triumph. Finding the retrovirus brought him only a sense of weariness, his energy of anticipation dissipated, much like the letdown that follows completion of a sustained effort. But there was more than that. He felt, too, the sodden gray heaviness of a moral exhaustion, the result of too long an association with misery. His mood recalled to him a movie he had once seen, a World War I movie, in which a German soldier, eviscerated by a piece of shrapnel, stumbles into a Frenchman's foxhole. The poor miserable Frenchman has to watch for hours while the German dies in agony.

You know not what you do. The phrase recurred again and again, uncannily appropriate, nagging insistently. What had happened to the children had been a warning. There was an old maxim in ecology that you never change only one thing, that one alteration inevitably engenders another, each new link invoking the next in an unending chain of consequence. The Aswan Dam prevented the flooding of the Nile with silt from the mountains of Ethiopia, which reduced the nitrogen content of the water, which diminished the food available for plankton in the sea off Alexandria, and the reduced plankton population reduced the fish population, so within several years fishermen's families were starving. Before the dam was completed no one imagined that such things would happen. Medvedev's attempt to achieve predictable genius had failed because, unpredictably, the virus itself had been changed. It no longer behaved the way it was supposed to. Even elementary biology classes taught that most mutations were disasters, ruthlessly eliminated by natural selection . . . as Yuri and his brothers were being eliminated.

The telephone broke the silence and jolted his revery. He and Irene had agreed to meet for lunch in Georgetown, to take several hours off so that Yuri could have a rest. It was just before noon, and she was calling to confirm the appointment.

"How's Yuri?" Mulligan asked. "Any more chest pains?"

"No," she answered sadly, "but something has happened, something inside of him. He doesn't seem to care any more. He's just poking through the books as if he's not really interested. I think he's given up."

"Maybe what I found today will be encouraging."

"You found it?" she was instantly attentive.

It suddenly occurred to Mulligan that his phone was very likely tapped, that someone from the CIA was listening to their conversation. "I'll tell you about it later, when we can talk privately," he said.

His driver took him to Georgetown. It is the loveliest part of the capital, with a gracious, eighteenth-century ambiance. Their route took them along narrow residential streets covered with arched canopies of old chestnuts and magnolias. Hundred-year-old roots gnarled and uplifted brick sidewalks. Huge hydrangeas planted behind fences in front yards concealed many of the houses but still yielded glimpses of gabled Victorian and porticoed Georgian mansions. Untidy gardens, seen through gateways, were patches of color, sprouting yellow and orange flowers in lazy, moist fertility.

They met for lunch at a restaurant Ridgely had known about, the Old Canal Inn, a renovated warehouse along the remnant of the Chesapeake and Ohio Canal. The day was warm, but the humid air only touched the skin enough to make one aware of its presence, instead of clogging it hopelessly. Their table was outside on a broad wharf overlooking the canal.

Irene's description of the change in Yuri had been accurate. A featureless passivity smothered the driving intensity he'd shown before. Yet he seemed curiously peaceful, as though he'd made an inner decision to stop struggling and was already saying goodbye to the world. He sat at the table with a distant, uninterested look, lost in his own thoughts. He seemed disdainfully indifferent to the rude stares of the other patrons in the restaurant and showed not the slightest interest when Irene pointed out a canal barge that was drawn by mules and overflowing with tourists, floating by majestically.

After they were seated at their table Irene clutched Yuri's hand tightly and looked eagerly at Mulligan. "Tell us," she said. "I know you found it this morning. You know how Medvedev did it, don't you? Tell us."

Yuri was looking at Mulligan with a cold, lustreless eye. A brief uninterpretable expression flickered like a candle flame over his deeply creased face. It was impossible to know what he was thinking. Surely he knew what the angina portended. Was that why he'd become listless, had lapsed into passivity? "It was ingenious," Mulligan said finally, "most ingenious. I was lucky to have found it."

"Will it help?" Irene let go of Yuri's hand and leaned toward Mulligan in eager anticipation, eyes shining. She was dressed in a sleeveless dress for the summer day, and her shoulders were bare, soft and graceful, just touched by the dark brown hair that framed a face now flushed with hope. "Will your discovery help Yuri?"

Mulligan shrank from the necessity to disappoint her. He shook his head somberly. "I don't think so," he said slowly. "I can't think how. What Medvedev did was to splice the genes he wanted to a virus, a retrovirus, and he infected the embryo with it right after fertilization. The virus was supposed to attach to the chromosomes, but it didn't. That's what went wrong."

Yuri's ethereal detachment crumbled. An expression of horror and disgust convulsed his face. *"An infection?* My brothers and I were an infection?" His voice was a current of self-loathing.

"It's not what you think," Mulligan said quickly. "The virus is just the means of getting the genes inside the embryo, sort of a transportation vehicle."

Yuri seemed not to have heard. He sat with his head bent forward, his face nearly touching the table, and mumbled something unintelligible. "Ivan, Gorgi, Andreyev." His brothers' names rolled from his throat in a low whisper of supplication and elegy. Suddenly he made a dismayed strangling noise and raised a hand to his neck. His face tightened as the pain forced him to concentrate on the vise gripping his chest.

Irene looked at Mulligan in frightened alarm.

"His heart," Mulligan said.

She fumbled hurriedly in her purse. "I've got his nitroglycerin here somewhere." In a moment she produced one of the tiny pills and placed it under Yuri's tongue.

They watch him closely as they waited for the drug to work. The thirty seconds seemed hours. Yuri's face stared up at them, with his lips drawn back in a grimace of pain, the misshapen yellowed teeth displayed in a twisted grin as his breath hissed through them. Then, slowly, the tension ebbed from his face, and his breathing became slower. He sat back in his chair with a sigh of profound relief.

The mad self-loathing seemed to have left him, too, as though the angina had squeezed it from him. The attack left him exhausted and limp. He nodded and smiled faintly when Mulligan asked him if he felt any better, then slowly closed his blue-veined eyelids.

"It's not a heart attack," Mulligan told Irene. "If the nitro works it's only another attack of angina, not a real heart attack." Not yet, he thought, not yet. But that can't be long now in coming. Very soon now we will lose him. "Let's get him back to the apartment."

Mulligan stood and picked Yuri up in his arms, surprised at how light he was. The boy's eyes remained closed, as though he'd withdrawn to an inner universe from which he'd be recalled only with difficulty. Only an occasional spasmodic twitching of his fingers indicated a remnant of feeling. In the car on the way back to Bethesda he curled tightly into a ball on Irene's lap.

He fell asleep soon after their return to the apartment. With a brooding suspicion that he might never wake again Mulligan laid him gently on his bed. The child shrank in sleep, sallow and dry. The bumps on his forehead stood out more than ever. Mulligan closed the door to the bedroom with a silent wish that the boy's suffering might soon come to an end.

He joined Irene on the couch in the living room. His thoughts were dominated by bitterness and a hard, inflexible fury. Everything had been twisted, perverted. He felt shame, too, a new and uncomfortable emotion, at the thought that his own theory had been Medvedev's inspiration. My Nobel acceptance speech will have to be an apology, he thought. He was surprised to find that his palms were wet with perspiration.

Irene sat for a long time without speaking. There was about her the sullen acceptance of fate, as of a prisoner who has already served a long term yet still has years to go. Mulligan waited for her to speak. "You know," she said at last, "how you're just ready for certain things to happen in your life? Like falling in love as much because you're ready to fall in love as because you meet just the right person."

"That's flattering," Mulligan said drily, attempting half-heartedly to lighten the atmosphere.

"You know what I mean. But I think I was just ready for those boys to come along. I'm thirty-four years old. Maybe it was the thought that if I was ever going to have children I couldn't postpone it any longer. For the last year or so I've had a feeling that I was missing something, something very important. Then Ivan appeared out of nowhere, and he seemed to need me so much . . . then Yuri . . ." Her voice cracked, and she shook her head in embarrassment to drive away the tears. "It's so stupid, really. I knew all the time that they were dying, and they're not mine, and they're so awful to look at, but still . . ." her voice trailed off.

Mulligan brushed a tear from her cheek, then held her in his arms. She had a musty odor of stale perfume. "This may seem irrevelant at the moment," he said, "but I love you. Very much."

She appeared almost offended by his words, and a swift look of distaste crossed her face, causing his heart to sink. "How can you go on with this, George? You won't go on any more, will you?"

Before he could reply there was a firm knock at the door. Mulligan rose and answered it. Ridgely stood there, with several men in the hall behind him.

"May I come in?" he asked in a pro forma way. "There's someone here for you to meet."

"Suit yourself," Mulligan said, and returned to stand near Irene. Ridgely left two men to guard the hall and entered with the third man dragging behind him in his wake. As usual, Ridgely seemed huge and florid, imposing beyond his right to be imposing. The other man was dabbing perspiration from his forehead as he entered; and he wore thick rimless glasses, so that Mulligan didn't recognize him at first. Yet there was something familiar . . . the man was short, thickset, with a broad, flat face, no neck, and close-cropped iron-gray hair.

Medvedev! Mulligan thought. My God, it's Yevgeny Medvedev!

Yet it was clearly a changed man. He had only the most superficial resemblance to the self-confident genius of the photograph Mulligan had seen. He appeared ruined and defeated, a man whose ego lies in shreds around him, who clings desperately to the decency of others as his only hope for salvation. His face had the stunned, bleak expression of the survivor of an artillery barrage. He looked as though he hadn't slept in weeks. Dark half-circles underlay eyes that were red and swollen from having been rubbed continually in an effort to banish fatigue. Anxiety or fear made perspiration appear again on his brow as soon as he had wiped it off. It was only with an obvious effort that he maintained a correct, upright posture.

"How the hell? . . ." Mulligan began, open mouthed, turning his head from Medvedev to Ridgely and back again.

"We've made a deal," Ridgely said somewhat nasally. "We've decided to exchange some information. There was always the chance that you might never find out how they did it. We decided we couldn't take that chance. There wasn't time." Ridgely spoke quickly before Mulligan could object. "So we approached our Soviet friends with an offer. Dr. Medvedev here was willing to make a deal. An exchange. What we know for what they know. He knows how he did it. You know what went wrong." He paused. "We trade. Then each of us will know what the other knows." Ridgely paused again, then spoke very slowly and deliberately. "And there's another thing. We're giving them back Yuri."

"You're *what!*"

Medvedev spoke for the first time. His English was heavily accented, mixing Russian and British pronunciation, but easily understandable. "You do know, don't you, what went wrong?" he asked Mulligan, sweating again. "I always had great faith in you, Dr. Mulligan, great faith. I am a great admirer of yours."

Irene had been transfixed by the sight of Medvedev. She rose to stand near the couch, staring at him, coiling inside, until with a shriek that might have issued from the throat of a Valkyrie she leaped at him. With her fingernails extended and hooked like claws she slashed at his face. "*Salaud!*" she screamed. "You bastard!" Before he could raise his arms in self-defense, two long gouges appeared on his left cheek. "How could you!" she cried. She kept on slashing at him, a whirlwind of fury until Ridgely, moving with surprising speed, grabbed her in a huge bear hug from behind and gently pulled her away. She squirmed out of Ridgely's grasp with a muffled "Oh, God," and rushed into the bedroom, slamming the door behind her.

"Leave her alone," Mulligan said curtly to Ridgely. "She'll be all right in a minute. It's been hard on her, all this. Just leave her alone for a while."

Medvedev dabbed at the scratches on his face with his handkerchief and looked at the blood curiously, as though he didn't know where it had come from. He wiped his forehead with the bloody handkerchief. "That was Dr. Sailland, I presume?" he asked. "She who was to save their lives? The one Ivan and Yuri ran to?" He smiled weakly and continued with heavy, self-deprecating sarcasm. "You might have introduced us properly, Dr. Mulligan, before permitting her to attack me."

Mulligan's own fury exploded. "She's right, though, isn't she? How could you?"

"Astonishing, really, that they made it to Paris," Medvedev continued, talking to himself as though he hadn't heard Mulligan at all. "Astonishing. All the way from Leningrad. They had more endurance and resilience than even we suspected."

"Proud of that, are you?"

"Shouldn't I be?" He looked at Mulligan with an expectation of agreement, seeking commendation, something to restore his self-respect.

"Jesus Christ!" Mulligan shouted. He grabbed Medvedev by his shirt and jerked him around like a street tough intimidating his prey. "How could you?" he shouted again, pushing Medvedev down on the couch. "Those were children, people, not some prize pigs that you bred to win the county fair. What kind of ghoul are you?"

Medvedev's bravado suddenly faltered, and he caved in utterly. He took off his glasses and wiped them with the bloody handkerchief before putting them back on. Light reflected from them as he looked up again at Mulligan. A shudder passed briefly through him. His voice was hoarse, barely above a whisper. "You may not believe this, Dr. Mulligan, but I've asked myself that very question dozens of times." He put the handkerchief back in his pocket and lifted his hands in a gesture of pleading, begging for understanding. "Why do men do things? I've thought it over so many times, so many times. Especially over these last few months, when everything went wrong. Why do men do things? I think in the end I did it because I knew how to do it. That's it, I think," he stated with some finality. "The fact that I *could* do it was, in the end, why I did it."

What is he talking about? Mulligan thought. What a self-serving excuse! There are lots of things that we know how to do that we don't do, like making supervirulent bacteria, or blowing up the Earth. Yet the possibility that something *potential*, a mere vision or idea, might compel men to render it *actual* was not one to be too lightly dismissed. Still, he was appalled and incredulous. "But surely you have ethics committees," he persisted, "some kind of oversight of human experimentation?"

"Of course we do." Medvedev sat up straight and sniffed, offended, as sensitive Russians always are to the charge of barbarism. "We're as civilized as you are. But this was a military project. We were prepared to accept some sacrifice."

My God, Mulligan thought, General Alexander was right all the time. They *do* want to make better soldiers. "But why not try animals first? Why start right off with people?"

Medvedev was eager to share the blame. "Well, that was partly your fault, Dr. Mulligan. I was testing your theory, after all. It was *human* intelligence we were after. Is there an animal model that could really test your theory? I think not. In any event, General Kermonov insisted that it be tried on human beings right away. He was always obsessed with the fear that you Americans might be trying the same thing and beat us to it. His interests were different, of course."

"Why did you make it a military project at all?"

"It was the only way I could get it done."

"Then why did he let you come here?"

Medvedev made a vague gesture of dismissal and twitched nervously. "He lost interest in the project as soon as it began to turn sour. Said I'd wasted a great deal of time and effort. He has no hope that it can be salvaged, so he doesn't care now what I do." Medvedev lowered his voice to a conspiratorial whisper. "Don't tell anyone I said this, but he really had very little insight into this—he's very short sighted, impatient . . ." Medvedev reached his hand out to Mulligan, to touch his arm, to dispel by physical contact the enormous philosophical distance between them. "General Kermonov doesn't understand at all what you and I understand . . . man is free at last! Free from the tyranny of heredity! Free from being a peculiar accident of evolution." He grabbed Mulligan's hand and held it in earnest entreaty. "Man has crossed the threshold and now controls his own destiny! Surely you see that? That is why you must tell me what went wrong! How to fix it!" Medvedev's eyes blazed with the fiery soul of a man possessed.

Mulligan stared at him. Yes, I *do*, he thought, I do see that, and it makes me deathly afraid.

"What about the mothers?" Ridgely asked, interrupting Medvedev's outburst with a more prosaic curiosity.

"That's easy," Medvedev said. He dabbed at his face again and saw that the bleeding had stopped, then returned the handkerchief to his pocket. Some color returned to his cheeks. "Possibly the easiest part. Do you mean to tell me that you couldn't find some young women who would be willing to let their bodies be used as little biological factories for a while? For a fee? Of course you could. What is it, after all? A tiny operation, virtually painless. Delivery nine months later. That's all. For ten or twenty thousand dollars I'm sure I could find some girls in half an hour who'd be willing to do that. No, the mothers aren't the problem."

"And the father?" Mulligan asked.

"I am the father." Medvedev said it simply, matter-of-factly, but his surface placidity was marred by a twitch that contracted one side of his face, forcing him to blink rapidly several times. His hand trembled when he readjusted his glasses.

Mulligan sat back as though he had been slapped in the face, staring in disbelief at Medvedev. How could he toy so with man's most profound emotions? "You mean . . . Yuri, Ivan, the others . . . they were your own sons?"

"The sperm had to come from somewhere." Medvedev attempted to restore his equanimity with a brusque rationality. "The point of the experiment, after all, was to see what the extra genes would do. It didn't really matter who the father and mother were."

"Jesus," Mulligan whispered. He felt a hollow sensation take possession of his chest. "Your own children."

Medvedev coughed slightly, clearing his throat. "I wouldn't say, I would be less than candid if I should deny that I've had moments of remorse about all this," he said, looking down at his hands as he spoke, bent forward with his head down in the posture of a penitent painfully articulating his confession. "When they started aging so rapidly, it was as though the clay that I had molded with my own

259

hands was turning to dust. When Gorgi and Andreyev died
. . . I must admit that I felt more than failure and disappointment. They were strange children, to be sure . . . one
approached them a little uncertainly, you know, not knowing what to expect . . . but still, I had begun to feel toward
them what I was . . . their father." He twisted his hands
together and a brief spasm of anguish crossed his face. "You
must believe me when I say that the progeria was a surprise.
What about it, then? Will you tell me what caused it? Will
you agree? We'll exchange information, we'll collaborate."

Mulligan tried to imagine Medvedev's feelings, the desperation and the despair, a man clawing at the edge of the
cliff to avoid falling into the chasm below. He'd been on the
verge of one of the greatest scientific achievements in history only to have seen it disintegrate before his eyes. And
his own sons! No wonder he'd been willing to risk everything and come to the United States.

The discovery of the error—that the retrovirus had failed
to attach to chromosomes—suggested a variety of possible
improvements. It would be more likely, for instance, that
the virus would properly attach if it had only one or two
extra genes on it instead of seven. Or the embryo could be
infected at a later stage of development with tissue-specific
retroviruses, so that the neurotransmitter enzymes could be
targeted specifically at the brain and the CPK enzyme at
muscle. Like any other scientific technique, Mulligan knew,
this one could be perfected.

Medvedev watched Mulligan's face carefully, ready to
probe for and grasp any opening. "Where is the evil?" he
asked, seeing Mulligan hesitate, voicing a question that must
have been in his mind for a long time. "In the knowledge,
or in the uses we make of it?"

Mulligan snorted in derision. "A fine unanswerable Russian theological question. But a little too late, isn't it? A little
after the fact?"

"Agreed, agreed," Medvedev said, hanging his head
down again like a penitent but only momentarily subdued.
"But what of Yuri? What has happened to him?"

With a slant of his head Mulligan indicated Yuri's bedroom. "He's in there, sleeping. You can see for yourself when he wakes up. He's a very old man now; his heart is giving way . . . coronary disease."

"Like his brothers. Dr. Sailland found no cure, then, for the progeria?"

"No cure. A treatment, perhaps. Only that. And she didn't find it. Yuri did."

"Ah, I see." Medvedev's eyes gleamed. "You educated him, then. We were always afraid to do that. Even the generals," he snickered, "such brave men, were afraid to educate them."

"It's horrible what's happened to Yuri." Irene' voice came from the doorway of the bedroom, a repelling chill in it like someone announcing a death to the rest of the family. She advanced into the room but disdained to look at Medvedev and spoke to the wall behind him. "Not only his heart, his mind has begun to decay. Only the studying and the chemistry helped him to keep his hold on reality. Otherwise he was torn by terrors we couldn't even imagine. At night he gives way to the most horrible visions. Now I think he's waiting for death, probably welcoming it. At least then the terrors will stop."

"But he found a treatment, you say, for the progeria?" Medvedev grasped at any straw.

"Possibly," Mulligan said. "Only possibly. An inhibitor for the CPK."

"Ah," Medvedev breathed. "I had the same idea. Especially when I discovered Dr. Sailland's articles in the literature. But by then it was too late. A CPK inhibitor . . . the synthesis of such a compound would require months. We had no time."

"You should be proud of your son, then," Mulligan said contemptuously. "He did it in just a few days. That much we'll readily grant you . . . he had a colossal intelligence." A wave of nauseated revulsion, as though he'd just stepped on a cockroach, passed through him. "I do know what went wrong . . . precisely," he said icily, feeling his contempt and antagonism solidify into an overwhelming hatred. "And I know how to correct it . . . but I won't tell you."

"That's the deal," Ridgely said authoritatively. "That's the deal we made. A simple exchange of information. They agreed to it; we agreed to it."

"And Yuri, too? You give him back? After all that's happened? After all he's done?"

Ridgely shrugged indifferently. "It's part of the deal."

"God, you wouldn't," Irene said, staring at Ridgely. "Not even you would do that."

"I would. I will," Ridgely said.

"No, you won't," Mulligan said. "You won't because I didn't agree." He rose to his feet and advanced threateningly on Ridgely, carried away by his anger. "I won't let you."

With a supple and practiced movement Ridgely reached under his left arm and pulled a large pistol from its holster. "Easy," he said to Mulligan, pointing the weapon. "Take it easy."

There was a moment of utter silence. Mulligan stared at the gun, its sudden presence chilling him, making him feel more than ever buffeted by cold winds. He noticed the horrified look on Irene's face and realized that they'd been like characters in a play from the theater of the absurd, exchanging snatches of disjointed conversation, unable to perceive the deadly narrative thread that held it all together.

The moment of silence stretched on, so that the sound of a door opening was clearly audible to all of them. Yuri stood in the doorway of his room. He stared silently at the tableau in front of him—Mulligan standing several feet from Ridgely, immobilized by the gun pointed at his chest, Irene behind him to the side, Medvedev seated on the couch. Yuri surveyed the scene in front of him with his usual staccato eye movements.

Medvedev rose quickly from the couch and took a short step forward. "Yuri!" His voice failed him and he couldn't speak further.

Yuri's face was a hoary mask of malignity; and old, so old that only the hatred radiating from it gave it life at all. He advanced warily into the room, leaning to one side, limping badly on the injured ankle. The only sound he made was the harsh rasp of his breathing. In his hand was a small, pyramid-shaped, tightly corked Ehrlenmeyer flask of colorless liquid.

Irene was the first to understand. "My God!" she whispered. "He's kept it with him! Don't do it, Yuri. Please don't do it."

He continued to limp forward as though he hadn't heard her, his gaze fixed on Medvedev, his head and shoulders jutting forward as he advanced. The curve of his back made his balding head appear even larger than it had before. His eyes narrowed to reptilian slits, deepening the wrinkles of the loose, sallow skin around them.

Mulligan started forward toward Yuri, then stopped, halted by the hatred radiating from him. Medvedev began to back away, wide eyed and paling, recoiling before his malevolence as though it were a physical force. He raised his hands in front of him in a meager gesture of self-defense.

Yuri advanced to the center of the room and stopped, alien and misshapen. "So we meet again, Comrade Yevgeny." A tremor of rage and agony passed through him. His words were punctuated by short quick gasps. "So far from our last meeting, and so much has changed."

Medvedev stared at Yuri as though he were a figure from a recurring nightmare now encountered in real life. A gagging, inarticulate sound came from his throat.

"We meet again," Yuri rasped, swaying slightly from side to side. "But now I know. I know why my brothers died. I know what I am. I know how you made me what I am." He made a shrill cackling sound, like a witch gloating over the triumph of evil, as the eggshell of rationality cracked and shattered. "An infection! A perversion! An infection! A perversion!" Into each word he poured the acid corrosion of his self-hatred and self-disgust.

Irene's voice broke through his chanting, louder now. "Don't do it, Yuri," she urged. "Please don't." She edged forward cautiously.

Yuri whirled around at her and hissed like a snake issuing a warning. Irene stopped.

"Don't do what?" Ridgely asked, moving toward the place where Yuri stood. He looked at Irene. "What's he going to do?"

"The inhibitor," Irene said, pointing to the tightly stoppered Ehrlenmeyer flask in Yuri's hand. "He's going to use it on him," she said, pointing to Medvedev.

Ridgely understood immediately. He pointed the pistol at Yuri. "Back away now," he commanded, his voice rising. "Back away!"

Yuri's movement was completed before Ridgely had time to react. He leaped forward and grabbed Ridgely's wrist with his left hand, a movement neither hidden nor subtle, merely too quick to prevent. His grip was like a vise, pointing the gun down, pulling and stretching Ridgely's arm outward. Then he pivoted swiftly and pushed the triceps up from beneath with his right hand. His hands were so small they looked like normal hands grasping a log. He pulled down at the wrist and pushed up on the triceps. Ridgely's extended elbow snapped like a stick. The man shrieked in agony, dropped the pistol, then lost control of his legs and fell whimpering and writhing to the floor.

The flask had fallen to the floor unbroken and Yuri now picked it up and removed the cork with his teeth. He glanced for a second, a second only, at Irene, as though to say goodbye, then poured some of the liquid into his cupped right hand.

"Oh, Yuri," Irene moaned softly. "Why, Yuri, why?" She sank into a chair and began to cry softly, her face buried in her hands.

Medvedev backed away again as Yuri advanced, attempting to circle, withdrawing until a corner stopped him. He shrank into the corner as Yuri came inexorably closer, staring uncomprehendingly but fearfully at the liquid in Yuri's hand. "There's something you should know, Yuri," he began, finding his voice at last.

"There's something I should know," Yuri mocked, cutting him short, the words squeezed from his throat in a croak that sounded like chalk scratched on a blackboard. "There's something I should know . . . I know too much!" he screamed at Medvedev, "and not enough!" He began to shake violently but with a piercing cry leaped high into the air.

As Yuri descended on him Medvedev shrieked loudly, hysterically, as though the words themselves would defend him, "I am your father! *I am your father!*"

Then Yuri was upon him, an impossibly quick and overpowering flurry of movement, uttering loud shrieks like some hideous vengeance from ancient legend. There was almost no struggle. Medvedev fell onto his back. His cries of terror matched Yuri's shrieking. With his cupped hand Yuri splashed the liquid onto Medvedev's face, then emptied the rest of the vial onto his chest. When it was done he became quiet, until Medvedev also stopped crying out. He then reached out to stroke the man's cheek, almost affectionately. "My father," he murmured. "My father." The madness and fury ebbed from his face. "It's done," he said with finality, standing up and stepping back.

Medvedev touched his cheek and stared at the film of liquid on his fingers. He felt nothing, neither pain nor stinging.

Irene spoke without looking up. "The molecule passes easily through the skin. It's already in your circulation. You'll be dead in a few minutes. So will Yuri."

Yuri collapsed first. Mulligan watched him with pity and horror. Muscle bundles weakened unevenly, and his legs wobbled before giving way. He slumped to the floor and dragged himself toward Irene.

"Irene!" It was the cry of a hurt child, the helpless dismayed reaching out of a child for help.

Irene knelt next to him.

"Don't touch his hands!" Mulligan shouted.

Yuri put his head on Irene's lap like an animal wanting to be petted and soundlessly looked up into her face. She stroked his head, tears welling up in her eyes. His face at last became composed, the long quiet of impending death absorbing his rage and hurt; and she continued stroking his head until his breathing stopped.

Medvedev sat on the floor, staring, disbelieving. He gazed bleakly at Mulligan. "Is this sufficient atonement?" His hand fell limply on his lap and he looked at it as though it belonged to someone else. "A transcutaneous poison," he whispered, his voice fading as the muscles weakened. "So deadly and swift." With a last effort he smiled grotesquely, the irony of the thought forcing it from him. "Only a true genius could have created this, you know. See how smart my son was!" His mocking laugh trailed off as his face first, then his neck muscles relaxed utterly in paralysis. He leaned forward and fell heavily and clumsily on his side before rolling onto his back. His mouth opened and closed in a wretched, fish-like gasp for air before his life finally ceased.

WASHINGTON, *June 27, 1985*

The Soviet Embassy, with some prodding from the State Department, assumed responsibility for Medvedev's corpse and shipped it back to Russia. A small press announcement said only that the noted Russian geneticist had been in the United States for scientific meetings and had died suddenly.

Yuri was buried in a small, private, nondenominational cemetery outside Washington. Both Mulligan and Irene insisted that the burial be at their personal expense. They were not certain whether a religious service was appropriate or not, so they did not have one, but, standing by the grave, watching the tiny casket being lowered into the ground, Mulligan felt the shadows of eternity and incomprehensibility. No one spoke them, but the words "ashes to ashes, dust to dust," came insistently to his mind. Irene cried softly and bitterly as heavy, reddish-brown earth was shoveled into the grave, her grief still sullied by remnants of outrage.

General Alexander was waiting to speak to them outside the cemetery. Mulligan had noticed him standing near the grave site. He had saluted, as soldiers instinctively do in the presence of death, acknowledging the force that gives definition to their virtues.

His self-assurance was evidently undiminished by the deaths of Yuri and Medvedev. In full dress uniform, the splashed color of battle ribbons on his chest, his weathered face firm and vigorous, he looked the very soul of valor and rectitude. He approached Mulligan and Irene as they walked slowly and silently out of the cemetery. "I came to pay my respects," he said, "knowing what this meant to you both." He bent his head lower to look into Irene's face. She turned away from him. "We always knew that the boy would die, didn't we, Dr. Sailland?" he asked softly.

"Not that way," she replied. "Not that way, not by his own hand, and not at the same time that he was murdering his father."

Mulligan was overtly snide. "You ought to be happy that he invented a brand-new poison for you," he said. "Transcutaneous, at that. Think of the possibilities."

"As a matter of fact," Alexander replied, not at all embarrassed, "I'm having what's left of it analyzed right now. But that isn't really what I came to talk to you about."

"I know what you came for," Mulligan said. He wanted to be vehement and to express his bitterness but found that he was too tired to summon the necessary anger. "I know what you want. You want now what you've wanted all along. You want me to tell you how they did it. So we can do it, too, maybe do it even better. Then the Russians wouldn't be ahead of us any more, would they?"

"It *is* important," Alexander affirmed quietly. "You know as well as I do that this is only the beginning, just a start. We're entering a new age. Sure Medvedev made mistakes, and the children all died very young from a terrible disease . . . I'll grant you all that. But he did it! Don't you see that? He did it! He produced a child faster and stronger and far more intelligent than any human being who ever lived before!"

Irene shuddered. "It's disgusting. You're disgusting."

Alexander flushed, momentarily unprepared for so frontal an assault, but recovered quickly. "I think I know how you feel," he said, smoothly falling back into the learned pattern of ingratiation.

"No, you don't," Mulligan stated wearily. "I don't think you do know how we feel."

"I know you know," Alexander said to Mulligan, accusing and goading. "I know you found out how Medvedev did it. I know you've thought of improvements. What is it you're so afraid of?"

Mulligan took a deep breath and held it for a few seconds before replying. He wanted to answer carefully. "I'm afraid of what you'll do, you or others like you," he said finally. "Nature makes mistakes, General, lots of them. Children are born with all sorts of genetic defects. That's one thing. But when men manipulate genes and something horrible happens . . ." his voice faded as a sense of foreboding settled heavily over him. Could Alexander ever be made to see the difference between tragedy and evil? Still, Mulligan was certain that the general would find someone else, some other biochemist to push ahead with the project. And Alexander already knew enough to make it much easier to do again. Better soldiers, better human beings . . . who decided what was better?

Alexander tugged his cap down and pulled his jacket smooth. He looked coldly at Mulligan, and his face hardened into obdurate command. "All the same," he said, "I'll expect a full report from you, complete in every detail, by the end of the week."

"Don't hold your breath waiting," Mulligan said.

"That's an order."

"Shove it. I don't work for you."

"You have for the last three weeks," Alexander said angrily. "Who do you think paid for everything? Who do you think arranged for the lab at the NIH? You owe me that report."

"So sue me," Mulligan said. "I won't do this any more." He took Irene's arm and they walked away. "I'll tell you what," he said to her, still angered and speaking perhaps more forcefully than he should have, "Why don't we get married and have children the old-fashioned way?"

Through her tears she nodded a happy assent.